BLOOD SPORT

BRITT REIGN

Cover Design by: Enchanting Romance Designs

Editing & Proofreading by: Darlene & Athena - Sisters Get Lit.erary

Formatting by: Cleo Moran, Devoted Pages Designs

Trigger Warnings:

- Domestic Violence
- Domestic Assault
- Death of a grandparent
- Suicide
- Mention of blood
- Explicit Sex Scenes
- Foul Language
- MMA Fighting/Violence
- Depression/Mental Health/Panic Attacks/PTSD
- NO ANIMALS DIE

Tropes:

- Friends to Lovers
- MMA Fighter
- Who Hurt You
- Big Guy/Petite Girl
- Forced Close Proximity
- One Bed
- Slow Burn Romance
- Kinks: Praise, Breeding, Breath

Playlist

1. You Don't Know What Love Means – NOTHING MORE
2. Hopeless – Too Close To Touch, The Word Alive
3. Another Way – Reimagined – Sleep Theory
4. Like That – Bea Miller
5. Rebel – Royal
6. Down Bad – Taylor Swift
7. Hero/Heroine – BOYS LIKE GIRLS
8. Creature – LANDMVRKS
9. Unsteady – X Ambassadors
10. Afterglow – Taylor Swift
11. Begin Again (Taylor's Version) – Taylor Swift
12. Down for the Ride – SLAVES, Jessie Abbey
13. Give – Sleep Token
14. WONDERWaLL – Bring Me The Horizon
15. Those Eyes – New West
16. Pieces Of Me – Ashlee Simpson
17. I Don't Want to Lose You – Luca Fogale
18. Blood Sport – Sleep Token
19. Don't Reach For Me – Knocked Loose
20. Cherry – Lana Del Rey
21. Emergence—Sleep Token
22. Work Song – Hozier
23. A Thousand Years – Christina Perri

*To those willing to walk through the depths of hell and back
to save themselves.
This one's for you.* ♥

Prologue

Sloan

Terror.

Pure Terror.

It's all I feel the second I see James enter through the bathroom door out of my periphery. My body immediately recoils in on itself at his presence.

James steps behind me as I'm finishing up my makeup, his whiskey eyes meet my violet ones in the mirror. They're slightly glazed over while mine are dull, lifeless. The dark circles shadowed underneath mine concealed the best they can be.

"You must look respectable in front of my peers, Reesey, not like a whore. How would that make me look? Do you taunt them on purpose? Want them to fuck you like a whore?"

James' words are like venom, always on a loop in my head as I apply a nude lip to make sure I don't stand out too much tonight.

I watch him in the mirror as he eyes me up and down

with a glint in his eye that I can't quite read. Immediately making the hair stand up on the back of my neck and causing the pit in my stomach to grow just a little deeper.

I'm not sure how much deeper it can get before I swallow myself whole.

I barely even recognize myself anymore. I've lost so much weight since being married to the infamous Dr. James McAllister. Not just from him controlling everything that goes into my body to make sure I stay the picture-perfect trophy wife, but also from the anxiety that eats away at me.

I'm living every day in hell, a shell of who I used to be.

I spend every second of every day monitoring the shifts in James' moods. It's like I'm constantly walking on eggshells. Never able to let my guard down. Not even for a minute.

When did I become this woman? Why did I let myself?

I look down, trying to avoid meeting his eyes.

I used to be so confident. So sure of myself.

Not this scared girl. This ghost of a woman that I don't even know.

The smell of whiskey already permeates the air around us causing my stomach to turn and my senses to go on even higher alert. James is even harsher when he's drinking. It's like the whiskey shuts his humanity off. Well at least the little bit he has, the part he saves for his patients and his peers.

Our guests should be here any minute. The second they arrive he will slip on the mask of doting husband and world-renowned orthopedic surgeon.

In others' eyes he's *"The perfect man."* I constantly hear *"You're so lucky to be loved by someone like him."*

I go to step away from him to exit the bathroom, but he

cages me in.

"Look at me," James all but snarls.

I look at him, leaning back against the sink, trying to keep the slightest bit of space between us.

When he goes to reach for one of the blonde curls hanging loosely on the side of my face, I take my chance and duck under his arm and make a run for it.

"Get back here you little bitch," James seethes as I rush out of the bathroom door.

No. No. No. I just needed to make it a couple more minutes before guests start arriving, and I'm safe from harm.

This long sleeved, black velvet, mermaid style dress is elegant and classy. Appropriate for his colleagues and it covers all of the bruises he's marred my skin with. However, it's not the best for escaping.

I run down the stairs to get to the door as fast as I can, which is a challenge in these stupid black red-bottoms with a six-inch heel. He demands I always wear them for his dinner parties, especially when there are other male surgeons from work. I must always maintain the look as his perfect arm candy.

"Reese Sloan McAllister, I said get the fuck back here!" James growls so close.

The thought '*Too close*' barely registers before he's gripping my hair and yanking me backward. A gasp leaves my mouth with a whoosh at the impact of him wrenching me back into his chest. This is nothing new to me, but that doesn't mean the pain hurts any less.

"I was going to be nice and flaunt my pretty little wife around the party tonight, but I think you'll have to stay hidden like the bitch you are," James snarls, dragging me by my hair to the cellar door.

"James, no. Please. I'm so sorry. I promise I'll behave," I beg.

"You should have thought about that before you tried to look like a whore, Reesey," James grits into my ear.

"Who did you curl your hair for, whore?" James questions menacingly while gripping my hair so hard I'm afraid he's going to rip it out.

"Answer me!" James snarls.

My arm feels like it's on fire where he grips it in a death grip. I'll definitely have another bruise I'm going to have to cover up at the hospital. If only they knew their favorite "Silver Daddy" was a monster.

"Who the fuck are you trying to impress, huh? I know it's not for me!" James growls with accusation.

"James, please. You're hurting me."

"You're hurting me!" James mocks condescendingly.

The doorbell chimes. I thank whatever guardian angel I must have, who's kept me alive this long.

"Saved by the bell, Reesey." James smirks, disgust oozing out of him.

"Now be a good little whore and stay fucking quiet. Oh wait, that doesn't matter now does it?" he chuckles sardonically shoving me into the cellar.

He slams the door in my face and locks it. There's no use attempting to scream or pound on the door because James soundproofed his basement before I moved in. He didn't exactly tell me, I learned the first time I upset him and I found myself locked down here.

It may be a finished basement with beautiful hardwood floors, but it's still a prison. Four gray walls. No windows. No furniture. No blankets. Nothing soft to sit on. It's not the worst place to be locked away but it's certainly not comfortable either. I've hidden in less comfortable places.

There is one steel, windowless door that leads outside. It's taunted me every time he's locked me down here. Because of course it doesn't just lock from the inside, it has several locks on the outside, that only James has a key for.

Each time James has thrown me in here, I've laid down in the center of the floor, staring up at the ceiling and daydreamed about ways to escape. I've dreamt about what a life would be like to be free. Free of the confinements of this marriage. Free of this house. Free of this prison I got myself trapped in.

Every early encounter I've had with James plays like a video in my head. I beat myself up about all of the red flags I had niggles about but always pushed to the back of my mind because everyone else thought he was such a catch.

I often lie here and wonder if James' ex-wife truly got into a car accident and died. Did he play a part in her death? Did she crash her car on purpose because he drove her to the edge of insanity—like he's done to me? Did she ever consider crushing peanuts into his food to kill him—like I've dreamt of doing numerous times? Did she think of ways to escape him—like I have?

Sometimes I feel like I'll never be free of him, and death might be the only way out.

That thought crosses my mind more often than it should. Even as a child hiding under my bed, hoping the screams from my parents would just stop. I wished for safety, for peace, for quiet, but never for death.

Some days James leaves me down here for hours, at times even, more than a day. He's playing his sick twisted games, leaving me waiting. The one good thing is I get time to dream of a better life away from him—that is until my very own nightmare has come back to retrieve me and take me back to my miserable reality.

If I run, I have a chance to live free of him. If I stay here any longer, I may die by the hands of this man.

I am done waiting for him to choose my fate.

I pushed him over the edge just enough tonight to get locked down here. But this time I was prepared with a copy of a key for my escape.

Tonight, I'm running as far the fuck away from this prison as my legs will take me. It's time I take my life back or at least go out fighting for it.

1

Beck

I rip open the door to the gym, heading straight for my heavy bag.

What the hell does Sutton think she's doing going on tour with August? She hardly even knows the guy.

It had been Sutton and I for years until that dark cloud just stormed in, stealing her from me?

I could seriously break everything in sight right now.

If I stayed there any longer and heard her spew any more nonsense, I would've really ruined what's between us.

"What did that bag ever do to you?" Sloan asks as she walks into the gym.

Just great. I thought I would be alone today. Looks like luck isn't on my side.

With Sloan in the room, I try to temper my anger so I don't scare her—but that's not likely.

"Don't worry about it," I grunt out as I slam my fists

over and over again into the heavy bag.

"Well, I'm a good listener, if you want to talk. Otherwise, I'll just be over here working on some of the techniques from class," Sloan offers as she begins stretching.

"You wouldn't understand."

"You'd be surprised what I understand, Beck. I know a broken heart when I see one. And you, sir, are the victim of someone ripping yours out."

"What did you just say?" I turn, ready to tell her to mind her own damn business until I see the haunted look in her eyes. The demons of her past are alive in her violet orbs.

I don't know what comes over me. The need to truly know Sloan overwhelms me. The desire to know what she's running from fuels me. For some reason I'm drawn to her.

"Let's talk then, Little Dove," I grunt, throwing her a pair of boxing gloves.

"Little Dove?" Sloan eyes me warily but starts to pull a glove on.

"Yes, you're tiny like a bird and seem innocent like one too," I offer, helping her with her gloves.

"I'm not that innocent. But we aren't talking about me. We are talking about you and that broken heart of yours," Sloan states quickly changing the subject.

"My heart isn't broken," I all but snarl and slam my fist into the heavy bag.

Sloan gasps and takes several steps away from me.

"Shit, I'm sorry, Sloan. I'm just... Sutton chose him. Fucking August. Over me. He has nothing to offer her. She barely knows him. Now she's leaving all of us for some guy she just met not that long ago. Sutton chose him over years of friendship with me. It's always been me and Sut.

And she just decided all of a sudden, she has a different dream. Sutton decided to go on a music tour with a nobody, throwing all of her dreams away. That café was her baby and now she's just handing the reins over to Quinn. And Quinn is backing her on this," I growl throwing several jabs into the bag.

"Let it all out. I'm going to stand over here out of the way. I am still listening though," Sloan states, leaning on a wall several feet away from me.

"Why the hell would Quinn think that this is a good idea? Sutton rarely trusts people and she's just going to trust this group of guys to keep her safe while she's on the road? How is that skinny emo boy going to keep her safe?" I slam punch after punch into the bag.

"What about Khaos? Is she just going to leave her dog behind too? Is she just going to forget about us?" I throw a roundhouse kick at the bag.

I'm drenched in sweat, pacing, and about to blow smoke like a bull. I'm seeing red. Completely lost in the thoughts spiraling out of control in my head.

Why am I not good enough for her?

Have I not proven to Sut how much she means to me? I have done everything to make her feel safe and Sut still didn't choose me.

Why didn't she choose me?

"Beck..." Sloan's soothing voice snaps me out of my head.

Looking up, Sloan's pained eyes meet mine and they look so fucking haunted.

"Fuck. I'm sorry." I squeeze my eyes closed and bury my head in my hands.

"Do you... Do you need a hug?" Sloan asks timidly.

"Yeah, Little Dove, I'd like that." I kneel on the floor and open my arms to her.

"What are you doing?" Sloan eyes me curiously.

"I can tell you're uncomfortable. I thought if I kneeled it would be less intimidating for you to hug me." I shrug.

Sloan blinks rapidly at me before hesitantly walking over and wrapping her tiny arms around my neck. I pull her gently into my arms and she stiffens slightly, before softening just the slightest bit.

When she pulls out of my embrace, I sit on the floor and start stretching. Sloan sits across from me with her legs in a butterfly position.

"Beck… I'm just getting to know everyone here and the dynamics of your friendships, but I don't think Sutton made this decision lightly. She doesn't strike me as someone who impulsively makes decisions. You can tell she cares deeply for all of you. She even welcomed me in with open arms. Sutton really sees people, not the mask we show to the world. So don't be so hard on her.

"We are allowed to have more than one dream. We are human. We are evolving every second of every day. We are allowed to change our minds. I think she's brave for trying something new. For taking a leap when she has no idea what the future holds for her. Not all women need protectors. We aren't all damsels. Sometimes the best things we create are made when we save ourselves," Sloan says with such conviction.

I just stare at her at a loss for words.

That was powerful.

"I just can't lose her, Sloan," my voice cracks.

"I don't think she'll let you lose her, Beck. I just think your relationship might look differently than you hoped.

And that's going to hurt like hell for a while. But eventually, when you see her shine like the star we know she is, you'll find peace too," Sloan declares, stretching her toes out to touch mine.

"Thank you, Little Dove." I give her toes a gentle squeeze of appreciation.

"It's going to be okay, Beck." Sloan flashes me the softest smile, getting up off the floor and extending her little hand out to me.

I sure hope so, Little Dove.

2
Sloan

Past

I'm huddled in a tiny nurses' station with Kailey and Maria. We share three computers and three phones in maybe a 400 square foot space. The close proximity and the high stress of our job will either make you friends or enemies but thankfully it has made us practically sisters. I don't think I'd survive the chaos of this place if it weren't for them.

"Have you seen the new ortho surgeon yet?" Kailey squeals, hopping in her chair and sliding over to me.

"I have not, but word is he's a silver fox," I say nonchalantly, shrugging my shoulders.

"He is definitely a silver fox!" Maria chirps, coming over and sitting on the desk in front of us, sipping on her daily iced coffee.

"And...a newly single one!" Maria and Kailey say at the same time.

"Jinx!" they both shout and then burst out in a fit of giggles.

"You two kill me," I start laughing at their ridiculousness.

"Why do we care if he's single?" I ask, eyeing them both suspiciously.

"Weee don't care, but you might," Kailey says slyly.

"Isn't a hot, world-renowned surgeon being single a red flag?" I ask.

"You think everyone is a red flag," Maria states.

"I heard he's a widow," Kailey whispers solemnly.

"That's really sad but that doesn't change my mind. I'm celibate, remember? Swore off all men. Doing the independent boss babe thing." I side-eye them.

"Yes, yes, we know. Dreams of being a nurse practitioner. You plan to leave little old us here. You don't need no man, Reese. We get it. But he could just be your sugar daddy," Maria says, wiggling her eyebrows.

"I don't need a sugar daddy. I am perfectly happy on my own. Thank you very much." I spin around in my chair and go to throw my feet up on the desk.

"Ladies..." says a very deep male voice, startling me. I immediately drop my feet and both girls' eyes go wide. We all jump up from our chairs and blurt out, "Doctor."

"Ladies, I'm Dr. James McAllister, the new head of Orthopedic Surgery. I was just making my rounds meeting everyone. I was told you three are the ones I need to keep happy if I want things to run smoothly," he says matter of fact.

"Yes, sir. One of us is usually here every day. We make

sure everything runs smoothly for everyone from pre-op to discharge," I say, reaching out to shake his hand.

He takes my hand gently, placing it between both of his rather large hands. I watch as his eyes quickly make a pass at my left hand. *Interesting.*

"Pleasure to meet you, Miss..." James says in a charming voice, causing my erratic heartbeat from almost getting caught talking about him to slow the slightest bit.

"Reese Archer, sir," I say, holding eye contact. His eyes are the color of bourbon aged whiskey, soft and kind.

"Reese, it's a pleasure," Dr. McAllister says, squeezing my hand tenderly, returning my gaze.

"That's Kailey and Maria." I nod my head toward the girls. They're standing next to me, staring at him with hearts in their eyes.

"Ladies, Reese, I look forward to working with you all." He nods, releasing my hand and walking down the hall.

"*Oh my gaaaah!*" Kailey and Maria squeal and start jumping around me when he's out of sight.

"You guys! We almost got caught," I grumble.

"OMG, stop! He was so into you," Maria squeals.

"He didn't even know we existed," Kailey says, bumping her shoulder into me.

"Not happening you two." I plop down in my chair and scoot up to my computer to start putting orders in for the next surgical case.

"It is *soooo* happening!" they both say giggling, walking down the hall toward the operating rooms. "See you later, Reese's Pieces."

"Later, babes," I shout back.

3
Beck

I'm leaning against the wall in the gym with my hands behind my head, one foot propped up against the wall. I'm lost in thought, when Asher walks up to me.

"How have you really been doing since Sut left?" Ash asks, handing me my gloves.

"I fucking miss her, but she chose him, so it is what it is," I grumble, tightening the strap on my glove a little harder than necessary.

"I get that this hurts man. I can't imagine how you're feeling, but Sut has been your best friend for years. I kept telling you, you needed to tell her how you felt before it was too late. I don't want to say I told you so, but…" Ash says, ducking as I throw a jab directly at his face for stirring the pot.

"Fuck off," I growl, throwing another series of punches.

Ash blocking every single one.

He's fast as fuck. I'll give him that.

"I'm not saying you shouldn't be hurting. It sucks. She didn't choose you. You can lick your wounds a bit. But are you really going to throw years of friendship away when that was all you had up until a few months ago?" Ash asks, backing away from me and dropping his gloves to his sides.

"She was mine and she just fucking left!" I snarl.

"Yeah, she was your *friend*. Not your girlfriend. And you act like she's leaving forever. Their tour is only a couple months. She isn't your father. Sut's coming back," Ash reassures me.

Who the fuck does Ash think he is right now bringing up my father and Sut in the same sentence?

"Sure, she comes back, but then what's that going to look like? Huh? Still doesn't make her any more mine. And don't bring up my fucking sperm donor!" I start kicking the bag.

"What do you mean? It's going to look how it's looked for years. You two hardly even kissed until a couple months ago. You were friendly. Affectionate maybe, but you never really crossed a line with each other prior to your trip to Vegas. It can literally be the same minus the actual physical intimacy. I don't think August is the type of person who is going to forbid her from hanging out with you," Ash reasons with me.

"How would you know? You don't know August." I alternate throwing punches and roundhouse kicks at the bag, while Ash leans against the wall just watching me intently.

Kind of like how Sloan did. Why am I thinking about Sloan?

"You're right. I don't know, August. But I know Sut. I know that she always does what she wants to do, not what people tell her to do. I know her heart is huge but she also trusts very few people and she trusts him. So, we have to trust her. You can do whatever you want but I'm not going to just cut off my friend of six years. I'm sorry, man," Ash says, glaring at me.

"When did you become a fucking therapist?" I growl.

"When did you become such a dick?" Ash snarls, shoving me backwards.

"Sut chose him...over us," I say, so defeated. I tear my gloves off and lean against the wall.

"Do you even hear yourself? No, man. She chose herself. Which she has every right to do. We didn't even know she could sing. Six years and we had no idea. I'm so fucking proud of her for putting herself out there. Sut's come so far from the unsure, timid girl we met all those years ago. You need to get your head out of your ass and support her. Or don't. But that's on you, if you don't." Ash shoves my shoulder and starts to walk off.

"Where the hell are you going?" I grumble.

"I'm going for a run. I know you're hurt. You feel rejected. Probably even abandoned. But you don't feel that way because of Sut. Maybe you do a little, but that's not the only reason. You're acting way out of character for you. You should be happy for her. She's doing something that a lot of people don't get to do. It's bad ass. We should be cheering her on, like she does everyone else. So, you might want to take a hard look in the mirror and see why this is really fucking you up so bad," Ash declares before heading out the door.

"Fuck!" I slam my hands down on the mat.

A

Sloan

Past

I'm zoned out, printing out discharge instructions on a patient when I'm startled by a deep voice.

"Miss Archer, can I have a word?" Dr. McAllister asks, poking his head around the corner right next to where I'm sitting.

"Alone," he offers, nodding his head to the hallway.

I chance a glance to Kailey who's smirking slyly but ignoring me as I hesitantly get up.

I follow him into an empty hallway just diagonal from my desk. A few gurneys litter the hallway and surgical trays are lined up against the wall but there is no other staff in sight. An uneasiness still settles over me.

"Is everything okay, Dr. McAllister?" I ask, worry lacing my voice.

"Everything's great, Miss Archer. I've really enjoyed working with you these past few months. You're a real asset to this department. I see why everyone thinks so highly of you," he says, smiling softly at me, his eyes never leaving mine.

"Thank you, sir. It's been a pleasure working and learning alongside you as well," I offer nervously, sweeping my hair behind my ear. My heart rate ticking up near tachycardic at the intensity in his stare.

"That's great to hear, Miss Archer. I was actually wondering if I could ask you a personal question?" he asks, leaning a bit closer to me.

My body betrays me and holds me hostage in his stare and closeness. Even though I feel like I'm about to have a panic attack, I reply, "Oh. Uh. Sure. What's your question?"

"Are you seeing anyone, Miss Archer?" he says, ever so charming, smiling softly at me.

"Am I...? Me? Am I seeing anyone?" I fumble with my words, taking a step back.

Down girl.

"Yes, Miss Archer," he chuckles. "Are you seeing anyone?" His chuckle is so deep and rich. It almost makes my toes curl.

We are celibate. Staying celibate.

"No, sir. I am not. But that's by choice," I say firmly. Partly to let him know that I don't mix business with pleasure, but also to remind myself that we don't have time for distractions.

We are not going to get lost in whiskey eyes or imagine our fingers running through luscious silver hair, Reese.

We are not going to throw away our dreams for a man like our mother did.

We have goals and are sticking to them.

Dr. McAllister leans in closer to me. His eyes never leaving mine.

My heartbeat picks up again.

He's so close. Too close.

We could get caught and I could get fired.

"If we only ever had one choice in life, Miss Archer; it would be a very unfulfilling life don't you think?" he whispers in my ear, startling me out of my head.

As quick as he appeared, he's turning around to leave. That's when I find his woodsy smell surrounding me and the slightest hint of... Is that whiskey? *There's no way.*

"Let me know if you decide to make a different choice, Miss Archer," he says with his back to me, walking toward his operating room.

I'm not sure if the butterflies raging in my stomach are from the close proximity or anxiety.

5

Sloan

Present

I'm making mine and Quinn's iced lattes before the morning crowd rolls in to WaggingWithWords. The bell chimes earlier than I would have expected, startling me.

It's so much quieter around here without Sutton and August. Sutton always had music playing or August sat on the stage and played for everyone. The bell seems so much louder without those sounds drowning it out.

The sound startles me so much that I accidentally uppercut my entire 32 oz iced latte all over Beck. I mean... All. Over. Him.

Iced coffee is dripping down his light blue T-shirt, soaking his gray sweatpants leaving nothing to the imagination. I gasp in embarrassment, tearing my eyes from his very well-endowed package only to find myself staring at his chest. A very well-defined and carved from stone muscular frame that's on display thanks to the coffee.

"Damn, looks like those classes are paying off, Little Dove." Beck lets out a halfhearted chuckle.

I notice that he's sort of stumbling with his dog, Mayhem by his side.

"Beck, why do you smell like whiskey at eight in the morning on a Saturday? Especially during your training season?" I question him. My eyes still not quite leaving his chest.

"I think I actually smell like coffee now," Beck retorts sarcastically.

Mayhem makes a groaning sound as he lays down next to where Beck's standing. He looks just as concerned for his dad, as I do. The poor guy looks like his heart was put through a blender. And don't get me started on his face.

Holy shit.

His left eye is almost completely swollen shut. He has a fresh cut on a fat lip.

"What the hell happened to your face?" I gasp.

"Yeah, Beck. Why don't you tell Sloan why your face looks like someone used it for a punching bag?" Asher chimes in mockingly, coming up behind Beck.

"Solid uppercut, Sloan," Asher explains, breaking out in a small smirk.

Beck groans, "Can you two not talk so loudly? Fuck."

"What the hell happened to your face? And your clothes?" Quinn chokes out, walking up to the counter from the kitchen.

"Sloan accidentally punched the hell out of that coffee right into Beck's chest," Ash chuckles.

"Will all of you please keep it down!" Beck groans again, covering his ears.

"Ash. What. The. Hell." Quinn snaps.

"Don't look at me. I didn't do that to his pretty face," Ash says, almost chuckling as he puts his hands up.

"You didn't stop who did though either," Beck grumbles.

"Man, you were literally begging that guy to hit you. You were being an asshat. Trying to start a fight. I wasn't getting in the middle," Ash declares, shaking his head.

"Why were you trying to...?" Quinn starts to question.

"Because of Sutton?" I ask timidly.

Beck looks so defeated. The pain radiating from him penetrates my heart as I gaze into his ocean blue eye.

"Beck, Sut still cares about you. You can't go around starting fights just because she left. She'd be so pissed at you right now," Quinn reprimands him.

"Well, she isn't exactly here right now. Is she Quinn?" Beck spits back.

"I've always said love is a cancer like it could kill a person faster," I mumble, attempting to wipe up some of the coffee.

"Damn. That's dark," Quinn murmurs, eyes a little wide.

"Sounds like some shit the musician would say," Beck mutters.

"Beck, you should get some ice on that eye and that lip. How's your vision? Any headaches? Dizziness? Think you might have a concussion?" I instinctually go into nurse mode, rattling off questions, before I realize they don't know I'm a nurse. Was a nurse. Almost a nurse practitioner. I would've graduated in three months before I ran. My heart breaks the slightest bit at the reminder.

"Sorry. My ex... Never mind. Just make sure if you have any of those symptoms you go to the hospital and get checked out," I ramble before tossing the washcloth on the counter, turning and heading toward the kitchen.

"Let me go grab some ice from the freezer," Quinn offers, following behind me.

I flinch when she comes into the kitchen. Guarded and waiting for her to start questioning me.

"Gosh, Sut would be soooo pissed if she saw him right now. I don't even think we should tell her. I think she'd feel guilty and it would ruin the tour for her. What do you think?" Quinn asks.

"Yeah, I would say we leave this little detail out for now. At least maybe until she gets back," I say, shrugging. Relieved she isn't questioning me.

"Yeah, good idea. I understand Beck's upset, but he also needs to get his temper under control. This was part of the problem for Sut. He has like two modes, totally in command and just rage-filled," Quinn says, shaking her head in disappointment.

"I'll try and talk to him. Beck's been opening up some while we train at the gym. I think he loves her, but I don't think he loves her the way he thinks he does. Let's just hope Beck can get his feelings under control sooner rather than later before he ruins his career," I murmur.

Walking back out into the café, I hand Beck some ice wrapped in a wash cloth. "Put this on your eye for no longer than 20 minute intervals. You can do that three times today. Try to get that swelling down. If you get dizzy or start to lose vision in that eye, please go to the emergency room," I offer, squeezing his hand gently.

"Yes, ma'am." He salutes me and tries to wink with his eye that isn't almost swollen shut.

"Get out of here before you scare the customers away, Beckett. Oh, and stop starting fights. You're better than that," I scold him and gently shove him toward the door.

Beck reacts dramatically, acting like I threw him out of here even though I barely touched him.

He stops right before pushing the door open, smiling as he says, "Thanks for the ice, Little Dove. Try not to punch anymore coffee on anyone today."

"I'll try not to punch coffees if you try not to punch faces," I chuckle.

"Deal." Beck nods and heads out.

6
Sloan

Past

$\mathcal{M}$y dream career has always been to become a nurse practitioner. My mother had a similar dream but never followed through because the men in our family held her back.

Over the last several years I have studied tirelessly, put in the clinical hours, worked extra shifts and overtime so I could apply to multiple NP programs. I have been waiting for an acceptance letter for what feels like forever and the moment's finally here. I send up a quick prayer to the universe hoping I'm accepted but I feel two sets of eyes boring into me as I open one of my letters.

"Soooo…" Kailey and Maria look at me with hearts in their eyes.

"Soooo…" I offer, pretending I have no idea what they

want to talk about.

I close the envelope and hide it.

"Girl! Spill," they squeal.

"Spill what exactly?" I smirk, trying to contain my giggles.

"Oh my gosh. Seriously. Don't make us beg," Kailey demands excitedly.

"Spill the tea about your date with Silver Daddy," Maria almost yells at me.

"Okay. Okay," I say with a chuckle. "It was fine."

"Just. Fine?" They both give me side-eye.

I burst into a fit of giggles.

"Okay, it was better than fine." I smirk.

"Dr. McAllister picked me up at my house. He opened the car door for me and even buckled my seat belt. James took me to Guilia for dinner and it was fantastic. The affogato gelato was out of this world. I had always wanted to go there," I sigh in bliss.

I can still taste the cinnamon on my tongue.

"Ooooh, so it's James now, is it?" Kailey smirks at me, giving me googly eyes.

"Ha-ha. Do you want all the details or not?"

"Go on..." Maria pushes.

"The whole time his entire focus was on me. I swear he was staring at me like he would prefer to eat me over the dessert. James asked me so many questions about myself. I'm so used to being the one asking all the questions. It was nice to feel like someone was actually interested in getting to know me for once." I smile at the thought..

James made me feel so important. So heard. My skin tingled where his eyes roamed my body throughout the night.

"Soooo, has the celibacy finally come to an end?" Kailey asks with glee in her eyes.

"Not yet. He kissed me good night. His lips were so soft. He was a really good kisser but right as it started to pick up steam he pulled away. James said he didn't want to move too quickly. He said and I quote, 'I want to take my time with you.' He was a total gentleman," I say sweetly.

"I honestly thought he wasn't interested after that but he sent me a dozen gorgeous, white roses to my house this morning." I smile, thinking about how gorgeous the bouquet was. The vase holding the roses is so intricately designed.

"Ahhhh. How romantic. From where?" Maria swoons.

"I'm not sure. They were just on my front porch in a beautiful vase with a card," I say, smiling softly.

"I don't want to get my hopes up, but I think I'd like it if he invited me on a second date," I sigh, contentedly.

"To breaking your streak of a lackluster love life," Kailey hollers, lifting her iced coffee in the air.

"Ha-ha. I am still going to get my masters. That's still my first priority," I say chuckling.

"Here's to living vicariously through you," Maria adds, lifting hers in the air.

We all raise our iced coffees and cheer.

"Here's to living!"

"Miss Archer. Ladies, what are we cheers-ing to this morning?" Dr. McAllister startles us, when he pokes his head into the nurses' station.

"Just to having a good Monday," I chirp. Hoping I'm not blushing as hard as I feel like I am.

"Cheers to that. Have a nice day, ladies," James offers.

"Hey, Dr. McAllister, thank you." I smile at him.

"Of course, Miss Archer." Hes winks at me and walks out of the nurses' station.

"He…" Maria begins to say, fanning herself.

"Is soooo dreamy," Kailey finishes Maria's sentence, swooning.

"Ha-ha. He is attractive, you guys." I laugh at their shenanigans.

"Cheers to *Silver Daddy*!" they both yell out, causing all of us to burst out giggling.

"You guys kill me. Every. Time. We almost got busted." My giggle turns into cackling.

"Soooo what were we opening?" Kailey eyes me skeptically and rips the envelope from under my keyboard. And I let her, because I'm so nervous I feel like I'm going to be sick.

Kailey and Maria stand in front me, as I sit in my chair. Kailey pulls the letter out of the envelope so slowly. Torturing me. I hold my breath as I wait for her to read it. I stare at her, trying to read her face first.

"*You got into Harvard, Reese's Pieces!*" Kailey and Maria scream in unison pulling me out of my chair into a hug.

I got in! My heart is so full.

7
Beck

As I walk up to WaggingWithWords, I notice Sloan outside as I approach. We've gotten more comfortable with each other from all of the hours we've spent in the gym, but I still notice when certain things make her flinch. I try not to walk up on her too quickly, trying to avoid doing something that triggers or alarms her.

"Everything okay?" I ask Sloan, keeping a bit of a distance. I notice she's quickly locking up and there's a sign on the door that they're closed for the day.

Sloan startles slightly but then turns and realizes it's me.

"You don't know?" Sloan asks solemnly.

"Know what?" I wonder confused.

"Sut's grandma passed away. The funeral and burial are this morning. We're all going to the cemetery," Sloan offers somberly.

"Shit. I had no idea. You need a ride?"

"I don't mean to overstep, but you aren't going to..." Sloan hesitates, looking everywhere but at me.

"I'm not going to start a fight, Sloan. You have my word," I affirm, trying to ease her mind.

Sloan hesitates, looking up and down the street. I'm not really sure what she's looking for. I think she may be stalling. Likely not comfortable being the one to drop this news on me.

Tilting her chin up gently. "Sloan, you have my word."

Sloan swallows, licking her lips and nodding her head okay. My eyes trace her mouth for just a second before she turns her head out of my grip.

"Let's go," I offer, putting my arm out to lead the way to my car. Opening the door for Sloan, she hesitates but gets in. I gently shut the door behind her, watching her noticeably flinch through the window.

I won't hurt you, Sloan.

"You wanna pick the music?" I ask, offering her the aux cord.

"Thanks," Sloan says so softly.

Sloan is so kind. So gentle. So calm. Even though she's so closed off and guarded. She's such a conundrum to me.

We drive in a comfortable silence with only the sound of *Hero/Heroine* by Boys Like Girls playing softly in the background. It's almost peaceful until I remember where we're going and the fact that I haven't spoken to Sutton since I stormed out of the café before she left for the tour.

Sutton may not even want me at her grandmother's funeral. I never even got to meet the woman that was so special to her. Sutton always kept this piece of her close and she didn't share much about her with any of us. We knew she visited her grandma at a nursing home and that she was her rock after Sutton lost her parents. But other than that, Sutton had a wall up when it came to her grandmother. I noticed she was always distant for a few days after her visits but then would bounce right back to being her bubbly, outgoing self like nothing happened.

We pull up fifteen minutes later. I was so lost in my head that I almost forgot Sloan was even in the car, she was so quiet.

"I'm going to stand back here, just in case she doesn't want me here," I tell Sloan, helping her out of the car.

"Is it okay if I go sit with Quinn and August?" Sloan questions concern in her eyes.

"Of course, Sloan. You sit wherever you want."

Wringing her hands, she says, "Okay. I'll see you in a bit."

8
Beck

The second Sloan said she was going to the cemetery today; I knew in my heart I needed to be here for Sutton, even if she might hate me for how I acted.

Seeing her again after so many weeks is like a punch to the solar plexus.

Leaning against a weeping willow tree, my chest still aches at the thought of her not being mine. I watch Sutton from a distance, just staring off into space, I know I made the right choice in coming here. *I fucking missed her.*

Sut looks completely disconnected from herself and her surroundings. I've never seen her so distraught before. Not even when I first met her all those years ago, when she always stood in the shadows at parties we attended.

I'll protect Sut, like I always do. Hold her up, so that she can fall apart in my arms. She's my best fucking friend.

I know I can be what she needs.

I'm slowly working on getting my head back on straight. That's all thanks to Sloan.

She has spent many days at the gym with me, helping me work through my heartbreak. We've developed a sort of friendship. I teach her self-defense and she gives me lessons on love.

Whenever we're together we talk for hours. Sloan confided in me that she had an abusive ex and was terrified to move to Pittsburgh to start over. But she still hasn't told me where she ran from though.

I can tell just by how skittish Sloan gets, that she definitely ran from someone dangerous because I catch her looking over her shoulder more often than not.

But our talks have helped me understand that I had to start looking at my relationship with Sutton from a different perspective. Her bringing August to meet her grandmother but not me, should've clued me in on how she was feeling but I was too far gone. I have always loved Sutton and I will always protect her. Though I can see now what Sutton meant about our paths being different.

When I first met her, she was timid and untrusting, kind of how Sloan is. I'm a fixer. A protector. Sutton seemed broken when I met her, and I wanted to be a safe space for her. I want to continue to be that for her, but I don't know where we stand in our friendship.

Us being friends allowed Sutton to heal her past wounds, allowed me to shield her. But our dynamic, where we felt so comfortable and safe with each other and the I love yous, may have blurred the lines.

Regardless, love isn't always enough to sustain a relationship and sometimes comfort becomes enabling. Sometimes it allows us to repeat patterns that actually need to be broken in order to move forward and I didn't realize that until recently.

Somewhere along the line, things changed between us.

Sutton bloomed into this incredible woman; built herself back up from her roots to her petals and flourished. Sut doesn't need anyone to save her anymore--she saved herself.

So, while I'm not sure yet if August is right for my friend, I'm going to trust her heart,

because Sutton always seems to find the good in everyone. I'm going to be here for her while she navigates this new path that she's chosen for herself. Because Sloan and Quinn are right. Sutton deserves happiness more than anyone we know.

I watch as Sutton walks up and drops a purple rose on her grandmother's grave. Khaos sits, leaning against her leg to offer his support.

Sutton's lips move but I can't tell what she's saying.

A gentle breeze blows through her hair and she places her hand over her heart as a lone tear streams down her face. It's as if she felt her grandmother in that moment.

When she turns around to head toward the cars, Sut spots me. Immediately taking off running toward me.

My heart instantly soars. She needs me on her worst day. *Not him.*

The second she's in front of me I'm pulling her into my

arms. A contented sigh leaves my body, at the feeling of Sut back in my arms.

"It's okay. I'm here. I got you, Sut," I whisper in her hair, squeezing her tighter to me as she silently sobs in my arms, shoulders shaking.

Looking over her head, I notice August sitting, whispering with Quinn and Sloan. Every so often he'd look back at us with what seems like sadness in his eyes.

"Come on, let's get you out of here," I comfort Sutton, kissing the top of her head and trying to turn her toward my car.

"I'm..." she croaks out.

Sutton glances back toward the hole in the ground, shoulders slumping forward, and then turns to follow me.

"Watch your head," I warn, as I help her get inside the passenger seat.

"What are you doing?" Quinn asks so softly from behind me.

I didn't even hear her walk up to me. Quinn glances first at Sutton, who's staring straight ahead, and then back to me.

"I'll keep an eye on her." I tell Quinn quietly, "I'm going to take her home and tuck her into bed with Khaos and Mayhem."

"Okay. I'm going to go pick up some takeout and then we will all be over soon," Quinn says, looking at me hesitantly and then back to Sut.

"Why are you looking at me like that?"

"Because you can't just try and swoop in and rescue her like Prince Charming, Beckett. Her and August are together. You better not take advantage of her vulnerability right now or that black eye you had a few weeks ago won't be the last one you have. Do you hear me?" Quinn snaps.

"August has to get back to tour, doesn't he? He isn't going to stick around to take care of her."

"That's not right, and you know it. August loves her. He has begged her to allow him to stay and to be here for her, but she doesn't want From Troy to lose their big chance," Quinn says defensively, getting in my face.

"Don't make me out to be the villain, Quinn. I'm just taking care of our girl," I explain firmly.

"We can all take care of *our* girl," she states, pointing at Sutton. She's still staring off into space while sitting in the front seat of my car, ignoring the argument between Quinn and me.

August walks up to the door and leans in. "Sunshine, come home with me. What are you doing?"

"August, I love you, but I can't right now. Please just go finish the tour. Let the guys know I'm so sorry. I just… I can't right now," Sutton hiccups on a sob.

"Forget about the tour, Sunshine. I love you," August whispers, pulling her tiny hands into his gently.

"No, August. Go follow your dreams. They were always your dreams anyway," Sutton sobs out, shoving him away.

"Sunshine…"

Sutton turns her head and stares out the window with a faraway look in her eyes.

"Sutton, please don't push me away." August's voice cracks with anguish.

August leans in and kisses the side of her head. "I love you, Angel. Please don't give up on us."

August opens the back door and pats the seat for Khaos to hop in.

"Take care of Mommy while I'm gone. I'll be back for both of you," August whispers into his fur. He kisses him on the head then softly shuts the door.

I feel like an onlooker witnessing a vulnerable moment that I shouldn't be.

Sutton only sobs harder. My heart breaking at how tormented she looks.

August turns to face me. "You better not lay a finger on her, Beckett. Sutton and I are not over," he demands.

"I'm going to keep her safe, like I always do. In whatever way Sutton needs," I declare.

"I will be back for her," August vows before hesitantly walking away.

"Do. Not. Take advantage of my best friend. So, help me Gods, Beckett. Sutton loves him. She loves him so much that she will let him go, so that he can make his dreams come true," Quinn growls at me before walking toward Sloan.

There is no way in hell I'm allowing Sutton to grieve alone.

9
Sloan

My heart breaks for Sutton and the all-consuming grief she's feeling at the loss of her grandmother. It's coming off of her in waves. I feel like a voyeur watching the love pouring out of everyone for Sutton. I've never felt a love like that before.

Even though the tension is thick right now with everything going on, Beck still showed up for Sutton today. Putting his own anger aside and putting their friendship first.

August's sole focus has been on Sutton. Just standing by her side as she feels every ounce of her grief, remaining an anchor for her.

Quinn is unwavering in her loyalty to Sutton but still a spitfire, keeping both men in line. Every day she reminds me more and more of my two best friends I left behind.

It makes me miss Kailey and Maria that much more. I rub my chest to try to relieve my own aching heart. They really were all I had prior to meeting James, but our friendship became stilted partly because of him, but also because I let him control who I could and couldn't spend time with to keep the peace.

At first, it started with weekend girls' nights decreasing. Eventually I was only ever able to see them at work. I could tell they were starting to get suspicious of James and I'm pretty sure he knew. And that's why my schedule started changing.

They justified these changes and said it was the honeymoon phase. It was normal to miss a few girls' nights, until I was missing all of them to avoid an argument or worse with James.

They were fine with it at first when they thought it was new love and were living vicariously through me. Kailey and Maria loved seeing the white roses and gifts he'd leave on my desk with the cutest notes. They wanted to hear everything about our dates.

They knew James and I were spending so much time together, so we could try to get to know one another. How we were unable to keep our hands off of one another. He was definitely handsy, even at work; which made me uncomfortable. But I'd let it slide because he promised me no one would say anything because of who he was.

I was naïve.

And of course no one would say a word about James. But that wasn't the case for me.

The rumors were that I was a gold digger. I took advantage of him for being a vulnerable widow. Just a pretty young thing he'd eventually get tired of and toss aside for the next pretty nurse who came waltzing in.

It got to the point where people believed I only had a job there because of James. That there was no way I got accepted into the master's program at Harvard on my own. It was all because I was with him. Not because I was actually intelligent and worked my ass off to get into that program.

Everything I did was dimmed because everyone at work started thinking I was getting handouts because of him. Not that I had actually been on the road to success on my own before even meeting him.

The sound of the car door shutting brings me back to reality.

"You ready to head back, Sloan?" August asks quietly.

I nod and start to walk toward the car.

"Everything okay?" Quinn eyes me suspiciously.

"Yeah... Yeah, I'm okay. Just feel for Sutton," I start to say. "And for August too," I whisper to Quinn.

Watching August get in the back seat of Quinn's car, after he opened the driver and passenger side doors for us first. I smile softly to myself, at his silent strength and love. August is larger than life on stage but off the stage he's such a calm, quiet, gentle man. Nothing at all like I'm used to.

"My heart aches for Sutton and August. August really loves her. Sut deserves a love like his and August deserves a love like hers. But her grandmother was everything to her and she isn't going to be ready to go back on stage or on tour while she's grieving. If they're meant to be, like I believe they are, they'll find their way back to each other," Quinn says somberly.

"I hope so. For them," I sigh.

Quinn stretches out her hand over the center console with her palm up toward me. "Let's go check on our girl."

I stare at her hand for just a couple seconds before

weaving my fingers through hers. "Let's." I give her the slightest smile. The tension in my chest releasing just the slightest bit at the feeling of maybe having a really great friend again.

If only I wasn't keeping so many secrets.

10
Sloan

Past

Sitting at my desk in the nurse's station putting in patient orders, Kailey and Maria plop in their chairs next to me.

"Wow. Dr. McAllister really went big with that ring. I'm pretty sure you could see that thing in Paris without binoculars." Kailey gasps dramatically.

"It's gorgeous! What is it? 5 carats?" Maria beams.

"It's... Something like that." I shrug, trying to avoid even looking at it.

My stomach is in knots from the anxiety it gives me to not only wear a ring of this size but the value of this thing, especially at work. I'm constantly terrified I'm going to ruin the diamond. Lose it. It might even fall down the sink when I wash my hands.

It is so gaudy and definitely costs a fortune. He often enjoys reminding me of that fact.

"Reesey, I had that custom made for you. It cost more than your car."

James loves that everyone can see it from a mile away. It's that big. Meanwhile, all I feel is the weight of it and the anxiety it induces.

"Why do I get the sense that you hate it?" Kailey asks, sobering.

"Because I do," I whisper aggressively, looking around to make sure no one else hears my outburst.

"It is kind of ridiculously large. Is he making up for something he's lacking, Reese's Pieces?" Maria giggles trying to lighten the mood.

"Ha-ha" I shake my head. Hoping they'll stop talking about it. It was too soon--is too soon--I still can't wrap my mind around it.

James had reservations for us at the restaurant he took me to on our first date. He had invited my parents, which I didn't know about until we got there. "It was a surprise."

It never even crossed my mind that he would propose.

We were having a really lovely dinner. My father hadn't said anything inappropriate and only had two drinks. My mother seemed like she was enjoying herself. James had been charming as ever but right before they brought out the dessert, he was down on one knee with this gigantic rock out for the entire restaurant to see asking me to be his wife.

"Reesey, I know we haven't been together long but when you know, you know, and I've known since the moment I laid eyes on you. I knew you would be mine forever. Will you marry me?" James asked in such a smooth voice, holding my hand in his, almost hypnotizing me.

My mother and father were smiling so big, tears streaming down my mother's face.

Other guests of the restaurant were eyeing us with expectation and love on their faces.

I stalled for just a moment and I swore I felt the grip on my hand get a little tighter, but I was too busy internally panicking to notice.

"Yes," I whispered.

"She said yes!" my mother cheered.

"Welcome to the family, son," my father said, shaking James' hand.

"In all seriousness, this did all kind of happen very quickly. You went from all celibate independent boss babe to hopelessly in love and getting engaged in what? Six months?" Kailey questions breaking me out of my thoughts.

"Yep!" I say popping the P.

"Soooo... What are we missing?" Maria inquires looking at Kailey and then back to me.

"I don't know. Am I broken? Do you think I'm broken?" I question, my eyes filling with tears.

"Oh honey, no. Why do you think that?" Kailey asks, gently squeezing my hand in hers.

"It's just... I care about James... James is great... He remembers every little thing I tell him. Always gives me those beautiful roses. When we've gone to restaurants, he's taken the initiative and ordered my meals for me. James even talked to my mom on the phone the other night when she called me to check in and they ended up talking wedding details." I sigh, picking at my fingernails.

"I'm pretty sure he told me he loved me after like a month. And I do love him but there's a part of me that always wonders… If we're moving too fast. If James is right for me. If I don't feel how he does. I'm not sure if I can…or if maybe that's something with time…" I try to keep more tears at bay.

"You can't put a time frame on love. Time is an illusion after all," Maria reassures me.

"I haven't really been in many relationships outside of this to really compare it to though. So how do I know for sure if he's the one for me?"

"Do you feel like he sets your soul on fire?" Kailey asks, eyes lighting up with mischief.

"Umm… I'm not really sure what that feels like?" I eye her skeptically.

"Do you feel like the world would end if he wasn't in your life?" Maria chimes in.

"I mean…no? But no one has ever really made me feel that way…" I offer guiltily.

"I can't really even use my parents for guidance. My parents didn't have the best relationship either. I think they love each other in their own way but I don't think they're soul mates or anything.

"My dad used fear to keep my mother in her place when I was younger. He threatened her if she'd threaten to leave. I know they spent some time in counseling and things got a little bit better, but he's still always controlled her in some way, shape or form. I've always tried to live my life so I wouldn't end up in the same situation as her. Unable to leave a man. Afraid to leave. I always thought if I could be so independent, I wouldn't need anyone. If I could do everything on my own, I could prove that women could thrive without a man," I say fiercely.

"You have. Look at everything you've accomplished," Kailey offers at the same time Maria says swooning, "And then you met Silver Daddy."

"Yes, I met Silver Daddy at a time where I still wasn't quite where I wanted to be in my career yet. I still want to and plan to become a nurse practitioner. I don't want a marriage stopping that. I haven't reached all of my goals yet. I wasn't ready for something like this. I do love him but I'm not sure how open my heart truly is to him, you know?" I worry, looking at them for guidance.

"I think you can still love someone and be focused on your career. You just need to have balance. Maybe it feels fast because he crashed into your life when you weren't looking for love, but isn't that what they say anyway? Love comes when you least expect it," Kailey says with so much enthusiasm.

"Maybe… Maybe I just need more time to understand the balance thing. Or maybe I really am broken…and just won't ever be able to love a man like they do in novels and movies," I mutter, a pit forming in my stomach.

"You aren't broken. You love your patients. You love us. You are full of love. You'll figure it out. You always do. And you have us to support you through it all," Kailey declares, giving me a side hug.

If I had known then that my intuition was screaming at me to run. That James actually would set my whole life on fire. That saying yes to a man I had only known for six months would almost ruin my life. End my life. I would have never lost my two best friends. My relationship with my parents. My career. Myself. I wouldn't have had to run. I wouldn't have had to hide.

11

Beck

*L*eaning in the doorway of Sutton's bedroom staring at her lifeless body lying on the floor next to her bed, breaks my heart just the same as it has the last twenty-nine days. It's been four weeks of this and my chest aches for her.

Khaos lies curled up against her, his forehead pressed against hers. He has barely left her side. I've had to coax him to eat just as often as I've tried coaxing Sutton to eat.

Walking over to her, I scoop her up off the floor and put her in bed, pulling the covers up to her chin. Khaos immediately jumps up and positions himself exactly as he was on the floor.

"August?" Sut barely croaks out. Splintering my heart into pieces. She cries out for him in her sleep sometimes too. I wish she'd say my name instead.

Sut seems to be having recurring nightmares too. A few

have seemed similar to the night we spent in Vegas when I had to gently rouse her from sleep.

Pressing my lips to her forehead I ask her, "Why do you keep laying on the floor, Sut?"

"Because you can't fall any further when you're already on the ground," Sut whispers, as another tear falls down her face.

"Oh, Sutton," I say, curling around her, brushing her hair from her face. Just wanting her to let me soothe her.

Sutton rolls toward me but she keeps distance between us. I just wish she'd stop doing that. Doesn't she know by now, I'm here. I am here for her every day. August left. He hasn't come back to check on her in four weeks. Four fucking weeks. I'd never leave my girl that long.

"Beck, what are you doing here?" Sut asks softly. "I appreciate you being here, taking care of Khaos..." she trails off.

"I'm here for you, Sutton. I will always be here for you. August had to go back on tour. None of us wanted you to be here alone. From Troy are still touring. Quinn said the tour got extended because they were selling out every venue," I tell her trying to keep my voice calm.

The sides of her mouth lift the slightest smile at the sound of that news. At the same time, I feel my stomach drop. It's still him. It's never going to be me. No matter what I do.

"Let me take care of you. You won't eat. You barely sleep. You just stare off into space. Every time I come back from the gym; you're lying on the floor with the dogs. You need to get some fresh air. Go back to work, or at least come with me to Vegas next weekend for my fight," I all but beg her.

"Sut, did you hear me?" I ask, noticing she's completely

zoned out.

"Yeah…let me just…" Sut starts to say, pushing up from the bed to head toward the shower.

"Yeah? You'll come to Vegas next week?" I ask, excitement lacing my voice.

"No… I'll try to go back to work." Sut turns her back and shuts the bathroom door.

Burying my head in my hands, I feel like this is my last chance to try to prove to her that I can be the one for her. I don't know what else I can do to show her.

*T*he sound of Khaos whining at the bathroom door pulls me out of my head.

I knock lightly on the door to let her know I'm coming in. It's been forty minutes and the water is still running. I shut off the shower which was now freezing cold.

Sutton just sits with her arms wrapped around her legs. Resting her head on top of her knees.

Turning my head away to try to protect her dignity, I wrap Sutton up in a towel and scoop her off of the floor of the shower.

"What are you doing?" she asks as I carry her into her bedroom.

"You were in there forever, Sutton," I mutter, worry lacing my voice.

"Beck. I'm fine. I'm going to get dressed and go check on things downstairs." Sut looks away, avoiding making eye contact with me.

I tilt her chin so our eyes can meet. "Sutton, please. Let me take care of you."

"Can you find my phone for me please?" Sut asks, flipping the comforter over and digging through her bedsheets for it.

I sigh, "It's on your nightstand."

Sutton scoops her phone up and starts to scroll through it like a woman unhinged. I watch her closely as her facial expressions change rapidly.

"Sutton... Do you think—" I start to ask.

She puts her hand up, as if to stop me from questioning her and then she slides down the wall and sits on the floor.

I notice her jaw drop and tears start streaming down her face. This is the first sign of emotion I've seen since we left the gravesite.

Sutton must be on From Troy's Instagram. They've blown up since the tour.

Not even a minute passes before she's sobbing. Shutting off her phone and lying it face down on the ground. Khaos immediately gets as close to her as he can and Sutton starts running her fingers through his fur as she sobs uncontrollably.

It takes everything in me not to pull her into my arms, but if Sut wanted me, she could have me, and she doesn't want me.

So, I walk out of her room, glancing back one more time as I leave my bleeding heart with the woman who's crying on her bedroom floor over the love of her life.

12
Sloan

I turn at the sound of a door opening behind me in the café as I'm making a latte for a customer. Beck rounds the corner and looks utterly defeated.

"Hey. Sut having a rough morning?"

"Something like that," Beck grumbles.

"I can keep an eye on her today if you want to go to the gym. Maybe get some fresh air. I can run her up some food in a bit."

"Sut's never going to choose me. Is she?" Beck's eyes are filled with so much pain.

"Beck… I…" I start to say.

"Just give it to me straight, Sloan. You're an outsider looking in. You have to see more than Quinn or even Ash."

Beck growls.

I start to take a few steps away from him without even realizing it.

"Fuck. I'm sorry, Sloan. My heart just fucking hurts. Sut cries out for August while she's sleeping. She won't let me hold her. All she does is stare off into space. Now she's up there sobbing. She won't let me help her. Why won't she let me help her?" Beck's voice cracks in agony.

"I don't know Sutton as well as you all do, Beck. I've only seen how much August loves her and how much she loves him. It's obvious Sutton loves you too, but it's different. She looks at both of you so differently."

"Why him though? I just don't get it." Beck mutters.

"I don't know, Beck. I don't have the answers. No one has the right to judge anyone's relationship from the outside. They aren't living it, that couple is. But I will say, Sutton is grieving. She just lost her grandmother. I'm sure it's also bringing up feelings from losing her parents. Sutton selflessly asked her boyfriend to leave her and follow his dreams, while she was grieving—is grieving. This isn't about you. And I know you're hurting because you love her, but you can't expect anything from her right now. Maybe you need to get some space, for your own mental health," I offer genuinely.

"I don't want space!" Beck all but shouts, causing me to instantly jump back and burn my arm on the milk steamer of the espresso machine. I grimace as the metal touches my skin and immediately pull my arm against my body.

"Fuck. Shit. Are you okay?" Beck asks, slowly walking toward me.

"Beck, I think you need to take a walk. Please leave. Quinn and I can keep an eye on Sutton today. I think we all need a bit of space," I say firmly.

"Sloan, no. I am so fucking sorry! Let me see it," Beck pleads, running his hand through his sandy blond hair.

"Beck. Please," I beg, trying to keep myself together.

My ghosts must be shadows haunting my eyes because the second Beck's pain-filled eyes meet mine, he nods his head in understanding, apologizing again. He heads toward the door, shoulders drooping, and leaves the café.

Twenty minutes later, I'm softly humming a Taylor Swift song when I think I hear footsteps.

"Hey... Need any help down here?" Sutton's quiet voice follows.

"Sut! Hi! You're... Yeah, actually. Would you mind helping me get some more macarons from the fridge please? We're running a little low," I ask. Hoping if I give her a small task, instead of questioning her she'll be more comfortable.

"Yeah, I can do that. I'll be right back." Sut gives me a small smile.

A few minutes later Sutton's stocking our pastry case.

"I think I'm going to go to Vegas..." Sutton says so quietly I almost miss what she says.

"For...?" I ask cautiously. Wanting Sutton to know I support whatever decision she makes as long as she's happy.

Sutton turns, her jade eyes meeting my violet eyes. "For... To get away... For August... If he'll have me..."

"August loves you so much, Sut. There's no doubt. It's written all over his face," I reassure her.

"But I-Ibroke us... August might not want me back," Sutton whispers, voice cracking.

"You didn't break anything, Sutton. You are grieving and that looks different for everyone. They say if you love someone set them free and if they come back it's meant to be. And I think you two are magic together." I squeeze her shoulders gently in reassurance.

"Hey Sloan..."

"Yeah?" I smile softly at her.

"Can you just keep an eye on Beck when I'm gone, please? I don't want him to feel alone. I love him, just not..." Sutton says, wiping one lone tear off of her cheek.

"I get it, Sut, you don't have to explain it to me. I'll keep an eye on him. I promise." I pull her to me and give her a gentle hug.

"Thank you," Sutton whispers, squeezing me like I'm a lifeline.

"Thank you. For being such an inspiration, sweet girl." I hug her just the slightest bit tighter.

13

Beck

Ash and I arrived in Vegas three days ago. Usually, we get here a few days early so I can try to adjust to the time difference. No one wants to get in the ring, lacking sleep from jet lag.

There's a knock on my hotel door. I open it, expecting to see Ash, but it's Sutton. I'm taken aback at the sight of her. She told me she was staying back to work when I stopped by to see her before I left. I notice that Sut's arms are wrapped around herself like she's barely holding herself together.

"Sut, baby, what happened?" I ask, going to pull her into a hug.

Except she backs away, shaking her head.

"Can I come in?" she barely croaks out.

"Yeah, of course." I open the door wider for her to walk through.

She starts pacing my room, chewing on her fingernails. When she realizes what she's doing, she stuffs her hands in the pocket of her sweatshirt.

"Sut. Talk to me." I step in front of her, gripping her chin, halting her movements.

"Beck, I love you," she starts to say, tears running down her face.

"I love you too, baby." I smile at her, going to pull her into my arms.

She shakes out of my hold. "Wait, Beck, let me finish, please."

"I love you, and I appreciate everything you've done for me since I lost my grandmother, but I'm not in love with you," Sutton's voice cracks.

"I'm so sorry, Beck. I never meant for this to happen. For years, there was this thing between us that I always wished was more, waiting for something that never was. My heart belonged to you. My rock. My safe harbor. My protector. My shield. You brought so much light into my life when I was drowning in my own darkness. You were always my one constant, your friendship unwavering. Loving you felt safe." She quickly pauses.

"Now, I've realized that's not the kind of love we need. We've been depending on each other for so long we couldn't see beyond that. I need someone who sees me, someone whose demons play well with mine—ours aren't the same. It would be so easy to allow myself to fall, and let you take care of me, but I don't need a protector. I learned I can protect myself. I need to face my demons, not hide from them.

"I will always love you, but as a friend. I hope one day you can forgive me. You deserve someone who is going to love you so fully. Someone who needs your strength and stability, and that warm, kind heart. It's just not me," Sutton says, voice breaking as tears stream down her face.

I watch her face contort into agony, knowing this must be killing her because the thought of hurting anyone always guts her.

"I love you too, Sutton. I've done a lot of thinking these past few months. And I've come to the same realization. You have been such a presence in my life for years. I think I clung to you, for your light, like you clung to me for safety and security. But we aren't meant for each other in that way. You deserve to be so happy.

"I see the way August looks at you and I understand now how he complements you. You're the sun and he's your moon. The moon loves the sun enough to let them shine so brightly. You should never be hidden in the shadows. I hope that we can still be friends. Obviously, that will look different moving forward, but I'm willing to try, because I do love you," I say as warmly as I can.

Sutton swallows hard. Holding my eyes for a beat, making sure I'm being honest with her, as her tears keep coming.

"You mean it?" Sutton barely asks above a whisper, chewing on her bottom lip.

"I mean it," I say, pulling her into a hug.

"I'm so sorry I'm doing this before your fight. I just... I wanted to make sure we knew where we stood with one another before I go talk to August," Sutton apologizes.

"I understand, Sut."

Nodding, she wraps her arms around my waist. And I rest my head on top of hers, just breathing her in. Not quite ready to fully let her go. Sinking into her warmth for just a minute longer since I may never get to hold Sutton like this again.

After a few minutes I break the silence, whispering in her hair, "I have to leave and get ready for my match. Go to

August's show. I'm sure he misses you."

Sutton untangles her arms from my waist and takes a piece of my heart with her.

Opening the hotel door for Sutton, she goes to step out and offers, "Good luck tonight, Beck."

"Thanks, Sut. Same to you." I smile softly at her and gently close the door.

The second the door is closed, I slide to the floor and bury my head in my hands.

My heart annihilated.

I just let it break.

Crying for the first time since my dad walked out on my mom and me all those years ago.

What feels like an eternity, but is only an hour later, I get back up and head out the door for my match against Kenzo King.

"*L*adies and Gentlemen, this is the main event of the evening," I barely hear the announcer say over the roaring of the crowd. The room sounds muffled, almost like I'm under water. I haven't been in the right headspace since Sutton walked out of my hotel room.

My chest shouldn't ache like this. I know that we aren't meant for each other. I've known for a few months but I just couldn't let go of the hope that August wasn't going to be it for her and she'd come back to me. We may have been what we needed for each other at one time, but we aren't those same people anymore. Sutton deserves the absolute best, and if that's August I need to accept that.

It's going to take me some time to truly process losing the chance of a future with her as my girl. But I'll do it for her to at least keep her in my life--whatever way that looks like now.

The referee comes to the center and explains the rules. He confirms that we understand. I think I nod. Then I walk back to my respective corner.

This is one of the biggest fights of my life and I've been preparing for this all year. But I don't even want to be here.

Numb. That's all I feel.

Not excited. Not exhilarated. Not ready to fuck his face up; which is something I've dreamed of doing.

I. Feel. Nothing.

I make my way back to the center of the ring barely noticing Kenzo King snarling at me. We touch gloves.

"Let's go!" the referee yells.

I start to bounce on my feet and before you know it, stars explode behind my eyes and the arena goes dark.

14

Beck

*B*eep... Beep... Beep...

Gods, my head feels like it's been put through a meat grinder!

Beep... Beep...

Why does it smell like Clorox?

Why is it so dark?

What is that groaning sound?

What is that fucking beeping?

"Beck..." a soft female voice.

"Sut?" I think I croak. *Maybe I just think it.*

"Hey, Beck... It's okay... Try to open your eyes," she whispers.

It doesn't sound like Sutton. But that voice is so soft. So soothing.

"Beck... Try to open your eyes. It's me, Sloan," she says softly.

"Beck, man. Open your eyes," Ash says more firmly.

"Maybe he isn't ready yet," that soft voice lulls me back to sleep.

Sloan? Why is Sloan here?

15
Sloan

$\mathcal{B}$eep... Beep... Beep...

The sound of the monitors, seeing Beck lying unconscious has my vision blurring.

I try to rouse Beck to bring myself to the present but it's too late.

Beep... Beep... Beep...

James corners me in the PACU, as I'm monitoring his patients' vitals, who's slow to wake up from anesthesia.

He presses his body against mine from behind. Breathing down my neck. Trying to run his fingers up my scrub top, reaching for my breast.

"James, please stop," I beg in a whisper.

I try to pull away but he has me trapped between him and the patient's bed rail.

His fingers leave my breast but he digs them so hard into my ribs I wince.

"Why would I stop? I can't get in trouble and you're mine to touch whenever I want," James snarls so low in my ear.

"Sloan…" A deep male voice startles me out of my panic. My eyes start to blink rapidly.

"Hey, Sloan. Are you all right?" Asher asks softly.

"Sloan, take a deep breath."

I inhale deeply, then exhale. My breaths start to slow as I focus on Asher's deep brown eyes. I take another breath.

"Sloan…" Asher soothes, his eyes never leaving mine.

"Yeah, I'm okay. Can we wait outside?" I point at the door.

"Yeah. Let's give Beck more time." Ash and I walk side by side toward the door leading into the hallway.

*A*sher and I have been sitting in the waiting room of Summerlin Hospital for what feels like an eternity. I think it's only been a little over twenty-four hours.

It's been so quiet you could hear a pin drop. The only sounds I've heard are the deep sighs leaving Asher's large frame every so often and an occasional page over the loudspeakers.

It's strange sitting next to such a powerful man and not feeling the slightest bit of fear. How did I get to this point?

Quinn and I had been eating today's leftover pastries, watching the fight on pay-per-view in Sutton's apartment, the dogs resting quietly at our feet when Beck took that nasty hit.

The second Kenzo's foot hit the side of Beck's head and he hit the ground immobile, the air whooshed out of both of our lungs. Our eyes bugging out of our heads.

Nothing but silence followed, permeating the room.

We watched speechless as Asher rushed into the ring with several paramedics before Beck was taken away.

Unresponsive.

The sight of the gurney finally snapped us out of our complete and utter shock.

Quinn immediately started blowing up Asher's phone and without even thinking about it I booked the first flight to Vegas I could find.

I'm not sure what came over me or why that was my first instinct. I really should've been more careful but I hadn't even questioned it. All I knew was I needed to help. I needed to be there for Beck.

"Asher said Beck isn't responding. He has a pulse and he's breathing but nothing..." Quinn explains in a panic.

"I booked a flight. I'll fly out there and see if there's anything I can do. At least maybe give Asher a break. We can take shifts. Do you think you can handle things here by yourself?" I'm talking so fast I'm making my own head spin.

"Oh. My. Gosh. Sutton. She probably doesn't even know yet." Quinn shrieks.

"Wait, you booked a flight?" She points a finger, looking questioningly at me. "Are you...sure?"

"Yes, I'll be okay. I figured it made more sense if you stayed. Someone has to watch the dogs and keep an eye on the café." I pause. "Oh gosh, I'm so sorry. I wasn't even thinking. Beck is your friend. You'd probably rather go. I can stay here." I start to panic.

"It's okay, Sloan." She gently squeezes my hand reassuringly. "That makes the most sense. That was fast and

smart thinking on your end. It never even crossed my mind to fly there."

"You're sure?" I ask.

"Positive. Thank you." She gives me a side hug.

I lean into it the slightest bit, letting her warm affection sink in and heal the parts of me. It makes me miss Kailey and Maria just a little extra because I'm feeling comfort for the first time in a long time.

"When is your flight?" Quinn asks.

"Umm"—I open my phone to check again—"shit, 9p.m. and it's seven-fifty."

"Let's get you packed and haul your ass to the airport. I'll call Sut on the way." Quinn jumps up and rushes to my room in Sutton's apartment.

"You're still in the United States. So, if you forget something, like underwear. No biggie," she says with a wink.

"Umm, why would I forget underwear?"

"Why wouldn't you? is the better question." Quinn smirks. "You're in Vegas, baby!"

"Q, I love you, but focus. One of your best friends is on his way to the hospital," I chastise her.

"Okay, fair point. I'm just trying to lighten the mood a little." She chuckles half-heartedly.

I'm packing panties in my carry-on suitcase when I hear her ask quietly, "Beck's going to be okay though, right?"

When I turn to face her, she has tears in her eyes.

"I'll make sure of it," I whisper, leaning my head against her shoulder.

"Why won't he just wake up?" Asher groans under his breath, snapping me out of my daze. Neither of us have hardly slept the past couple days.

"Maybe he just needs a little more time." I gently squeeze Asher's forearm.

"It's been three days, Sloan. How long does it take to wake up from these things?" Asher asks, squeezing the back of his head with both hands. Defeat in his eyes.

"Everyone's different. He's going to be okay though, Ash," I offer gently.

"You can't promise that. You heard the doctor. They said they don't think he should fight again. If he takes another hit like that he could die. And if he hears them say that, he's going to wish he died. This is his life, Sloan." Asher's voice cracks in agony.

"Beck is going to have to rest for a while. He'll eventually have to recondition again. The doctor said he shouldn't fight but that doesn't mean he has to quit. It's just a suggestion. Beck could recover." I state, trying to console Asher.

"Beck 'could' recover, but he could also have brain damage. The doctor even said Beck could have memory loss." Asher leans his head against the wall.

"Ash..." I whisper. "There are so many possibilities and outcomes for this and it's incredibly scary. No one wants Beck to lose his dream or his memory. The most important thing is that he is alive. The doctor said Kenzo missed his temple by a centimeter. Beck could've died, but he didn't. It may be a tough road but we will all get him through this. Physically he will recover. I'm more worried about how this will affect him mentally." Resting my hand on Asher's back.

"Sloan, what if he forgets Sutton left? What is he going to do with all of his bottled-up anger? Beck needs an outlet to stay level headed and that's hitting things and working out hours a day. Beck is going to be a bastard to deal with," Asher sighs. "You saw how he was when Sutton left the first time. I'm surprised the bag at the gym doesn't have a hole in it."

"I know. Maybe he can get a therapist, find something low impact he can do to keep himself busy," I offer.

"Yeah, right. Beck will go to therapy when pigs fly," Asher sighs.

"Mr. Ward?" The nurse pokes her head in the waiting room.

"That's me," he responds, walking toward the nurse.

"Mr. Scott is awake. Speak softly. No screens," the nurse states.

"Yes, ma'am. Thank you." He nods, ready to follow her.

Asher stops abruptly, turning to hold his hand out for mine. I stare at it for just a second before I gently slide my hand in his.

A whisper of a smile graces Asher's lips, as his very large hand engulfs my very small one and he holds it so gently. The gesture almost brings tears to my eyes.

It's as if he knows that this little bit of trust I'm giving him is huge for me. He gives me the slightest little squeeze in appreciation as we make our way to Beck's hospital room hand in hand.

I feel a sense of calm like I haven't felt in a long time washing over me. *I am safe.*

16

Beck

The second Asher and some tiny girl with jet black hair enter my hospital room, I jump down his throat with questions.

"What the hell happened, man?" I bark. Giving myself an instant headache with the tone of my voice.

"You might want to lower your voice so you don't give yourself a migraine. The nurse told us to be quiet, asshat. Probably means you should keep your voice down too," Asher voices, giving me shit right back.

"Why am I here?" I ask, irritated that so many cords and tubes are attached to me.

"You don't remember?" Asher questions eyeing me suspiciously and then looking at the petite girl next to him.

"You aren't going to introduce me to your friend?" I grit out, eyeing her suspiciously. "You have a girlfriend I don't know about?"

"Hi, Beck..." the girl starts, her voice so soft and soothing. Almost familiar even.

"I'm Sloan. I'm friends with Sutton and Quinn. I've taken your self-defense class with them," she says, her unique colored eyes tracing my face as if she knows me.

"Beck. Your fight with Kenzo King..." Asher begins.

"Fuck. Get me out of here! I need to get back to the gym to keep training. It's in a few weeks. There's no way that asshole is taking my belt," I grind out.

Sloan and Asher share a look between each other before they both look at me solemnly.

"Beck..." he says, leaning against the windowsill as a doctor walks in.

"Good evening, Mr. Scott, I'm Dr. Hadley. It's good to finally see you awake. You had us worried there for a bit. You sustained a pretty serious concussion. You had lost consciousness for quite a while. Thankfully you did not sustain any skull fractures or intracranial hemorrhage when we reviewed your CT scan," he informs me.

"I'm sorry, what's an intracranial hemorrhage? Layman's terms, doc." I try to make a joke.

"It just means you didn't have a brain bleed or a fracture, Beck. That's a good thing," Sloan answers softly.

"Yes, what your friend said. Your scans are all okay. You were unconscious longer than we would've hoped. We watched the video of your injury and you were hit incredibly hard and very close to your temple," he continues.

"What video? What injury? Did you swing too hard at me at practice, Ash?" I ask sarcastically, looking over at Asher, who looks weary now that I really look at him.

Dr. Hadley clears his throat, "In any case, we're anticipating some short-term memory loss but it shouldn't last for more than a few weeks."

"Memory loss? What memory loss? My memory is

fine!" I say appalled.

"Actually, Beck, man," Asher utters, scratching the side of his head like he's uncomfortable. "You already had your match against Kenzo and lost. And you...umm...don't remember."

"You also know me fairly well," Sloan says so faintly I almost miss it.

"What? I lost to that fucker. He took my belt," I growl and go to stand up, ripping at the tubing in my arm.

"Mr. Scott, please sit and calm yourself down," Dr. Hadley instructs, trying to gently push me back down on the bed.

"Get your hands off of me!" I yell.

"Beck. Man, relax." Ash grabs me by the arm and shoves me back down.

Dr. Hadley takes a step back and that's when I notice Sloan is scrunched up against the furthest wall away from me in my room. She looks terrified as she begins to sit in a chair, wrapping her arms around her knees.

Is she scared of me?

"Sir, please take a breath. All of this commotion is not conducive for your healing. You sustained a pretty severe concussion, but it doesn't appear there was any permanent damage. However, with the location of your injury and the length of time you were unconscious there are some concerns. You will need to rest for several weeks. No heavy lifting. No fighting. No running. Limit screen time and loud sounds," the doctor states firmly.

A wave of nausea takes over me, and I vomit before I can respond.

Great.

Dr. Hadley jumps back to avoid getting sprayed. But I

end up with vomit all over myself.

Walking into the bathroom, he comes back out with a cool washcloth, handing it to me, before continuing. "Typically, we'd have you rest the first 48 hours. It's been 72, so you can get up and start doing some light walking. If you go outside, please wear sunglasses. The lights can trigger a migraine. The nausea and vomiting could persist for a few more days. I do not recommend getting back in the gym and training for at least a month."

"A month! What the hell am I going to do for a month if I can't go to the gym?" I bark at him.

"Beck, you can still teach the self-defense classes. You just can't participate," Sloan offers from the corner she's still tucked away in.

"How am I supposed to teach if I can't show you what to do?" I all but growl at her.

"You have us work with each other. You don't have to exert yourself!" Sloan bites back.

"Will either of you make sure he follows up with a neurologist back in your hometown?" Dr. Hadley asks. "I imagine you won't be staying in Vegas for a month."

"We're in Vegas?" I ask, turning and trying to look out the window. The second I turn my head another wave of nausea comes over me.

This time Sloan must notice I'm going to be sick because she's running toward my bed and shoving a bedpan under my face as I projectile vomit into it.

"Thanks," I grumble. Taking another fresh washcloth from her hand that appeared out of nowhere to wipe my face.

"You'd make a great nurse with those reflexes," the doc points out and looks at Sloan smiling.

"Thank you, sir. I actually—" Sloan starts to say.

"Can I take a shower?" I ask Dr. Hadley, interrupting her.

"Please do. I am planning to discharge you tomorrow. Get some rest," he says, pointing at me. "And please keep him in line," Dr. Hadley directs Sloan.

"Yes, sir." Sloan salutes him.

Asher chuckles and bumps shoulders with her.

"Prick," I groan under my breath.

"Let's get your stank ass in the shower." Asher whistles.

"I will get myself in the shower, thanks." I glare at him.

"There's a great neurologist in Pittsburgh not far from the café. I will call and see if they can get you in to be seen in a few weeks," Sloan offers.

"I don't need to be seen, Little Bird..." I groan, getting myself up out of the bed and walking to the bathroom. I'm feeling a bit dizzy as I make my way to the sink.

"You remembered," Sloan whispers, walking cautiously behind me.

"Remembered what?" I question, meeting her eyes in the mirror.

"Well...you usually call me, Little Dove, but that's close." Sloan smiles softly at me.

"It makes sense, you are so pint-size and fragile looking. Easily broken," I scoff.

Sloan is in my face so fast. "Just because you're hurting, Beckett, doesn't give you a right to be a dick."

And just as fast she came up beside me, she ends up walking out of the bathroom and slamming the door shut behind her.

"You really are a dick. Sloan flew all the way here to

help you. Since we've met her, she's tried staying in the shadows and she got on a plane for your ass. Quit pushing people away with your shitty attitude," Asher says through the door. Then I hear the door to my hospital room open and close for the second time in just a few minutes.

I'm met with silence and my horrifying reflection in the mirror.

"Fuck!" I press my head against the cold mirror in the bathroom.

My face looks like hell. Bruises of all shades from purple to yellow litter the right side of my face and ear.

How the hell am I going to get through these next few months?

And why the hell isn't Sutton here?

17
Sloan

Beck has been a bear to deal with since we got back from Vegas a couple weeks ago. Eventually he did apologize for his dickish behavior. After he was discharged from the hospital, the three of us stayed two extra days in Vegas cooped up in one hotel room until Beck wasn't having dizzy spells and nausea anymore.

Usually, I wouldn't be comfortable sharing a room with a man, let alone two. Two very fit men who could break me in half, except I've never really felt safer. Watching them lay in the same bed so I could have my own is probably the cutest thing I've ever witnessed. I giggle just thinking about it.

"Ash, you wanna be my big spoon?" Beck chuckles and then groans.

"Awwww, does chuckling make your head hurt, punk?" Asher grits out, trying to stretch out without touching Beck.

"Remind me again why the fuck we're sharing a room

when you make so much money?" Asher asks, shoving a pillow between him and Beck.

"Well since I lost this last fight and won't be fighting anytime soon. I gotta save money," Beck offers with annoyance lacing his voice.

"Actually, we're sharing a room to keep an eye on Beck," I whisper.

"I could've kept an eye on myself, Little Dove," Beck grumbles.

"Yeah, yeah. Everyone go to sleep. I'm trying to sleep," Asher sighs.

Beck thankfully slept most of the plane ride back to Pittsburgh.

Asher and I talked quietly amongst ourselves.

We tried to come up with a plan to keep Beck as active as possible without overexerting himself. But every idea we've suggested Beck has shot down.

Beck's tried to show up at the gym to work out several times and has been kicked out by one person or another. Which has only pissed him off more. He thinks we're all "ganging up on him."

Quinn said he's been stopping by the café multiple times throughout the day, driving her crazy because he's bored. She made him wipe down some tables and re-organize a few of the bookshelves to make himself useful, getting him out of her hair.

A few of the trainees have said that Beck keeps trying to give them advice on their workouts but he's nitpicking every little thing, irritating them too.

Every time Beck runs into me, he responds like a Neanderthal with grunts because he's sick of being told what to do.

Even Mayhem seems sick of his shit at this point. Rolling his eyes and letting out annoyed whimpers when his dad lashes out.

*W*alking into the gym to work out myself, I notice Beck lacing up his shoes. He heads toward the treadmill, but one of the younger athletes immediately notices and rushes over and beats him to it, "Sorry Beck, I gotta warm up. Boss's orders."

Beck immediately throws his fist into one of the padded walls and lets out a deep frustrated growl, "It's been three and a half weeks. Give me a fucking bone."

I flinch when his fist hits the wall. But I end up smiling because the young athlete is laughing as he starts jogging on the treadmill, hollering out, "Mayhem probably has one you can borrow!"

Beck snarls at the poor kid, before he heads toward the front door. The second he's out the door he takes off running down the sidewalk.

"Shit," I whisper under my breath. I decide to follow Beck, just in case something happens to him.

Beck starts out running at least a little slower, but about ten minutes into his version of a jog he really starts ramping up his pace. I try my best to keep up with him, but his legs are probably three times the length of mine and I can't even if I tried.

"What the hell are you doing?" Beck yells, stopping abruptly.

I almost crash into him, but he puts his hands out to

stop me from colliding into his frame.

"I should be asking you the same thing," I yell back, looking up at him.

"Why do you have to be so small, Little Dove?" Beck groans.

"Excuse me?" I bite out.

"Your legs are so damn short. You can't keep up with me! I'm not going to just let you run in this park alone, but you're slowing me down and I need to fucking run. I have too much cooped up energy," Beck yells out, before he takes off in a jog again.

"So, you knew I was following you and you kept running anyways," I growl, running after him.

"Of course, I knew. Do you think I run this slow regularly?" Beck questions sarcasm laced in his tone.

"This isn't slow. Quit running from your problems. The doctor said you can't do more than jog this week, Beckett. Why are you so damn stubborn?" I holler.

"Why doesn't anyone understand I need to let off steam? I need to workout or my thoughts catch up to me," Beck blurts out and then immediately looks ashamed.

I stop abruptly on the sidewalk in the park. Bent over at the waist trying to catch my breath.

"Are you okay?" Beck asks softly, walking up to me.

"Cramp. Not..." I let out a deep exhale. "Not a runner."

"So why are you running with me then?" Beck questions.

"If you won't take care of you then I'm sure as hell going to," I say, taking another deep breath.

"I don't need to be taken care of," Beck grumbles.

"Everyone needs to be taken care of," I cry out.

"What if I run with you on my shoulders? Then I can run and don't have to worry about leaving you in my dust," Beck jokes and reaches for me like he's going to try to lift me up.

"Nope. Absolutely not. Don't you dare. Keep your hands to yourself, Beckett," I shout.

"Shit. Okay, sorry." Beck backs off. "No need to shout."

"Beck. You are running when you were told not to. You have tried to go to the gym daily, when you were told not to. You literally just said you don't want your thoughts to catch up to you. That you need an outlet to let off steam. What if you actually talked about your thoughts? Sometimes releasing it is the best thing you can do," I offer, sitting down on the grass, crossing my legs.

"What the hell are you doing? Get up," Beck barks at me.

"No." I shout at him.

"What do you mean, no?" Beck comes closer to me.

"How does it feel?" I ask.

"How does what feel?" Beck looks at me so confused.

"How does it feel for me to defy you? For me to tell you no? For me not to listen to you? Over something so benign?" I ask, lying back, looking up at the sky.

"Sloan. Get off the ground. It's filthy," Beck barks.

"Answer the question, Beck," I say, pretending to do snow angels in the grass to irritate him some more.

"I don't need to answer your question," Beck says frustrated, running his hand through his sweaty blond hair.

"And I don't need to get off the ground," I say matter of fact, looking up at him.

"It's not the same." Beck throws his hands in the air.

"It is," I affirm. "You want me to do something and I want you to do something but neither of us agrees with the other because we're both being stubborn. You're running from your past and so am I. You don't like being told no. I'm tired of not being able to say no. You don't like to give up control. I am trying to take back my control."

"Fine," Beck says, lying down next to me.

"Fine what?" I ask quietly, rolling over onto my side to face him.

"I'll stop trying to do too much," Beck says so softly I almost don't hear him. "But I want you to train with me."

"Why?" I sit up questioning him.

"Because I know you're running from something too and I want you to feel ready if your past comes back for you." Beck sits up and leans his shoulder into mine.

"Okay," I whisper before a squeak leaves my body and I'm being lifted into the air.

"Put me down!" I smack Beck's shoulders.

"Let me give you a piggyback ride back. It's low impact resistance training." Beck winks at me while he's still holding me in the air.

"Ugh. You're a caveman," I squeal.

"I know," Beck says so quietly, still holding me suspended in the air like I weigh nothing.

"Fine. My legs are tired from trying to keep up with your ass. Squat down, please," I push on his shoulders to get him to lower himself so I can climb on his back.

Beck gives me a little boost and then he's off and jogging again. Carrying me like a baby koala on his back. Giggles erupt from me. A sound I don't think I've ever heard myself make.

"You have a great laugh, Little Dove. I need to hear it more often," Beck says sweetly as he continues to run.

Warmth and something like hope, spreads through me. As a fissure in my heart fills in with the slightest bit of glue. I hold onto Beck just a tad tighter and let myself give in just the littlest bit to the feeling of safety that washes over me being held in his strong arms.

"I'm starving!" Beck says as I hear his stomach grumble.

"Take me back to the café and I'll whip us up some breakfast." Gripping his neck a little tighter.

"You better eat with me, Little Dove."

I growl at him and dig my nails into his chest.

"Please eat with me?" Beck asks sweetly.

"Okay." I ruffle his hair, smiling to myself.

"You're a feral, little thing," Beck comments with a chuckle.

"You're a Neanderthal," I joke back.

Beck laughs and I sink a little deeper into his hold.

18

Beck

We head upstairs into Sutton's apartment where Sloan has been staying since she left for tour.

I've started remembering bits and pieces of the conversation Sutton and I had prior to my fight with Kenzo King but I can't remember all of it. Maybe that's for the best.

Just like I still can't remember the fight since it happened so fast. Perhaps I never will.

Looking around with fresh eyes, I notice the apartment looks tidier. I'm not surprised since Sloan tends to clean when she's anxious.

"Can you put the ingredients in the fridge, please? I'm going to shower really quick and then I'll make us some omelets and coffee," Sloan says, gently putting her hand on my back.

"I can start cutting some of the vegetables while you shower," I offer.

"That would be great. Thank you." Sloan smiles before she walks down the hall to the spare bathroom next to her bedroom.

I catch her out of the corner of my eye staring at me for a

brief minute before I hear the bathroom door click shut.

I wonder what that was about?

The sound of the water running has my mind remembering Sutton showering in the hotel room in Vegas. She was almost mine, but that feels like an eternity ago.

And now she's his... I feel my heart cave in on itself.

My phone ringing startles me out of my thoughts and I just miss slicing my finger with the knife as I'm chopping up green bell peppers.

"This is Beck Scott," I answer on the third ring, irritation lacing my voice.

"Hi, yes, Mr. Scott, this is your landlord, Mrs. Hazel. I was calling to let you know that we unfortunately had a water main break that has flooded your entire floor. We are evacuating the building and planning repairs but it could take a few weeks. I knocked on your door but only heard your dog barking," Mrs. Hazel continues.

"Is Mayhem okay?" I question anxiously.

"Yes, Mr. Scott. He is currently sitting on your sofa. I'm sorry for going in without you being here but I was worried he may be in danger. He's quite the ham. I'm not sure if you're able to come get him. We are hoping to get everyone out of here today. We are waiving your rent this month and next to help offset any hotel fees you may have," Mrs. Hazel says nervously.

"That won't be necessary for me but thank you, ma'am. I am on my way," I say, hanging up the phone.

I'm making my way down the hallway to the bathroom to let Sloan know when she opens the bathroom door.

All the air leaves my lungs at the sight of her.

Long black hair is braided down her back. A sage green crop T-shirt shows off her tapered waist and porcelain skin. Tight black leggings cling to her toned legs. Her little feet are bare, toenails painted the softest pink. Those big lavender doe eyes appear almost innocent staring up at me.

So innocent. So vulnerable. So...gorgeous.

"Hey, is everything okay?"

"Umm..." I clear my throat, snapping myself out of just staring at her.

"Beck, you're making me kind of anxious." Twisting the hem of her T-shirt in her hands.

"Sorry, yeah... My landlord just called. Apparently, my apartment flooded. They need me to go get Mayhem and try to find a place to stay."

"Oh my gosh. Is he okay?" Sloan gasps. "Let me grab some shoes. I'll come with you."

"Yeah. She said he was okay. They're just trying to clear everyone out. You don't have to. I'm going to call Ash and see--" I start to say.

"I'm sure Sut would let you stay here instead of getting a hotel. They won't be back for another couple months," Sloan offers while cutting me off.

"You... You'd be okay with that?" I ask, eyeing her curiously.

"Yeah, if you are. I'm not sure if that's weird. Staying in her room or staying here with me, but you stayed here when everything happened with her grandma. I don't see why not. Obviously it's up to you and to her since this isn't even my place. I'd love to see Mayhem more too because I miss Khaos—" Sloan is rambling and talking so fast, wringing her hands.

"Little Dove." I interrupt her, gently stroking her cheek with my thumb.

She blinks rapidly up at me, "Yeah?" Sloan's almost breathy.

"If Sut is okay with it, that would be great. You can help keep me in line." I wink at her to ease some of the tension.

A knock on the door startles us both.

Instinctively I step in front of Sloan and walk toward the door to answer it. Trying to keep her hidden behind me while I answer the door.

I'm not sure why I feel so protective of her all of a sudden.

When I turn around to smile at Sloan, she's already disappeared into her room.

"Aaaand what do we have here?" Quinn asks slyly when I open the door to her shit-eating grin and she pops up on her tiptoes, trying to look over my shoulder to see if anyone is in the room with me.

"I was just heading out, Q. Mind your business." I bop her on the nose with my index finger.

"Actually, we both were," Sloan says, stepping up beside me. I never even heard her sneak back out here.

Quinn looks at both of us suspiciously, eyes going back and forth between the two of us.

"My apartment flooded. I have to go get Mayhem," I tell Quinn walking past her in the stairwell.

"I'm going with him and calling Sutton on the way to see if she'll let him stay in her room," Sloan informs Quinn.

"Ohhhh, I love it. What a great idea," Quinn squeals running down the stairs after us, texting someone at the same time.

"Q, you're going to eat shit, if you don't watch where you're going," I scold her.

"I've walked these steps plenty of times while tipsy, Beckett. Mind your business." Quinn says, bopping me on the nose like I did to her.

"Wait, love what?" Sloan and I ask in unison.

"This is about to be a forced close proximity romance for my two besties," Quinn squeals, aggressively typing on her phone.

"That is like a top fave trope for me. It's perfect. Perfect. Perfect!"

"Quinn…" Sloan and I say at the same time again.

"See! You're already starting each other's sentences. Just you wait and see." Quinn squeaks, pulling Sloan under one of her arms and me under the other.

The three of us squeeze down the rest of the stairs. "See you later soon-to-be love birds." Quinn blows us kisses as we leave.

We're not even five steps down the sidewalk before Quinn comes running out of the café. "Sut said no banging in her bed, but welcome home!"

Sloan and I share a look before we both burst into laughter.

"She's insane." We both start cackling.

"And just FYI," Quinn shouts. "That leaves a lot of other surface area to use for science."

"For science?" I question, laughing at Quinn's dramatics and the look of terror mixed with, is that mischief, from Sloan.

"Welcome home." Sloan nudges me in the side trying and failing to hold in more laughter.

"Home, sweet home, Little Dove." I tuck her under my arm where she fits perfectly, as we continue to walk to my apartment.

The smallest sigh leaves her and I feel her sink just a little closer into me.

19
Sloan

The sight of Mayhem laying on the sofa while Mrs. Hazel gives him belly rubs has me giggling the second we walk into Beck's apartment. He's sprawled out on his back, tongue sticking out to the side of his mouth with the goofiest grin on his face.

My giggles are snuffed out by the sight of at least a foot of water filling up his living room. It almost makes it seem like the sofa is floating with Mayhem and Mrs. Hazel sitting on it.

Which has me giggling again.

"Something funny, Little Dove?" Beck lets out a small huff, eyeing me with curiosity.

"They just look like they're floating. I'm envisioning this couch was on the Titanic and it went overboard and these two are just sitting on it so they don't drown. But really Mayhem is just loving life, eating up all of the attention without a care in the world," I ramble in between muffled laughter.

Mrs. Hazel looks around and starts laughing too. "It really does, dear."

"I'm really sorry this happened, ma'am. I hope you have insurance. Did anyone get hurt?" I ask.

"Thankfully almost everyone was at work. Just had to make some phone calls to some unhappy tenants but hopefully everyone can find a place to stay," Mrs. Hazel says solemnly.

"If you need help with anything, please let me know. I have some down time right now in my training so I'd be happy to help if needed," Beck offers, kindly.

I smile softly at his kindness and patience with his landlord.

"Well at least I don't have to worry about you, Mr. Scott. I imagine you can stay with your pretty girlfriend?" She smiles adoringly at me.

"Sloan's not my..."

"Beck's not my..." Beck and I say at the same time.

"Ahhh. Time will tell, my darlings. Anyways, let's get you all out of here." Mrs. Hazel jumps up from the sofa.

Mayhem lets out a disheartened sigh.

"Come on you goober. Let's get out of here." I chuckle, clipping a leash into his collar.

"If you want to take him outside, I'm going to grab some clothes—" Beck starts.

"Okay. I'll grab some toys and dog food out of your kitchen and meet you outside." I smile at Beck and then flinch, realizing I interrupted him.

"I'm... I'm sorry for...interrupting you," I offer, my eyes cast down.

"Sloan," Beck whispers, lifting my chin. "You have nothing to be sorry for. Thank you for helping me."

Beck kisses the side of my head and then disappears down the hall. Leaving me standing there staring off after him, tension immediately leaving my body at that smallest affection.

Once I fill a few grocery bags with essentials for Mayhem and some groceries from Beck's fridge, I grab the leash and head outside.

Sitting on the stairs of Beck's apartment complex with Mayhem's body pressed against my leg and his sweet face resting on my lap. I close my eyes and tilt my face to the sun and let the rays warm my cheeks. It's a beautiful fall day. Not too warm, not too cool.

I've always loved dogs, but James hated animals. They were too messy and took time away from him.

I'm running my fingers through Mayhem's fur, taking in this moment of peace when the hair on the back of my neck stands at attention. My eyes immediately shoot open as I look around anxiously. Not a soul is walking along the sidewalk and Mayhem still rests calmly at my side. My distress doesn't appear to have set off any alarm bells for him.

Breathe, Sloan. James has no idea where you are.

"Ready?" Beck startles me when he comes out of the apartment door.

Shooting up from the stairs, "Yeah…yeah…ready," I stammer

"You okay?" Beck tilts his head.

"Yep!" I start walking down the stairs. Mayhem's lead rests in my left hand.

"Here, let me take those." Beck gently removes the

grocery bags from my right hand.

"It's okay. I got it. You're carrying enough," I offer, reaching for the bags.

"Little Dove," Beck whispers firmly.

My eyes immediately meet his. As if that slight firmness from him calls to me.

"Okay, but I'm hanging on to Mayhem."

"Yes, ma'am." Beck winks at me.

I elbow him right in the gut and take off running with Mayhem. When I turn around to check on him, Beck's pretending to be bent over in agony.

Mayhem and I make our way back toward Beck when I notice a white rose laying on the stairwell two doors down from where I had been sitting not long ago.

I'm frozen to the spot.

All the hair stands up on my skin.

My heart starts beating rapidly.

My vision starts to get splotchy.

My ears are ringing.

My chest feels tight. Am I even breathing?

No.

No.

No.

Not possible.

20

Beck

When I look up and see Sloan walking back toward me, her face goes from humor to terror in an instant.

"Hey, what is it?" I ask, immediately pulling her close to me.

Sloan is trembling in my arms. Her skin is pale, like she's seen a ghost.

I rub small circles on her back and run my hands gently through her hair to try and calm her. "Take a deep breath through your nose and then blow it out, Sloan. I'll do it with you. Ready?"

I breathe in and out, but she's unmoving, a statue.

"Come on, Little Dove. Please? Deep breath in." I inhale deeply and finally feel her do the same against my chest before blowing out. "Now exhale."

"Good girl. Again." We inhale in unison and then exhale.

"One more time, baby," I encourage and feel her take another breath.

"Please talk to me. What happened?" I ask quietly, gently running my hands up and down her arms to try to stop the trembling.

"I…" she starts.

"There was…" She can't seem to get her words out.

"A white…" Sloan starts to cry.

"The rose?" I whisper, pulling her closer to me.

Mayhem presses his head into her legs from behind her, as we cocoon her between us.

"Yeah." Sloan hiccups.

"My ex. H-h-he used to…" Sloan breaks in my arms. Sobbing and shaking.

"It's okay, Sloan. I have you. You're safe. It's just me. Not him," I promise into her hair, keeping her close to my chest.

Her tiny fists dig into my chest through my shirt.

I feel her tears, my shirt sticking to my skin where they soak through.

"I got you, Little Dove. I got you," I continue to promise her.

"Can w-w-we…" Sloan starts to ask.

"G-g-go please?" Sloan whimpers.

"Yes, baby, come on." I pick up the groceries with one hand. I tuck her under my other arm holding her close to me while we walk back in silence. Mayhem heels perfectly, walking as close to her as he can get on her other side.

When we get inside, Sloan makes sure every lock on each door is locked several times. I put Mayhem's food away in the kitchen and my groceries in the fridge that she thoughtfully packed.

I run my duffel bags to Sutton's room as fast as I can so

I can get back to Sloan.

She's mindlessly cracking eggs into a bowl, staring off into space when I come back into the kitchen. I gently place my hand over hers as she's about to crack another egg. Her fingers are trembling beneath mine. I wrap my arms gently around her from behind, as she lets the egg fall onto the counter and flinches.

I reach for a towel, wiping her fingers off and then tuck her arms around her waist as I hug her, pulling her in so she leans back against my chest. I rest my head on the side of hers as I just stand there holding her.

I let her know that she's safe. Bringing her to the present moment and trying to pull her out of her thoughts that she seems to be trapped in. After a few minutes pass and I finally feel her melt into me. I gently kiss the side of her head. "Why don't you go sit on the couch with Mayhem. I'll make the omelets and coffee. How about you pick out a movie for us to watch?" I whisper in her ear.

A single tear falls from her eyes and lands on my forearm wrapped gently around her waist.

"Okay," Sloan whispers. "Thank you."

Sloan slowly pads over to the living room, never turning to meet my eyes. I watch as she pulls a baby blue throw off of the back of the couch, wrapping it around herself. The second she lays down Mayhem curls up and rests against her feet.

As I start making the omelets and turn Sutton's fancy latte maker on, I notice that Sloan has stopped scrolling and has Ten Things I Hate About You up and ready to press play on the tv.

"Oooh, that's a good throwback."

When Sloan turns to answer me, her eyes are a little brighter and the color is back in her cheeks.

"It's my comfort movie," Sloan says softly, running her nails through Mayhem's fur.

I bet they'd feel good in my hair.

"Well, it's a great choice." I walk over to bring her a veggie omelet and a toffee nut latte.

Sloan takes a sip of her latte and the tiniest moan leaves her. "How did you know?" Sloan asks.

"Know what?" I play dumb. I've watched Sloan make her and Quinn these lattes for the past few months. I know it's her favorite.

"That toffee is my favorite?" Sloan smiles at me, taking another sip.

"Well, you see… One time this girl threw a solid upper cut of coffee on me and it smelled really nutty, so I just sort of guessed," I say, trying to lighten the mood.

"That was an accident. You scared me that day," Sloan shrieks, gently punching me in the arm.

"I know, Little Dove. I'm only teasing you." I nudge her shoulder with mine as she presses play on the movie.

She takes a few bites of her omelet and is silent for a few minutes. "This is perfect. Thank you, Beck."

Sloan puts her plate down on the coffee table and picks up her latte taking another sip.

"Of course, Little Dove."

When she faces me, I turn my body to face her, so she knows I'm willing to listen to whatever she's about to say.

Sloan eyes me suspiciously before asking, "No really, how did you know?"

"Because I see you, Little Dove," I say, staring in those eyes before turning to watch the movie.

"I couldn't have these with my ex. Hazelnut and toffee

nut were always my favorite lattes, but he had a nut allergy. So I used to have to get caramel or vanilla, which was fine but not my favorite. It's nice to be able to enjoy them again." Sloan fumbles with her words.

I watch as she fidgets under her blanket out of my periphery before I pretend to cough and lift up my arm. Within seconds Sloan's nestling under my arm, resting her head on my chest. I pull the blanket up over her and tuck her in.

"You deserve to enjoy all of the little things you want," I whisper.

Mayhem snuggles up against her feet on the other side of the couch while Sloan burrows in closer to me. The fact that I'm able to bring her comfort, softens my heart even more for her.

I'm convinced Sloan is asleep by how softly she's breathing but then I hear her whisper, "I see you, too, Beck. Thank you for this."

21

Sloan

The sound of the water running has me slowly fluttering my eyes open. For a second, I forget where I am. My heartbeat and my breaths start to pick up in a panic. Why is there water running?

I sit up from the warm cocoon I fell asleep in, when Mayhem pokes his head through the blanket, I just accidentally tossed over top of him in my panic. I forgot he was here. That means...

I exhale a deep breath and take a moment to center myself.

Beck is in the shower.

Not James.

Why would a random white rose just be sitting on those stairs? James always used to leave me white roses. Growing them on his property was something he prided himself on. I was never allowed in the garden, but he always made sure there were fresh roses in the house for me every few days or left on my desk at work. Always white. James refused to grow any with color. He said it tainted the pureness of them.

I'd felt like someone was watching me when I was standing on the staircase of Beck's apartment. And then that rose appeared.

There's no way James found me. How could he when I didn't leave a trail? I brought cash with me when I left except for— Fuck. I wasn't even thinking. James would've gotten an alert that I bought a plane ticket with the credit card. But it wouldn't show where I flew out from, would it?

I'm spiraling into a panic attack when footsteps pad into the living room. I realize I still haven't even gotten up from the couch.

"Hey, is everything okay?" Beck asks cautiously.

I hear him but I can't form words.

His large hand grazes my chin, tilting my head up to look into his eyes.

"Little Dove, you're worrying me."

Blinking rapidly at him, "I... What if...what if he found me? I have to leave, Beck."

I go to jump up off the couch but in seconds, Beck is lifting me in his arms, cradling me. He sits back down on the couch where I had been sitting, holding me in his arms.

Why does he feel so good? I never felt like this with James. And Beck is a force, so much taller and thicker and stronger than James. Why am I not afraid of Beck like I am James?

"Talk to me, Little Dove. No more running," Beck requests.

"I... My ex... James used to grab me too hard, leaving bruises. Sometimes he'd shove me down, grab me by the hair and scream in my face. I had to hide so many marks he left." Beck goes rigid behind but he holds me tighter in his arms.

Beck's unyielding strength gives me the courage to open up a little more to him than I did before.

My voice starts to crack. "I was afraid of J-J-James. I had to walk on eggshells all the time, especially when he got d-d-drunk. Sometimes I still feel like he's watching me, like he's going to f-f-find me. There are times I feel like I c-c-can't breathe. I'm paralyzed in fear like he still has his hooks in me. I hope I never s-s-see him again for as long as I live." I struggle to get the words out to Beck. Trying to fight back the sob that wants to break free.

Beck is a statue behind me. Anger coming off of him in waves as Beck growls out, "You never deserved that, Sloan. No man has any right to ever lay their hands on you. He will never touch you again. I swear to you he won't get the chance."

"You can't promise that, Beck. What if James found me? The rose... Maybe I need to leave. I never should've stayed this long," I whisper with tears streaming down my face.

"Yes, I can, Little Dove. I will do everything in my power to keep you safe. Do you want to be on the run and have to look over your shoulder the rest of your life? No, it's time you take your power back. It's time you learn to protect yourself. Let him find you after we've trained together. Let me train you so that you are prepared with an arsenal in your back pocket. An arsenal that James won't see coming if he finds you and I'm not there to protect you myself," Beck almost begs. So much determination on his face.

"How am I going to be able to take down a guy though? He was always so much stronger than me and he always made me feel so weak. If he wasn't beating me down with his fists, James was breaking me down with his words," I say ashamed, curling in on myself.

"Sloan. You. Are. Not. Weak. You may be pint-size, Little Dove but you are so fucking brave. So strong for getting out of a bad situation. I will train you as hard as I train our athletes. Train you like I train for fights and add self-defense techniques from the class. Ash even knows some knife training skills that we can incorporate. I'll have Ash create a nutrition plan for you too, to make sure you're getting enough nutrients to build muscle," Beck offers, so adamant in his desire to keep me safe.

"You will not control my diet!" I lash out, jumping up from his lap, storming out of the room into the kitchen to get space.

When I step into the kitchen, I grab a bottle of water to keep my hands from shaking. Beck is still sitting on the couch looking at me dumbfounded. Like I slapped him across the face.

"Umm, I'm not sure what I said that's upset you," Beck starts cautiously. "But I'm going to go and give you some space."

"You said you'd get Ash to create a nutrition plan for me, like I can't feed myself. My ex monitored my diet like a hawk. You nor Ash will be doing the same," I growl.

Beck looks completely taken aback by my outburst. He looks at me with understanding for a couple of minutes before he nods and starts to head upstairs to Sutton's room.

When he gets to the top of the stairs, Beck says, "Komm," tapping his thigh.

"Pardon," I shriek.

Before Mayhem hops off the couch and runs up the stairs after Beck, quietly shutting the door once he disappears through it.

He was talking to the dog... Ha... I really am losing my shit.

I'm pacing the kitchen when I get a text from Quinn.

Quinn: You 2 love birds make out yet? 😉

Sloan: Ha, never gonna happen. Had our first fight though.

Quinn: WHAT? WHY? I will come stab that asshole so fast!

Sloan: He wants me to start training with him for his rehab and to better my self-defense skills. Get this, that asshole said he wants Asher to make me a diet plan. Like how dare he try to control my diet!

Quinn: Umm...did he say why?

Sloan: Does it matter? No man will control my diet again!

Quinn: So... I agree... But hear me out... I'm really sorry if your ex was a dick and did that to you. You never deserved that. No woman does. But... Beck and Ash train really hard. So hard that they eat double the normal calorie intake most people eat. I know, because most of our smoothie line is based off their meal plans for athletes to help keep them at peak performance shape. So if he wants Ash to make you a plan and he wants you to train WITH him… I think he really is just trying to make sure you'll be eating enough so you can recover.

Sloan: Ugh…so I'm the asshole?

Quinn: Wounded warrior maybe? Not an asshole. Sending you a hug. <3

Sloan: <3 Hugs. Thank you.

After texting with Quinn, I take a few deep breaths. Running through the conversation with Beck in my head. Beck was really just being thoughtful and I projected and bled my own wounds all over him.

Taking one last deep breath, I make my way over to the stairs and quietly take them up to Sutton's room. I gently knock on the door when I reach it but there's no answer.

"Hi…" I start.

"I'm… I'm sorry for snapping on you. You didn't deserve that. My ex… I couldn't eat anything unless he approved of it. He ordered my meals at restaurants. Cut me off at parties in front of people. It… Never mind. It doesn't matter." I rest my hand against the door.

"I thought you were doing the same thing. It doesn't excuse my behavior. The second you mentioned my nutrition, my mind immediately screamed no and shut down. I know you aren't him and that you're just trying to look out for me. I'm really sorry, Beck," I apologize for my behavior.

I stand there for a couple more minutes in silence before I realize he isn't going to open the door. Turning to head down the stairs, I'm almost at the last step, when I hear two light taps on the door. My eyes immediately land on the door, but it remains closed. But I feel like that's Beck's way of letting me know he heard what I had to say, making me feel like it will be okay.

22

Beck

I'm not ready to see Sloan yet, so I hesitate to open the bedroom door. While I understand that she was triggered, I don't appreciate being yelled at or to be viewed so negatively by someone, especially when all I was trying to do was help. Sloan should know me well enough by now to know I wouldn't try to intentionally control her diet.

The kitchen and living room are spotless when I pad into the area. It's an open floor plan so you can see everything except the bedrooms.

Even though it's Sutton's place, Sloan has left little touches lingering around. A few extra books that look like thrillers sit perfectly stacked on the edge of the coffee table. A contrast to all of Sut's romance novels in a perfect rainbow on her bookshelf.

Her baby blue crocheted blanket lies over top of Sutton's lavender throw on the back of the sofa. The throw Sloan had us tucked under on the couch last night before our argument.

I wonder if that's her favorite color. I meant to ask her because it's mine, too.

A few potted plants sit on the windowsill and on the kitchen island. Sut used to struggle to keep plants alive, though she always tried.

Sloan's bedroom door is still shut, so I throw on my running shoes and quietly leave.

"You look like you're doing the walk of shame," Quinn laughs, startling the hell out of me, when I walk through the door of the café.

"Yeah, no, get that idea out of your head," I grumble.

"Oh, come on. Sloan's beautiful."

"Sloan is beautiful, but I literally love your best friend. Are you really that okay with me just moving on that quickly?"

"Did you just hear what you said? You *love* my best friend. Not you're *in love* with my best friend. I love my best friend too. And not to dig the dagger in further but *our* best friend is traveling the world with *her* boyfriend. The man that she is in love with and who is in love with her. So honestly, yes, I would love it if you moved on."

"There's something seriously wrong with you." I side-eye her.

"We knew that already!" Quinn grins manically.

I roll my eyes, laughing at her being outrageous.

"But seriously, Beck, I love all of you. You all deserve to be happy. I actually think you and Sloan could be great together. That is if she can work through some of her issues and if you can work through some of yours," Quinn says, shrugging her shoulders.

"What do I need to work through?"

Quinn looks at me like I'm an idiot. "Um…your temper

for one? Not fighting people outside of your job. You are kind of a control freak. You definitely have some daddy issues like abandonment, maybe some mommy issues too," she says, tapping her chin like she's trying to think of more things to add to the list.

"Okay. I get it, Q," I sigh, running my hands through my hair.

"Here's your shake and your cold brew." Quinn hands me my daily favorites without me having to ask.

"Thank you," I reply, attempting to smile.

"So should I make Sloan work today to give you space or...?"

"She told you?" I ask, surprised.

"The CliffsNotes"—Quinn shrugs—"I tried to tell her that you weren't her ex and I think she knows that too. But we don't know how dark her past is so we can't hold it against her. Maybe she hasn't really had time to get out of survival mode and work on her triggers. Try setting some boundaries and be there for her. Sloan has a good heart, but I think she had a bad man really fuck with it."

"Thank you." I pull Quinn into a side hug.

"Get out of here, big boy. Too much affection for me." Quinn smacks me on the ass and shoves me toward the door.

I laugh at her antics. "Later, Q. You can let Sloan know I'm at the gym."

Quinn blows me a kiss. "I'll give our girl the choice."

*A*n hour later while I'm spotting one of our younger athletes on bench press, Sloan walks in.

She's hiding in a giant gray sweatshirt that comes down to her knees but her snug black leggings still show off her lean legs.

When Sloan notices me, she heads over toward the gym equipment.

"Hey," Sloan whispers, wringing her hands in the sleeves, keeping her eyes on the ground.

A sweatshirt that stops me dead in my tracks, because it has my old high school wrestling logo on it.

"Why are you wearing my shirt?" I question her, irritation in my voice.

"What?" Sloan squeaks.

"That one. It's mine from high school," I state a bit more firmly than necessary, walking up and tapping on the logo.

"Um...I didn't know that? Sutton left it behind and said I could wear any of her clothes so I didn't have to buy any. I-I-I d-didn't know," Sloan stutters.

"She... Sut left it behind," I say almost above a whisper.

"Beck. I am so sorry. I didn't know it was yours. I just grabbed it from her pile she left folded in the laundry room. I really had no idea," Sloan says, gently wrapping her fingers around my forearm.

My ears are ringing, I can barely make out what Sloan's saying. My vision is tunneling, knowing that I've been left behind.

"Beck." Sloan squeezes my arm a little tighter and starts rubbing small circles on my lower back with her other hand.

"Beck. Look at me," Sloan demands, snapping me out of my spiral.

My blue eyes meet her lilac ones and I think we can feel the pain oozing off of each other in waves. Sloan wraps her arms around my waist and squeezes me into a hug, digging her nails into the skin of my lower back.

I pull her tighter into my chest and rest my head on the top of hers, just breathing her in. She smells nothing like Sutton, more florally. Sutton always smelled more like vanilla or coconut. The scraping of her nails on my skin, keeps bringing me back to the present moment, almost grounding me.

"I'm sorry I yelled at you last night. I promise to be better about not lashing out. I know you were only looking out for me. I'd like to sit down and talk to Ash," Sloan says softly, continuously rubbing small circles into my back.

"I'm sorry I just freaked out about my sweatshirt. It just threw me off. I gave that to Sut years ago. It's just weird seeing someone other than her in it," I offer honestly.

"I understand. I'd take it off but I only have a sports bra on, and I'm not comfortable..." Sloan starts to say.

"It's okay, Little Dove. You can keep it." I run my fingers through her hair.

I feel her sigh into me a little deeper as she says, "Thank you."

Sloan definitely likes having her hair played with. Or maybe she needs these hugs as much as I do.

"So, what's on the schedule today? Lifting? Running? Yoga? Shadow boxing?" Sloan asks, perking up a bit. Trying to break some of the tension in the room.

"Have you done any lifting before?"

"Not much. I was more of a Pilates and dance class

kind of gal." Sloan smiles sheepishly.

"I can definitely see that. We'll start out light then. See what you're most comfortable with. I like to do lower weight, higher reps for women. I tend to lift a bit heavier myself personally but will keep it a little lighter so I'm not straining. I do recommend going a little heavier for glutes and quads though for you, if you're up for it," I suggest enthusiastically, excited to start working with her.

I strive to always be at my peak performance. It's a passion of mine to help coach others to reach their own max potential as well. It's empowering, watching them challenge themselves and succeed. I push them to their limits until they can overcome it.

I'll be forever grateful to the coaches I had in college and undergrad. So, I pride myself on being a good role model for our trainees.

My goal is to push Sloan to her limits. Even if she hates me at first.

I'm not sure the type of person Sloan is running from but with how terrified she's been and what she's told me, I don't want to take any chances.

My goal is to make sure she's confident in her own strength. That Sloan could look at a man my size or Asher's and know with absolute confidence she has a chance to fight her way out of a bad situation. With physical strength and discipline comes mental fortitude. If the time comes that Sloan has to face her monster head on. I will make sure she is ready, mind and body.

"You're the boss. I'm the student. Let's get started, coach." Sloan winks at me.

The way Sloan's staring at me like she's putting her trust in me, playful, with her guard down, has the ice around my heart melting just the slightest bit. The disappointment from Sutton leaving my sweatshirt like she left me behind is not as bad now.

$\mathcal{S}$loan's stronger than she realizes. And stronger than she looks for being so petite.

I had her warm up on the treadmill for twenty minutes and then go straight into a chest and quad circuit. Benching 65 pounds and squatting 85 pounds. I was pretty impressed with Sloan, this being her first time lifting.

We ran through some jump rope exercises, pushups, jumping jacks, high knees and planks. No breaks, one exercise after the other, and she killed it.

Her balance might even be better than mine. Must be all of that Pilates she's used to.

Walking over to the pull-up bars, I hop on and just hang there for a minute, dangling from the bar.

"I'm gonna pass on that one, Beck. I couldn't even do pull-ups in high school when they used to test us. Always failed that one. Continuous A- in gym class." Sloan laughs, taking a sip of her water.

"Ah, but I have a trick, Little Dove. Come here." I drop one arm and crook my finger for her to come here, dangling from the other.

"Show off," Sloan teases, walking over to me.

Pulling up with one arm, to do a one-handed pull-up, I wink at her. "That's showing off."

Sloan giggles. And it's the cutest thing I think I've ever heard. It almost steals my breath.

Reaching back up, holding on to the bar with both hands, "Hop up," I say, staring at her in a childlike wonder.

"Pardon?" Sloan chokes out.

"Hop on to me like you would if I was giving you a piggyback ride. Except on the front," I smirk at her.

"Beck, no. I'll…" Sloan starts to say, nervously giggling now, looking around the room like she wants to escape.

"Little Dove," I entice her.

"How do you expect me to…?" Sloan starts to question, scanning me from fingers to toes.

Hopping down, I scoop her up, wrap her legs around my waist and jump back up on the pull-up bar. Sloan immediately crawls up my waist to my chest. Clinging to my chest, she wraps her arms around my neck like a baby sloth does from a tree branch.

"Hold on tight, Little Dove," I whisper in her ear.

Her breaths start to come out rapidly but she holds on tight, as I start to do pull-ups with her wrapped around me. Her warm breath grazes my neck, leaving goose bumps in their wake.

"Show-off," Sloan grumbles under her breath.

"What was that?" I laugh, pretending I couldn't hear her. Trying to ignore the sensation of her lips so close to my neck.

"I said you're a show-off, Beckett Scott," Sloan growls.

Fuck. Her growl is sending shivers down my neck.

"*Oooh shit.* I get a full name scolding. There she is. Show me that fire. Now put your hands on the bar between mine," I command her. Trying to tease her. While trying to think of anything but her pliable soft body against mine.

Maybe I should've thought this plan out first.

"Beck, I'll fall," Sloan hesitates.

"You won't. I have you. Trust me," I reassure her. "Just place one hand at a time, between mine. You can do it."

I widen my hands a little bit to give her more room. Sloan's tiny hand pokes out from my sweatshirt as she reaches up onto the bar.

"Good girl. That's it."

I feel her body tremble around me. I'm not sure if it's from fear or from me calling her a good girl. But Sloan reaches up with her other hand, letting go and trusting me. Sloan's legs squeeze tighter around my waist. I count backwards from twenty in my head to try to keep myself from getting hard.

"I got you. Now on three, pull up with me, my weight will give you a boost," I instruct.

"On three..." Sloan whispers, exhaling a deep breath like she's terrified.

"One... Two...Three..." I count, pulling us up on the bar.

I watch her face light up with joy as she pulls herself up with me.

"Ten reps, okay?"

"Yes. One... Two...Three..." Sloan counts pulling herself up again, relaxing her legs slightly around my waist. She has a smile on her face and determination in her eyes. Her brows are furrowed and sweat beads on one of them.

It's kind of adorable how focused she is.

"Well, this is cute," Ash rags, coming up next to us. His eyes gleaming at the sight of Sloan wrapped around me. Good thing she's facing my chest and can't see the look in his eye.

Sloan squeaks and lets go of the bar, startled by Asher's

outburst. I barely keep us from falling but I land on the ground still holding onto her with one arm, using my other arm to sort of balance with my hand still on the bar. Once we are both stable, I place her gently down on the mat.

"Jesus, Ash. Warn a girl," Sloan says, grabbing at her chest.

"Sorry, Sloan," Ash says, grimacing. He walks closer to her, pulling her into a side hug.

"What are you two up to?" he questions, eyeing me suspiciously.

"Sloan wants me to slow down because of the concussion. I said I would, only if she would work out with me. So, we're working out. What's it to you?" I glare at him.

Asher raises his hands up like he means no harm. "I'm just curious. Chill man."

"Actually, this is perfect timing," Sloan says, breaking the tension between us.

"What is?" Asher and I both question.

"Beck thought you should create a meal plan for me, since I'm going to be training with him. Do you have time to come up with one for me?" Sloan asks sweetly.

Asher softens toward her. "Of course I do. Wanna head back into my office?"

"Yeah, if we're finished?" Sloan questions me.

"Almost, Little Dove. We gotta stretch first or you're gonna hate my guts tomorrow."

"How do you know I don't already hate your guts after that terrifying encounter?" Sloan says sarcastically, pointing to the pull-up bar.

"Smart ass." I nudge her gently with my elbow.

"Make sure you do some hamstring and tricep

stretches." I point at her as she slowly sits down on the ground.

"Yes, boss." Winking at me.

Sloan spreads her legs wide and folds herself in half to touch her toes.

My mouth goes dry, *she's hella flexible*. I cough, adjust myself and turn my head. I start to stretch myself to try to distract myself from how limber she is.

Fuck.

"Is it cool if I ask you some questions while you stretch?" Asher asks Sloan but stares at me with a gleam in his eye like he knows what I'm thinking.

Prick.

"Sure," Sloan hesitates.

"So in order to create the perfect plan for you, I'll need to know your height and weight. I'm not sure how comfortable you are sharing that with me or if you'd need me to weigh you," Asher states warily.

My eyes immediately meet Asher's and then her. Watching Sloan's body language change drastically from the start and end of that one sentence has me watching their interaction intently while I continue to stretch next to her. Sloan went from almost euphoric to deflated in an instant.

"Um..." Sloan starts.

"If you aren't comfortable, I could try and figure something out..." Asher utters tentatively watching her closely too.

"No..." Sloan trails off, looking down at the ground and then away. I can feel the anxiety coming off of her.

"Little Dove, I can step away if you'd be more comfortable," I offer.

"No," Sloan says firmly, turning and looking at me. "I mean, stay please. Um... Can I finish stretching and then we can talk about it together in your office? I just..." Sloan stumbles through her words.

"That's fine, Sloan. Take your time. I'll be in my office. Just knock when you're ready," Asher offers, gently squeezing her shoulder when he gets up and walks toward his office.

"Sloan, if you aren't comfortable with the nutrition plan. You don't have to do it. I didn't suggest it to be hurtful. My workouts are just demanding on my body, so I know they will be on yours. What you may normally eat won't be enough to keep up with your muscle recovery. I don't—in no way, shape or form—want to control what you eat. Neither does Asher. He just makes suggestions for how many calories and how much protein you should try to meet every day so you stay healthy and strong. You can eat whatever you choose in that capacity, it's just like a roadmap to make sure you stay on course with your goals," I try to explain to her so she knows I don't have an ulterior motive.

Sloan is so beautiful, petite but slightly underweight, and I would never ask her to change her body. After watching Sutton struggle with her body for years, I learned even more so to be so careful when discussing food and body image with others. We never know who suffers in silence. Even some of our incredibly fit athletes suffer from body dysmorphia and anxiety-induced eating disorders.

"I know you both are being helpful, Beck. I'm just scared..." She falters as tears start to stream down Sloan's face. "I haven't weighed myself in a long time but I know when I left, I was too thin, starving so I could be as empty as I felt. I try not to look in the mirror anymore because I hated that ghost of a girl that was always staring back at me. She's not me. I want to take my life back, you know. I just...I'm trying to figure out how." Sloan's crying harder now.

I scoop her up and pull her into my arms. I carry her back into my office, so she has privacy to break down, away from the prying eyes of others working out in the gym.

"You are beautiful, Little Dove. You deserve to feel just as strong and beautiful as you are, but on your own terms," I offer softly, running my fingers through her hair to soothe her.

"But you call me Little Dove, like a fragile little bird. You even said that in the hospital," Sloan spits out, while she continues to cry.

"I was hurting when I said those things to you. So angry at myself for getting myself knocked out and put in the hospital. You are tiny compared to me, like a little bird, but you are far from fragile. I'm sorry I ever made you think that you were." I kiss the side of her head gently.

"Thank you," Sloan whispers through her tears.

"For what?"

"This. Just letting me cry. Without holding it against me."

"Any feelings you have are valid, Sloan. I would never hold them against you." Holding her close to my chest.

"I'm ready now, but I'd like for you to stay with me while I talk to Asher, please?" She looks up at me with the saddest eyes.

"Always, Little Dove." I kiss the side of her head, gently releasing her from my hold.

Standing up, she reaches for my hand. I take it gently in mine and we walk out the door and head toward Asher's office. Sloan leans her head gently against my shoulder on the short walk there.

My protective instincts kick in and are on overdrive for this girl. "Do not make her cry," I growl out to Asher the second we walk through his open door.

What is this girl doing to me?

"Yes, please come in! I just love a growly Beckett Scott," Ash says sarcastically with the tiniest hint of mischief sparkling in his eyes. Like he knows something I don't.

"And I promise not to make you cry, Sloan. Not because asshat told me not to but because I don't want to make you cry," Asher assures her.

She giggles and sits in the chair across from Asher.

I make a note to stand directly behind her with my arms crossed, watching like a hawk to make sure he doesn't upset Sloan.

"So dramatic. Can we get on with it?" he sighs, rolling his eyes at me.

Sloan turns and gives me the side-eye but continues to laugh at my antics.

"Please." She smiles at him.

I love this girl's laugh. When did I start to love this girl's laugh?

23
Sloan

It's a cool, crisp fall Sunday. The leaves on the trees lining the street are painted gorgeous shades of red, orange and gold. The air smells fresh through the open window with the slightest hint of rain from the drizzle this morning.

Asher and Quinn are meeting Beck and I this morning. We're taking a mini road trip to Ohio for the day to go pick pumpkins and do all the fun fall things. I never got to have days like this. Days with friends, going on little adventures, doing anything festive.

It was never prestigious enough for James. He wouldn't be caught dead at a pumpkin patch. Skiing in Aspen absolutely but never a pumpkin patch or apple orchard. It didn't matter to him that I couldn't ski to save my life. I never did anything I wanted to do, never did anything so mundane as a day out with friends. And there wasn't a chance in hell James was letting me go anywhere with the girls alone. That's why I have been looking forward to this day since we started planning it.

I'm dressed in a cute pair of light blue ripped mom jeans that Quinn and I found at the thrift store last weekend. I paired them with a pale blue and forest green flannel over a cream turtleneck. The perfect pumpkin patch attire. Something straight out of a Pinterest board.

I'm staring at myself in the mirror for the first time in a long time. Really seeing myself. Something I promised Asher and Beck I would start doing.

"I love you," I whisper to myself with my hand gently placed over my heart, *"I'm enough."*

I'm appreciating the rosiness that's back in my cheeks and the light shining back at me in my eyes when I hear a tap on the door that has me almost jumping out of my skin. A squeak leaves me as Beck pokes his head in the door.

"Hey, it's just me. I didn't mean to startle you. Wow, you smell good," Beck offers, gently squeezing my shoulder. "And you look stunning, Little Dove."

My skin tingles where his fingers graze my shoulder.

When I turn to face him, Beck's wearing a sky blue and navy plaid flannel with a dark blue pair of jeans. Jeans that hug his thick thighs just right. His dirty blond hair is styled messy and a couple days worth of facial hair peppers his chin and cheeks. Beck looks good with a five o'clock shadow. Beck looks good all the time and always smells incredible, so woodsy. I sigh to myself.

We kind of look like a couple. And there's a part of me that doesn't hate it.

"Thank you." I smile softly at him. "You look nice too."

"Thank you." Beck kisses the side of my forehead. Our eyes meeting in the mirror. "You almost ready?"

"Yep. Let me throw on my boots and I'll be good to go," I say excitedly.

Beck's blocking my way out of the bathroom. His eyes look heated but mine must be haunted because Beck steps out of the way so I can pass. Immediately recognizing that I'm about to start panicking at being trapped, or rather feeling trapped.

"Little Dove..." Beck gently grabs my wrist on my way out of the bathroom.

"Yeah?" My voice breathy but anxious.

Beck tilts my head up so our gaze meets, his eyes are filled with so much heat. "May I kiss you?"

I start to nod my head yes, unable to look away from his gorgeous ocean eyes.

"Your words, Little Dove. I need your words."

"Yes. I'd really like it if you'd kiss me, Beckett." I smile softly at him. All anxiety from a few minutes ago melting away.

There's something about the way Beck speaks to me. So firm, yet so gentle, I can't help but cave to anything he asks of me.

He cradles my face in his palm, tilting my chin up as he gently presses his lips to mine. Tentatively at first like he doesn't want to spook me.

He kisses me firmly with the slightest bit of pressure. I wrap my arms around his waist to hold him tighter to me, encouraging him, letting him know I'm not fragile and that I want this just as much as he does.

Beck wraps his other arm around me, pulling me closer. The feel of him cradling me so close, grounds me in this moment. He takes the kiss deeper as we explore each other.

The softest sigh leaves my body and I relax into his hold. I surrender every ounce of control over to Beck as we sink deeper and deeper into this kiss. One that tastes like comfort, as the background world just fades away.

It's nothing like I've experienced before. It's not a heated kiss. It's sweet. There's no rushing. Just two people exploring one another, not needing anything more than this moment of peace and reassurance. This moment of feeling wholly safe in another is something I've never felt before.

Kissing Beck is warm and inviting. Like slipping into your favorite sweatshirt on a cool fall day. Like he's home. Like I could do this with him forever.

The sound of Mayhem barking has us finally separating. I gently press my fingers to my lips, smiling to myself.

That's the best kiss I've ever had. My heart still feels like it's melting.

We turn to find out what he's barking at and see that he's just staring up at us, tail thumping excitedly against the floor.

"I think he felt left out." I giggle. "I'm going to go put my boots on now."

Beck laughs, kissing the side of my head, before heading toward the kitchen. "I initially came in to let you know that I made us some lattes and packed some protein muffins to take with us. Q said they'd be here in ten but that was probably five minutes ago."

He made us lattes.

Such a small thing to do, but it warms my heart every time he does something so kind for me, without me having to ask or having to owe him anything in return. I'm not sure he even knows how much I truly appreciate it.

The only time James ever did nice things for me was before I was his wife. Looking back on it, they weren't even really nice. More so, controlling. Like ordering my meals without even letting me look at the menu. Making me a black coffee every morning but always throwing out my creamers and trying to make me think I just forgot to buy them. Putting white roses on my desk at work so others would see how great of a guy James was, but if I got myself flowers for the house, he would throw them away. James would "clean up after me" if I didn't clean fast enough for him but act like I owed him something for doing that.

With James it was always something. Always conditional. Always controlling.

I'm sitting on the couch putting my boots on, when Mayhem whimpers and rests his head on my lap, snapping me out of my spiraling thoughts. I will not let James ruin this day. I scratch his head, quietly thanking him for being here and so loyal to me. His presence is like a comforting shadow.

I walk over and pull out a stool at the island, sitting down to take a sip of my latte. Mayhem curls up at my feet on the floor. Sighing at just how good Beck makes a toffee nut latte and how much I love his dog. I take in this moment—being taken care of and feeling at peace.

Beck is such a strong, stable presence. Almost unshakeable. Sometimes I feel like I could lean on him for a lifetime.

"I'm glad you like it." Beck chuckles.

Blinking rapidly, I snap out of the little bubble of bliss I was just lost in.

"Mmm...it's so good I might just steal yours." I smirk, reaching for his jokingly.

"I'd give you mine, if you really wanted it." Beck smiles softly at me, reaching over grazing his knuckles over mine. My heart swoons just the slightest bit.

There's a loud knock on the door that has me almost leaping out of my seat.

"*Let us in love birds,*" Quinn shouts through the door.

Our eyes meet in an instant and we both burst into laughter. My hand covers my racing heart and Beck reaches for the other, giving it a gentle squeeze.

"See you later, Sweet Boy." I kiss Mayhem on the nose and ruffle his fur through my fingers.

"Be good," Beck offers, petting Mayhem too before we head toward the door.

"*Do I hear kissing?*" Quinn screams through the door.

"Would you quit harassing them, Q," Ash berates her.

"Yes. Kisses to my boy," Beck responds, winking at me, before he opens the door to Quinn with twinkles in her eyes and Asher wearing a shit-eating grin. "Now wipe those looks off your faces."

"Hi guys." I wave awkwardly like we've been caught red-handed. I peek out underneath Beck's arm in the doorway.

"There she is," Quinn coos, pulling me into a hug and tugging me down the stairs with her. "Tell me *everything!*"

"Quinn there's nothing to tell." I laugh. "I swear we were kissing Mayhem goodbye."

"At the same time? So, like maybe your arms brushed? Or your lips maybe? Accidentally? For like a second?" Quinn asks like she has the zoomies.

"You really need to go back to the true crime novels. All of those romances are going to your head." I giggle.

"Ugh, my romantic life is pathetic. That's why I escape into these dreamy stories of six foot ten men with ten-inch cocks and best friends they like to share their girls with but if anyone else touches her, they're..." Quinn runs her finger across her throat and then starts giggling.

"Goodness," I whisper breathlessly, my cheeks probably flushed pink.

"See! So, I have to live through you. Beck's over six foot and Sut said he's..." Quinn starts to say.

"I'm gonna stop you right there." I gently cover her mouth with my hand to avoid hearing her discuss Sutton and Beck together.

Out of respect for Beck and Sutton... Not that... There's no way I'm jealous...

"You ladies, ready to go?" Asher comes up behind us putting his arms around our shoulders.

"Let's do it. I've never been to a pumpkin patch. I'm actually really excited." I smile up at them.

"Really? Never?" Beck questions, his eyes softening when they meet mine.

"Never." I shrug, a little sad.

"Well, what are we waiting for? Let's make this the best day ever!" Quinn squeals.

As we walk toward the car together, a sense of calm washes over me. This is really starting to feel like home. I get in the back seat with Quinn and stare out of the window, as the guys get in the front, with Asher driving.

My eyes catch sight of a large vase of white roses just sitting on the windowsill in an apartment complex not far up the street, causing me to shiver.

No.

There's no way.

A gentle grip on my knee has me shooting up in my seat.

"Hey, sorry. You okay?" Beck asks softly, questions in

his eyes.

"Yeah…" I gulp, looking back out the window, but I don't see the roses anymore.

Am I seeing things?

"You're trembling. Here." Beck hands me a coffee thermos. "I made you another hot toffee latte since we were going to be outside most of the day. Thought you might want a second one."

"Thank you." I smile, grateful. I take the cup from him, gently brushing my fingers against his, just so I can feel a little more grounded. A little bit more connected to him.

"You sure you're okay?" Beck eyes me cautiously.

"Yeah, I'm sure." I offer a hesitant smile.

No. I'm not sure actually. Can you tell? I want to scream but try to remain stoic.

Beck looks over at Quinn who's also eyeing me suspiciously, like neither of them believe me but they aren't going to push.

"Okay. I'm here." Beck gently squeezes my knee again before turning back around in his seat.

Quinn reaches across the seat and gently laces her fingers with mine, without saying a word.

Hero/Heroine by Boys Like Girls starts playing a few seconds later, allowing the remaining anxiety to wash away.

Beck is here.

Quinn is here.

Ash is here.

James is not.

I am safe.

At least I hope I am.

24

Beck

The two-hour car ride to Van Buren Acres in Ohio was weirdly quiet but also kind of peaceful.

Leaves crunch under our boots, as Asher and Quinn walk ahead of Sloan and me to the small red barn where we pay for our entry.

"Wow! This is so cute!" Sloan looks around in awe. Her eyes are lit up and she's beaming. The ghosts in her eyes from the beginning of the car ride, gone. I still don't understand where they came from. Sloan looked so elated while we were getting into the car.

"Where do we start?" Quinn asks, clapping her hands together in glee.

"Want to do the hayride first so we don't have to lug anything on it? I imagine you gals want to take some pumpkins home," Asher suggests.

"Always thinking ahead, Ash. Love that idea!" Quinn jumps up on his back and kisses his cheek. His reflexes quick to grip her legs when she wraps them around his waist.

Is Asher blushing?

"Get over here, Little Dove." I reach out for her hand.

Sloan eyes my hand for a second.

"Please?" I ask sweetly.

Sloan grins and laces her fingers with mine.

"Oh my gosh! Are those baby pigs?" Sloan squeals.

"They're racing. Take me to the piggies, Ash." Quinn giggles, giving Asher a tap on his ass.

Asher grumbles but takes off in a sprint with Quinn on his back. Quinn throws her head back laughing.

"Jesus, Q. Don't whip back so hard or we'll both go down," Asher gripes.

"Relaaaax, Ash. You got us," Quinn coos, pulling herself closer to him though.

Sloan and I burst into laughter as we run for the fenced in area where the little pigs are racing.

We all watch as two little brown and white and two little black and white pigs about the size of a corgi dog race each other to the finish line.

"Oh my gosh. Their snorting noises are so friggin' cute," Sloan chirps.

"They're so cute. I wanna take one home," Quinn squeals.

Ash and I just smile at the girls and how excited they are.

When I turn to watch the last straggling pig cross the finish line, I'm stopped in my tracks at how breathtaking Sloan is. Her guard's down and she's glowing with childlike joy. The biggest smile I've ever seen her make, lights up her entire face. Those lavender eyes sparkle in the sunlight.

"Little Dove," I whisper, gently wrapping my arms around her, as she leans against the fence still watching the pigs running around.

"Beckett." Her eyes meet mine. She's radiant and relaxed, something I'm not used to seeing from her.

I could get lost in her.

"Your smile is beautiful. You are beautiful," I barely choke out.

"Thank you," Sloan says so softly under her breath. Twisting toward me in my arms, she stretches up on her tiptoes, kissing my chin.

I lean down and kiss the tip of her nose. The clearing of two throats from Asher and Quinn have us breaking out of our little bubble.

"You ready for that hayride now?" Quinn asks, pulling Sloan out of my arms and linking their arms together as they take off skipping toward the line.

"What are we going to do with them?" Asher chuckles, shaking his head.

"What do you mean?" I ask confused.

"Don't play dumb man. You like Sloan. I actually think you'd be good for each other," Asher offers as we walk and talk, a few feet behind the girls.

"We aren't together. We're just friends," I say in denial.

"Yeah. We see how that "just friends" worked out for you last time," Asher rags sarcastically.

"Fuck off and mind your business. If you're gonna run your mouth, you gonna tell me what's going on with you and Q?" I shove him.

"Chill man. I'm just saying. Don't leave your head stuck in your ass for six years again," Asher pushes.

"You're an asshole. Don't avoid the question," I growl.

"Are you two coming or are you about to have a boxing match in the middle of a *family* farm?" Quinn hollers over to us.

"Coming!" Asher and I both yell back at her, giving each other the side-eye. We slow jog to catch up to them.

*A*fter the hayride, we each picked out pumpkins to paint for when we get back to the apartment tonight. They're safely stowed away in the car because the girls didn't want to carry them and frankly, neither did we.

We got some apple cider slushies and apple cider donuts to eat on the walk over to the sunflower fields. The donuts are out of this world. I miss training but damn have I been missing out on some things—like sugar.

I walk next to Sloan through the sunflowers, our shoulders brush every so often bringing me back to the present.

My thoughts drift to Sutton and how she always reminded me of sunflowers. But I've thought less and less of her these last couple months. Quinn mentions her from time to time just to tell us how the tour has been going. It sounds like she's doing really good and I'm happy for her. Khaos is also internet famous, which has been funny to follow on social media. I haven't found the need to follow From Troy's page and I've avoided looking at Sutton's. But I miss Khaos, and his posts they've created for him can make anyone laugh even on their worst days.

Quinn also told me August plans on proposing. She wanted me to know because she imagines it will go viral with the way he's doing it. Always such a flashy fucker. Apparently, August also asked Quinn to tell me so it didn't send me over a ledge. I should be pissed at the fucker but I respect that he extended that decency to me.

"This is so good," Sloan says, sipping her slushie.

It's adorable when Sloan's eyes light up when she's really enjoying something. Her eyes are always telling a story even when her mouth isn't.

"Yeah, it is," I offer, my mind still wandering off.

I keep finding things I like about Sloan..

"Hey, are you okay?" Sloan asks softly, tapping her drink gently against mine.

"Yeah, I'm fine."

"Did something happen with you and Asher? You've seemed a little distracted since whatever was going on before we walked over."

"I said I'm fine, Sloan."

"Okay," Sloan whispers, not pushing any further and continues to walk quietly next to me.

A few minutes pass and I'm lost in my thoughts. Questioning if Asher and Quinn are right. Do I actually have feelings for Sloan or do I just like the idea of trying to keep her safe? Is she just filling a void? Are we keeping each other company since we're too broken, lonely souls? Maybe Ash is right. I shouldn't make the same mistakes I did before.

I think I have a thing for emotionally unavailable women. Maybe Q was right, too, about my "issues" as she likes to call them.

Stopping in the middle of the field, I owe Sloan an

explanation for my change in mood. "Fuck. I'm sorry. I just... Sunflowers always reminded me of Sutton." I pause, thinking maybe it's a bad idea to bring Sutton up.

"It's okay, Beck. You can talk about her," Sloan reassures me.

"The more I think about it though, I see now that Sutton wasn't for me. Our friendship was easy but I think it was because I always wanted to try and help Sutton. If I was helping Sutton, I wasn't having to work on myself. I wasn't having to sit with the void inside of myself, if I was trying to make her laugh or make her smile. It was also a way for me to avoid having to commit to anyone but my career.

"My dad left when I was in my early teens and my mom was a miserable person after that. So, I never really thought relationships could work. I used my career as an excuse to avoid relationships and I sort of used my codependency on Sutton's happiness to fill the companionship I sometimes wished for.

"I guess sometimes I worry I'm doing that with you, but you also sometimes make me face things that I usually would have avoided. You keep me in line." I pause to get my thoughts together.

"And now"—running my fingers through my hair—"it's just standing next to you watching you just take all of this in like it's magical, stirs something inside me. It makes me question if maybe there is something more between us than we realize, but I don't want you to be a rebound? Is rebound even a thing if you weren't actually together? I don't know. And I also don't want to be a rebound from your ex. I just want us to be on the same page because I really liked kissing you this morning and I want to do it again. But only if it's something you want too," I ramble out.

Sloan reaches for my hand, weaving our fingers together. "I'm so sorry your parent's relationship tainted your view on what a healthy relationship could be. I've also always been a bit skittish of commitment because even though my parents are still together, they've never seemed terribly happy," she says, her eyes never leaving mine.

"For what it's worth, I hope to stick around, Beck, I really like it here with you all. But if my ex finds me, I can't promise anything. I don't want to be on the run forever. I enjoy spending time with you, Beck. I loved kissing you, and I feel safe with you, more than I have with anyone else.

"I don't want to label anything between us, when I'm still trying to figure myself out and your heart is still mending. I'm open to seeing where life takes us. But I also won't be your second choice. So please be gentle with my heart and only choose me, if you're truly choosing me. I'm not going to be a placeholder for Sut." She voices her thoughts.

"You aren't a placeholder. That's what I'm trying to tell you. Sunflowers always reminded me of Sut, but standing out here with you, all I see is you, Little Dove," I say. Gently running my fingers through her hair, as I gently press my lips to her forehead. I linger there for just a minute as I feel Sloan's tiny arms wrap around my waist, holding me close to her.

This moment—her—feels right.

25
Sloan

$\mathcal{B}$eck's tucking me under his arm, directing us out of the sunflower field toward Quinn and Asher to the corn maze.

This has become my new favorite place to be. In his warm embrace. What is this man doing to me?

My heart is still beating rapidly, at his confession.

Beck wants me. Not Sutton.

When we catch up to Quinn and Asher, Quinn loops her arm with mine, pulling me away from Beck, as we get in line for the maze.

"Girl, spill!" Quinn whispers.

"There's nothing to spill," I giggle.

"Lies. All lies. You're blushing." Quinn pokes my cheek.

"Nothing happened, Q. We were just talking." I shake my head at her antics.

"We're next, Q. Little Dove, stays with me," Beck

declares, intertwining our fingers together.

"We're going in as a group, Beckett," Quinn sasses.

"I know. But Sloan stays with me."

"Come on, Q." Asher grabs her hand, walking ahead of Beck and me.

We wander through the corn maze, the air is thick with the earthy scent of damp soil and the musty scent of crushed cornstalks. Towering walls of green and beige extend high above me overhead, creating a maze of narrow, weaving paths that disappear into the dense brush. It's deathly silent, other than the rustling of the leaves swishing softly in the breeze as the stalks brush against each other. It's eerie and kind of terrifying.

The sun has set. The soft, fractured glow of the moon overhead is the only bit of light illuminating the path but everything is getting darker the deeper into the labyrinth we go.

Asher and Quinn must have gone a different way because we lost them a little bit ago.

"Marco!" Quinn shouts from who knows where.

"Polo." I laugh, but the hair on my arms is standing up.

I can't see where the hell they went. My own hand isn't hardly even visible in front of my face. Why did I think a maze in the dark was a good idea? Especially when I've been so on edge lately.

Beck's been walking in front of me, my hand clutched in his. Taking us to every dead-end corner I think this place has. I almost stumble into him every time we meet a roadblock.

"She can hear me!" I hear Quinn shout.

"I think every human and animal on this farm can hear you, Q." I hear Asher laugh out loud.

"I seriously *hate* you, Ash!" Q's voice seems much closer than it was a minute ago.

"Marco," I chirp.

"Polo! There you are," Quinn squeals, pulling me in close. She links our arms together, making my hand leave Beck's. "Let's try to get out of this thing. I feel like we've been in here for hours."

"I think the whole thing is a bunch of dead-ends. I don't even think there's an exit. It's all a lie," I giggle.

Quinn and I are trying to find the exit while clinging to each other. Tracing our fingers with our free hands through the cornstalks as we walk. Hoping it might give us some sort of sense of direction.

I keep reaching out my hand in the hopes of finding Beck, but somehow he and Ash got separated from us. Quinn and I are walking into what seems like another dead-end wall. But the wall moves.

A blood curdling scream rips out of my body when a hand grips my arm, which has Quinn screaming too.

"What the fuck? They don't have actors hiding in here," Quinn squeals.

My ears start ringing and my heart beats rapidly in my chest out of fear. I only freeze for a second before I twist my wrist so hard out of the grip and throw four punches and a knee at whoever is standing in front of me.

A loud groan is all I hear before I take off running with Quinn's hand in mine. Brushes of cornstalk hit against my arms and face but I don't care. I need to get the hell out of here.

The adrenaline coursing through my blood stream has me pumping my legs so hard. I don't think I've ever run this fast. Quinn keeps up, running next to me. Her fingers laced in mine, keeping me somewhat present in the moment. We finally make it out on the other side of the maze in what feels like an eternity but really is only a couple minutes. We're both bent over panting. Our eyes searching the exit of the maze for the guys to show up.

"What just happened? Where the hell did the guys go?" Quinn says in between deep breaths.

"Someone grabbed me. What if my ex..." I drop to my knees and start sobbing.

My vision is starting to go black. I'm not even sure if I'm breathing. I might be hyperventilating.

"Oh, honey." Quinn pulls me tightly in an embrace and I cling so tight to her.

"You're safe. You got us out of there. You kicked ass. I'm so proud of you. Shh, I got you, Sloan. Deep breaths, sweet girl," Quinn coos in my ear, rubbing small circles on my back as I continue to full body sob in her arms.

"What is happening?" Asher barks when he finally makes it out of the maze.

Beck is walking behind him slowly

"Hey. Sloan, it's okay. What happened?" Asher softens, kneeling down to question me.

"I...I felt..." I stammer. "I felt...someone grab me...I... did what you guys showed me..."

"Fuck," Asher hisses under his breath, his eyes wandering back to Beck.

"Why the hell are you..." Quinn starts, looking over at Beck. "Oh shit."

"What?" I barely get out, looking up.

Why is Beck holding his groin?

He hobbles closer to us and everything clicks into

place. "You!"

"Fuck, Sloan. I'm so sorry, I wasn't thinking. I thought it would be funny to hide and scare you girls," Beck apologizes, so much guilt written on his face.

"Are you kidding me, Beckett?" Quinn yells, gently releasing me from her arms. "I should kick you in the balls myself for being so fucking stupid. You know she's been skittish since the moment we met her."

"Lower your voice, Q. There are kids around," Asher reminds Quinn.

"You stay out of this." She shoves her finger into Asher's chest.

Getting up from off of the ground, I walk toward Beck.

"What the hell is wrong with you," I yell, punching him in the stomach.

"I said I was sorry," Beck huffs.

"Sorry isn't fucking good enough, Beckett. You know you can't do that shit to me. I thought the worst possible thing—that James found me! That he was grabbing me, and I was so fuckin' terrified it never even crossed my mind it could be you," I berate him.

"Fuck. I thought it would be funny. I knew you were with Quinn. I knew you weren't alone. It was a prank. I wasn't thinking. I'm sorry," Beck apologizes.

"You should know better, Beck." I let out an exasperated sigh.

"I know, I fucked up. I really am sorry." Beck's voice breaks.

"I can't right now." I shake my head in disappointment—at Beck and myself.

Turning away, I start walking back toward the car. I need some space. I don't want to make a bigger scene. My heart is still racing and my hands are trembling. If I was anyone else, that would've been a funny prank.

Lost in my thoughts, I realize I'm at fault too. I probably need to tell all of them more about my past so they can understand. But I'm not sure how much to tell, how much is safe to share. I just need a minute to gather my bearings.

The panic attacks started not long after I started dating James. Being around him always gave me so much anxiety, both at work and home. It always took me a few minutes to regulate my breathing, for my ears to stop ringing and my vision to stop tunneling. Usually, I was able to come back to myself from the attacks, though it's better without James around.

"Sloan, wait up," Quinn says, catching up to me when I'm only a few feet from the car. "I'm sorry if I said something that hurt you. I didn't intend to. I love Beck but he just doesn't think sometimes. Too many hits to the head."

"I'm right behind you," Beck grumbles so close behind us.

"I know," Quinn snaps at Beck.

A loud sigh leaves Beck. Followed by a chuckle from Asher that quickly turns into a groan from Beck jabbing him in the ribs.

The car lights up and turns on when we get close and I pause. Halting in my tracks.

"Automatic starter, it's okay, Sloan," Asher assures me.

Beck opens the car door for me so I climb in. I slide all the way across the back seat so Quinn can slide in after me, except Beck's large frame fills the seat next to me. He pulls the door shut, locking it.

"What are you doing?" I squeak out.

"Yeah, Beckett. Get in the front." Quinn berates him through the window.

"Sit in the front, Q. I need to talk to Sloan," Beck commands.

"You get in the front," Quinn says, hitting the window with the side of her fist.

Asher rolls down the passenger window. "Sugar, get your ass in my front seat."

"What did you just call me?" Quinn rips open the front door and jumps in, reaching across the center console and grabbing Asher by the shirt.

It's the most mischievous grin I've ever seen on Asher's face. "Ooooh, so scary! You heard me, Sugar. Now sit."

"You both need a swift kick in the dick," Quinn snarls.

"You know I love it when you talk like that to me, Sugar. Now buckle up," Asher demands, removing her hand from his shirt.

"Make me," Quinn snaps back.

Asher chuckles deviously, "You're such a brat."

He gently situates Quinn in her seat, putting her seat belt on for her before he pulls out of the parking lot.

I'm trying so hard not to laugh at the tension between them I almost forget that Beck's sitting next to me, just staring at me. I sigh, turning to face him.

"I am really fucking sorry I scared you. You're getting way too good at those upper cuts," Beck states, rubbing his stomach and grimacing.

"I'm sorry I freaked out," I offer.

In all honesty though, it didn't even register that it could've been Beck. I was getting so anxious that we weren't finding our way out of there and it was so dark.

Sometimes the dark plays tricks with your mind.

The car is awkwardly silent as we drive down the highway back to Pittsburgh. After what feels like an eternity of Beck's eyes searing a hole into the back of my head while I keep my head turned away, Quinn breaks the silence.

"Would you be comfortable sharing at least some things with us? We can't help keep you safe if we don't know anything. We've just kind of gathered you're running."

"You don't have to tell us everything. We don't want you to have to relive something traumatic. But if you can at least tell us who he is or what he looks like, it might help so we can be on alert," Asher adds gently.

"I promise you, we only want to keep you safe. We would never judge you for anything you may have had to do to get here. I'm actually really fucking proud of you that you fought and didn't freeze earlier. Even if it was me who's ass you kicked." Beck goes on to say.

"You are important to us, we want to have your back if you need us. We want nothing more than for you to be able to keep yourself safe, to feel empowered as a woman again. But we also want to be an extra set of eyes to keep a look out for you," Beck explains.

"I'm not asking to be insensitive but are we safe? We will vow to protect you always, but we should know what we're up against. Is he just going to come after you or do you think he'll hurt anyone to get to you? You know I watch a lot of true crime so I gotta ask," Quinn hesitates.

"It's okay, Q. I know you're just worried. Honestly, I'm not sure. I hope he wouldn't hurt any of you. He... James... His name is James. He never laid his hands on any of my friends from work, as far as I know, but he did manipulate our work schedule. When James started noticing the girls were getting suspicious of the change in me, they started treating him differently. So, he made sure we hardly worked together anymore," I say, my heart breaking at how much I miss Kailey and Maria.

"So, does he know where you are?" Asher questions, his eyes meeting mine in the rearview mirror.

"I don't know. I hid a bag in the woods and ran when I had the chance. I filed divorce papers and a restraining order the day before I left. I had only been using cash."

"So why do you think James has found you?" Asher asks.

"I've had this weird feeling like someone is watching me."

"How do you figure he tracked you down?" Quinn asks, but quickly answers her own question, "The plane ticket!"

I let out a deep exhale, agreeing, "The plane ticket."

"What plane... Oh," Beck sighs.

"Yeah, that's the only time I used my credit card, but he had access to all of my accounts when we were together. James was very controlling." My chest starts to feel tight just at the thought of him.

"So, you're worried buying the ticket might've tipped him off to where you are?" Asher asks.

"Did you run from far?" Quinn questions.

"Ish...not super far but a few states," I answer half-heartedly.

"Okay, so James is controlling, potentially violent, but will be more so hunting you? Not us?" Quinn asks nervously.

Chills break out on my skin out of fear of him hunting me, hunting any of us. "Hopefully not you, definitely me. That day we went to your apartment because of the flooding, Beck, the reason I sort of panicked was because I saw a white rose on the steps. James used to leave me white roses all of the time because he grew them. I thought maybe he had found me when I saw that."

"But that was a few weeks ago. Has anything else unusual happened?" Beck asks.

"Not really. There have been a few times when closing up the café I've felt like eyes were on me, but there wasn't anyone around. I found a rose laying on one of the bistro tables one afternoon at the end of the day. I thought I might've seen white roses on a windowsill earlier when we left, up the road a bit but then they were gone. I don't know if my anxiety has my mind playing tricks on me or what," I ramble.

"First of all, listen to your intuition. If you think you feel something or you see something, anxiety or not, your body is warning you. Second of all, I will kill that motherfucker. There's gotta be a sinkhole somewhere nearby—" Quinn twists in her seat to face me, squeezing my knee.

"What's he look like?" Asher interrupts Quinn, who looks ready to hunt James down.

"Uhh... Average height. Probably like 5'10". Silver shorter hair. Usually, clean shaven. On the leaner side. James typically would ski and swim. Older, like 50ish," I offer uncomfortably, wringing my hands in my shirt.

"Damn girl," Quinn chokes out, I'm assuming at his age.

Beck reaches over and gently unwinds my hand from my shirt, threading his fingers with mine. "It sounds like we really need to start revving up on the self-defense skills, Little Dove. More fighting, less lifting and we may need to get a couple of the athletes to help. It might be difficult for you at first. If we can mock-up scenarios in the gym with a couple different-sized guys and different ways they could potentially grab you, you'll be more prepared especially mentally I would just worry with James having such a hold on you, that if we aren't more aggressive in training you, you'll just freeze up. You need to be ready if he tries to abduct you. You need to take that bastard down if he comes for you."

"I'm so tired, Beck. Tired of running. Tired of hiding. Tired of living in fear. The weight is getting to be too much." I dip my head down, not meeting his eyes.

Beck lifts my chin, so his eyes meet mine. "I hear you. I wish I could face your fears for you. I hope that he never finds you, but you and I both know he probably already has. And I want to be the one to protect you when that moment comes. But if he lies in wait and hunts you when I'm not there, you will know how to fight. And you will fight like your life depends on it. Because it does. You are powerful, Little Dove. Don't ever forget that. You need to see what I see. You need to believe in yourself. Not the illusions he's fed you."

"Okay," I whisper.

"But..." Beck starts, wiping the tears from my cheeks, that I hadn't realized were falling.

"But?" my voice cracks on the question.

"I'd really love it, if you'd let me help you carry some of that weight for you. You don't have to do it all on your own anymore. I have you." Beck kisses my forehead gently.

I rest my head on Beck's shoulder. He brings his arm around me, pulling me in and holding me close to him. "Okay."

"I'm ready. It's time I take my life back. I'm tired of living my life always looking over my shoulder," I agree, sinking into his strength. Allowing it to seep into my bones.

"We start tomorrow then," Beck confirms, squeezing my hand I have resting over his heart, gently.

"Tomorrow." I squeeze his hand back.

"For what it's worth, I really am fucking sorry for scaring you earlier," Beck says genuinely.

"I know you are." I kiss just below his ear, where my head rests.

26

Beck

I'm sitting on the mats in the gym in a small circle with Asher and three of our other fighters going over a game plan for training Sloan, when she walks in.

Fresh faced, her long black hair up in a messy bun on the top of her head, in a pair of tight black leggings and an off the shoulder light blue sweater. Sloan's stunning.

"Hey. I got your note," she says softly.

"Did you eat your breakfast and stretch?"

"Yes, boss." Saluting me.

The guys start laughing before I glare daggers at them, and all but Asher immediately go silent.

"Ahhhh…so he bosses you all around too?" Sloan rags.

"You fit in so well, Sloan." Asher smiles at her.

I want to wipe that smile right off of his smug face.

"Are we ready or not?" I grumble.

"Ready, boss," Sloan giggles.

I internally groan at her calling me boss. So obedient.

With just the right amount of sass.

"You're gonna get your ass spanked red if you keep being a smart ass, Little Dove," I grind out, just to see how she reacts.

"Pardon?" Sloan squeaks.

The guys immediately scurry off to various corners of the gym. During our meeting this morning, I asked the guys to work on sparring with each other in the background while I coach Sloan. We agreed when I say "double hook" loudly, that's their cue for one of them to drop what they're doing and come after Sloan. We went over either grabbing her by the elbow to take her away, putting her in a headlock or grabbing her by the neck and pushing her into one of the wall mats.

I suspect her ex is untrained, but violent, and would likely be more aggressive in grabbing her. And if he's even more pissed off that Sloan ran, he may not hold back at all and just try to either torture or kill her. Which means James will likely go for her neck or her hair, but I don't want the guys pulling her hair. If she can get out of a neck hold, Sloan will be able to get out of a hair hold.

The guys are wearing pads, just in case Little Dove fights like hell like she did last night. My abs are actually still sore.

I'm so fucking proud of her.

The rhythmic thumping of gloves hitting pads and sneakers scuffing the rubber floor plays like a soundtrack behind us as we start to instruct Sloan.

"Okay, Little Dove, I'm going to put you in some controlled scenarios and show you how to get out of them. Ash is going to attack me first, so I can show you how to get out of each hold. Then you and I will reenact each scenario and you'll need to fight to get out. Don't be afraid to hurt me," I explain to her.

"Okay…" Sloan says hesitantly.

"You got this, Sloan," Asher encourages. "Rough him up a little. He deserves it."

Sloan chuckles as she walks over toward one of the walls off of the mat. Sloan leans against the blue padded wall watching Asher and me closely. Discomfort written all over her face as we get into position.

I'm standing in the middle of the mat staring Sloan in her eyes, when Asher grabs me roughly by the elbow tugging me backwards. I watch her eyes flinch before I immediately drop my weight to the ground in a squatted position, I start yelling "help." Twisting my arm and thrusting it downward, I'm able to loosen Asher's grip and then use my thumb and pointer finger to rip his hand off of me, and get out and run.

We show Sloan this a couple times before I run over and grab her by the elbow without warning and start yanking her away from the wall. She yells out but immediately drops low into a squat and uses all of her might to rip my arm off of her elbow. She even stomps on my foot and tries to trip me for good measure.

"Perfect! Nice work, Little Dove!" I applaud her.

"Okay, next is going to be a choke hold. You're going to hate this. It's not going to feel great on your neck and I'm sorry for that. Unfortunately, this is the most common way a forceful man tries to abduct a woman or an abuser tries to harm his victim. It's probably the most important one you'll need to know," I warn her.

"Okay," Sloan whispers, her eyes wide, face going a little pale.

Asher comes toward me, both hands wrapping around my neck. Squeezing fairly tight. Reaching upward, I shove my hands up through his arms and slam mine down over top of his to get him to break the hold.

"I don't want to do this one specifically to you, but I want to show you how to get out of a headlock. Your ex may not want to face you or may try to grab you from behind to startle you," I instruct, trying to be as open with her as possible.

Asher comes up from behind me and gets me in a headlock, his inner elbow pressing against my throat. Dropping as low as I can again, I turn my head toward Asher's armpit into his body to relieve the pressure off of my throat.

"Always turn your head into the hold. I know it doesn't seem like it makes sense but it takes the pressure off of your airway," Asher instructs her.

Using my hands, I start to pull his arm at the wrist and then elbow to break his hold.

Asher comes back to squeeze tighter, so I keep my head twisted inward toward his body to keep him from being able to choke me. Then I use my left hand and grab his pinky finger on the hand of the arm that he has around my neck, pulling it outward.

"Fingers do not want to be pulled all the way out to the side. The pinky is the easiest one to dislocate, which will have him dropping his grip. So yank that hard," I tell Sloan. "Biting as hard as you can is also another option. Either way as long as you keep your throat safe, there are a few ways to try to break out of the grip, duck and run."

"Apparently you can bite through a human's small finger like a carrot. Our brains just don't let us. Think I could try that?" Sloan chuckles.

Her anxiety is apparent so I figure now is the best time to holler out, "Double hook!"

"Fuck, really?" Asher whispers exasperated.

As Luca, one of our fighters, runs over to Sloan.

Luca completely catches her off guard and gets her in a headlock from behind.

Her scream is ear-piercing.

Asher glares daggers at me.

And the sound she makes is a dagger to my heart.

But within seconds, Sloan's dropping all of her weight, turning her head inward and cranking on Luca's finger, scraping her nails down his wrist, and biting at him like a rabid animal.

Luca releases her, cussing, but pride shines in his eyes.

"Damn, Sloan! That was some quick reaction. I'm impressed," Asher raves.

"What the fuck, Beck!" Sloan storms over, shoving me as hard as she can.

I barely budge. Which seems to piss her off even more, so she shoves me again. "What." And then again. "The." And then her two little fists are beating into my stomach before Sloan's bursting into tears. "Fuck!"

I pull her close to my chest, trying to console her.

"That was cruel! You didn't even warn me!" Sloan screams at me as she continues to throw jabs at my stomach.

All of the guys, including Asher make a run for it out of the gym at her outburst.

Grabbing her wrists gently to get her to stop hitting me, I tell her honestly, "It was cruel but I'm not sorry. From what you've told us, I believe that James is a monster. A situation with him won't be controlled, Sloan. He may actually try to hurt you. Try to kill you.

"When you run from a narcissistic abuser and they find

you, they want you to suffer. James is going to be beyond furious that you left him. If he's tracking you and leaving flowers to scare you, James wants to hurt you. I don't know your ex, but if someone as strong and resilient as you ran, I imagine you're hoping like hell he never finds you. I just needed to make sure you would fight like hell to protect yourself. And you did. I want you alive, my beautiful girl. So, I'm sorry that I had to scare you. But I'm not sorry that you know what to do now."

"I hate you," Sloan cries.

"No, you don't. You hate this situation."

"Why do you have to keep pushing me?" Sloan says defeated, tears continuing to stream down her face.

"Because you can bend, but you will never break, Sloan. You won't let yourself. You're too fucking powerful for that." I gently run my hands through her hair, trying to soothe her.

"I'm not!" Sloan snaps, shoving my hands away.

"I'm weak! I let him…I let him turn me into someone… someone I'm not. I don't even know who that fucking girl is anymore!" Sloan points at herself in the mirror. Completely disheartened.

I grip her wrist, gentle but firmly with one hand. Tilting her chin up with the other, so her eyes meet mine, so she knows how serious I am. "You. Are. Sloan. Archer. You are so fucking powerful."

"Then stop treating me like I'm a fragile bird," Sloan yells.

I walk away from her, leaving her on the mat staring off at me.

"Where the hell are you going?" Sloan growls at me.

Mmm…there she is.

Once I get to the front door, I lock the door and flip the sign to *Closed*.

I ignore her yelling at me because I know it'll get her worked up. I like it when my Little Dove is riled up. I love to antagonize her, to push her. I love when she's filled with fire, even if it's directed at me. My guess is she had to hide this fire inside of her with her ex, had to dim herself for him. I imagine this is who she was always meant to be. Who she was before he sunk his talons into her. But now it's time for Sloan to fight back.

"What are you doing?" Sloan questions as I lean against the locked door staring at her.

"Answer me, Beckett!"

Sloan hasn't left the spot on the mat. She just stands there staring back at me, fire blazing in her eyes. Her hands framing her hips. She looks almost wild. And all I want to do is throw gasoline on her. See if we can set this place ablaze with the tension that's been building up between us. I want to see if I can use her anger and turn it into passion.

"Little Dove," I rumble. "My eyes are up here." When I notice her eyes are staring at the growing bulge in my gray workout shorts.

Sloan's eyes snap to mine in an instant, as if a magnetic field pulled them to mine. Lust shines in her eyes through the tears.

"You aren't fragile," I assure her, taking one step closer to her.

"You aren't weak." I take another step toward her.

"Then prove it," Sloan snaps, taking the bait, just as I hoped she would.

"Okay, Little Dove. How would you like me to do that?" I start to prowl toward her, hungry for her.

"I want you to break me, Beckett," Sloan challenges, almost panting. "Ruin me."

"If I make it to that mat, I'm going to fuck you, hard, Little Dove. Is that what you want? Make you forget your shitty ex ever existed. Erase every scar he ever left on that delectable body with my mouth. Prove I can break you, but that you can handle it," I growl.

"Yes, I want that," Sloan breathes out.

"Good girl, using your words," I hum in approval. "I need to be in full control, Little Dove. I will never do anything you aren't okay with, but I expect you to do as I say. Everything I do is for your pleasure. To push your body to its limits until you come harder than you've ever come before. I will happily ruin you, Sloan. So, stop me now if you don't want this."

"I want you, Beck," Sloan barely croaks out.

"Lie back on the mat for me then, Little Dove," I instruct.

"Should...we go somewhere more private?" Sloan questions, hesitation in her eyes.

"No, baby. I don't care who sees. Let the world watch."

"Okay." Sloan nods. Her eyes filled with so much trust.

"If anything gets to be too much and you want me to stop, just say "stop" and everything stops. The word "no" will not make me stop though, okay Sloan?" I grin.

"Got it, boss." Sloan smirks, nervously.

I groan at her bratty obedience. So fucking perfect.

"I got you, baby," I reassure her. I hover over her on the mat, just staring at her, as she lies below me. Taking her in. Raven hair sprawled out like a halo around her head, violet eyes piercing me.

I kneel down over top of her, I slide my knee between

her bent legs. Just barely grazing her pussy with my knee. Sloan lets out the smallest whimper.

Leaning forward, I pull Sloan's face up to mine and slam my lips down on hers in a searing kiss. Sloan kisses me back, her lips are pillowy, soft and full.

I wrap some of her hair in my fist, tugging it lightly to get a better angle. Sloan lets out a moan at the light tug of her hair, allowing me to slide my tongue between her lips and swirl it with hers. I release her lips so I could kiss my way down her slender neck.

Reaching my hands under Sloan's light blue sweater, I pull it up and over her head, as I continue to kiss my way down her neck. I take a little nip of her collarbone, which has her groaning. Sloan sneaks a nip of her teeth just below my ear which has me groaning and leaving goose bumps where her lips graze, just like they did in the car the other night.

Kissing my way down her chest, I take one of her pert nipples into my mouth through her sports bra while I grind my knee against her pussy again. I feel the heat of her core through her leggings.

"Beck."

I continue to leave open-mouth kisses down her toned stomach to her hip bones. I dig my teeth into her flesh, loving the way my teeth marks leave an imprint. I'm marking her as mine. Sloan writhes underneath me.

"I've got you, Little Dove. Stay still or I'll spank you."

Sloan's pupils dilate, but she stays silent, keeping still. I sit up, leaning back sitting on my feet. I tuck my thumbs in the waistband of her leggings and tug them down. Sloan shimmies her hips to help me get them off of her faster, making my mouth go dry at the sight of her. Sloan's completely bare under her leggings.

"No panties?" I groan.

"Too many layers for working out."

"Mmm…so you've never worn any? Never mind." I bite my fist just staring at her.

Fucking perfect.

Sloan smirks at me, reading my mind. "Nope."

"Good girl." I nip her inner thigh. "I'm never going to be able to focus while training you now, if I know you're bare for me all the time."

"Please touch me, Beckett," Sloan moans.

"You trust me, baby?" I ask without really giving her time to answer, before I'm reaching under her thighs and lifting her up, placing her on my shoulders.

"Oh my Gods, Beckett. What the hell are you doing?" Sloan yelps as I carry her over toward the pull-up bars.

I feel her fingers dig in my hair and tug. Using the strands of my hair to stay up right.

It feels so fucking good.

"I got you, Sloan. But do me a favor, baby, and take your bra off while you're up there, please?" My voice is muffled. My mouth is not even two inches from her pussy, that's dripping—for me. I hold back a groan.

"Yes, boss," I hear the sass in her voice. So, I bite her inner thigh again.

Sloan yelps, but then I see her sports bra tumble to the ground out of the corner of my eye.

"That's my good girl. Now hold onto the bars, so I can eat this pretty pussy," I grind out before swiping my tongue through her soaking folds.

"Fuuuck, you taste like fucking heaven."

Sloan moans and relaxes into my hold, allowing me to

dive in. I'm devouring her like a man starved, like I don't need oxygen to live. I swipe my tongue back and forth through her folds, sucking her clit into my mouth hard until I hear her gasp. Her wet heat is coating my lips and chin. I could drown in her and not give two fucks. I dig my big hands into her tight little ass, spreading her wider with my grip and diving my tongue deeper into her pussy. I alternate tongue fucking her pussy and flicking my tongue over and over on her clit.

"Come for me, Little Dove," I barely get out before she cries out in pleasure. Her thighs clenching around my head so hard, she almost muffles the sound of her ecstasy from my ears.

"Good girl." I kiss and nip her inner thighs until she comes down from her orgasm.

"Let go of the bar, baby. I got you."

Sloan let's go and I feel her thighs tighten around my neck and shoulders. With my hands still gripping her ass, her legs wrapped around my neck, I carry her over to the weight bench. As I gently lay her on her back, she smiles up at me with a dazed look on her face.

"Hi gorgeous." I smile, taking her in while she lies sprawled out for me.

She's fucking stunning. Relaxed. Trusting. *Mine.* I think for just a second.

"Hi." Sloan blushes.

I know I won't ever be able to use this bench without thinking about what I'm about to do to her.

Mirrors line the entire wall. I want to watch Sloan's face contort in pleasure as I fuck her from behind. I want her to watch as I take her and bend her to my will. I want her to see what she does to me, that even though I'm in control she holds all the power. I want her to see how fucking gorgeous she is—how fucking powerful she is.

"Lie back baby, I'm still hungry," I growl and swipe my tongue through her mess just to taste how fucking delicious she is again. Clean up the mess she made for me.

"Wait," Sloan breathes out, running her hand through my hair, almost pushing my head away.

"That's not the safe word, baby." I dive back into her dripping pussy.

"I know, Beckett. I... I want to taste you, too," Sloan says nervously.

My eyes meet hers, questioning, "Are you sure? This is supposed to be all about you."

"I'm sure. This is for me. Please? Can I taste you?"

"I have a better idea. Let's taste each other," I suggest, pulling the bench forward.

I walk to where her head rests, tugging my gym shorts down and tossing them toward the other end.

Sloan's eyes go wide when my cock bounces free from my shorts. Hard as granite for her.

"Lean your head back slightly off of the bench," I command. She scoots backwards slightly, following my instructions and does what I say.

"Good girl, now open up for me." I run my thumb over her lower lip, pressing down slightly, as it falls open.

I stroke my cock a few times, before lining up the tip with her lips. I press forward, slowly pushing in. Her mouth is so fucking warm and wet. It feels so fucking good. Too fucking good.

Sloan starts to bob her head, taking me in deeper. Sucking on the head of my cock, almost making my eyes cross.

I lean forward so I can cup her breasts into my hands, squeezing and kneading them.

Sloan moans and the vibration around my cock almost has me seeing stars.

I trace my tongue down her stomach and when I reach her pussy, I begin to suck and flick her clit with my tongue. Holding myself up on one elbow while I gently thrust my cock into Sloan's mouth. I slide my index finger through her wet folds, adding my middle finger and rubbing her G-spot as I continue working her with my mouth. Sloan groaning along with feeling the back of her throat clench around my cock, as her pussy does the same around my fingers, makes me moan in ecstasy.

Sloan's legs slip off of the bench, spreading wider for me.

I need a second to recover, her mouth feels so good. Standing up, my cock slides out of her perfect, satiny lips, slapping my lower abs. I'm so fucking hard for this girl.

Sloan pouts at the loss.

Mmm... Little Dove is just as hungry as I am.

"Little Dove, I just realized I don't have a condom. I've never..." I start to say. Rubbing my hand down my face.

"I'm on the pill. I was checked before I left. I haven't been with anyone for a while. I'm good, but if you're not comfortable..."

"Stand up, baby," I command.

Sloan stands in front of me. Gently grabbing her by the throat, I pull her to me and smash my lips down on hers, before I spin her around to face the mirrors behind her.

Our eyes meet in the mirror.

"I want you to watch me take you, Little Dove. Want you to see what you do to me," I rasp.

"Show me, please," Sloan whispers, never breaking eye contact with me in the mirror.

"Put your right knee on the bench and lean forward onto your elbows. Keep your left leg on the ground, legs spread me for baby."

She gets into position and I step up behind her, towering over her. I tilt her head up, her eyes meeting mine, studying my every move.

"Good girl," I whisper, stroking my hand gently down her back.

She melts into my touch.

Once I reach her pussy, I run my fingers through her folds, just to make sure she's still ready for me. My Little Dove is soaked. Her body trembling.

Stroking myself a few times. "Are you ready, baby?"

"Yes. Please, Beck."

Lining up my cock with her center, I slowly push into her. Sloan's so fucking tight, I barely make it in an inch.

"Relax, baby. I have you." I spread her ass and spit down between her cheeks to my cock.

Her eyes go wide and flare with heat. She rocks back on me, taking me a little bit deeper. We both sigh and groan. Sloan spreads her left leg a little bit wider for me.

I run my hand up her back, massaging her shoulders gently to get her to relax onto me. Reaching for her hair, I wrap it in my right fist, tugging her head up so our eyes meet in the mirror, as I thrust deeper into her.

We both let out a deep moan, as I continue to move deeper and deeper until I bottom out inside of her. Sloan starts to grind her hips on my cock and her eyes fall to where we're joined in the mirror. Watching as I slide in and out of her.

So fucking perfect.

"Harder, please," Sloan begs.

I tug her hair harder, tilting her head to the side so I have access to her mouth. I slam my lips on hers, while I slam my cock harder inside of her soaking wet pussy. I give my Little Dove exactly what she asks for.

Licking and nipping my way down her neck. Sloan smells divine, like a field of lavender. My left hand digs into her hip, pulling her onto my cock, bouncing her up and down on it. Our eyes never leaving each other in the mirror.

Droplets of sweat form on our skin. I trace my tongue to taste every inch of her. I reach forward with my right hand cupping her breast, pinching and tugging on her nipples.

"Rub your clit for me, baby," I grind out in her ear, as I bite her lobe.

Goose bumps pepper her skin.

"Mmm...does my good girl like that?"

"Yes, more please." Sloan breathes, reaching between her legs. Her fingers graze my cock as she makes small circles on her clit. Her pussy starts to clench around my cock almost sending me over the edge.

"Eyes on me, Sloan, when you come," I barely grind out before pulling her off my cock and flipping her over onto her back.

"Where do you want my cum, baby?" I ask, barely holding it together.

"Mmm... Inside me, please, Beckett." Her words surprising me.

I bend her legs until her feet are almost behind her head, slamming into her once, twice, while stroking her little nub with my thumb. She explodes, her core clenching so hard, soaking me, setting off my own release.

I crash my lips down on hers as I fill her with my cum. My legs are quivering and Sloan's trembling beneath me as I collapse forward on top of her. She's still bent in half, so I try to hold up some of my weight with my elbows braced around her head.

"Fuck," we both barely breathe out.

Sloan drops her legs, wrapping them around my waist as I'm still buried inside of her. I press my forehead to hers, just breathing her in.

"That was..." she whispers.

"You were incredible, Little Dove." I kiss her forehead, her nose and then her lips.

Sloan's face immediately drops when I stand up and grab my shorts off the floor.

Sloan is quiet as I scoop her up into my arms, carrying her to the showers in the locker room.

I maneuver her in my arms as I remove my shorts and reach into the stall to turn the showerhead on. Once the water temperature is hot enough, I step in under the spray of water.

Sloan stares up at me in silence, her eyes soft, dazed, as I gently set her down on her feet. She's tracking my every move.

Squeezing my bodywash into my hand, I lather it before turning her away from me and rubbing her shoulders down to her toes. Massaging, washing, rinsing, and kissing as I go. Sloan melts under my touch.

"I don't have the best shampoo here. I might have to wash your hair when we get home," I whisper in her ear, kissing the side of her head. Just holding her in my arms under the water.

"Thank you, Beckett," Sloan barely croaks out.

Turning her toward me, her eyes look glassy yet grateful. I gently stroke her cheek, kissing her lips gently.

I could kiss her forever...

Turning the water off, I grab us clean towels off of the rack next to the stall. Wrapping her up, I scoop her back up in my arms, carrying her out of the shower.

"You don't have to carry me everywhere, you know?" Sloan chuckles.

"I know I don't have to, but I want to, Little Dove." I cradle her closer to my chest.

I place her back in the middle of the mat where we left her clothes. Pulling her sweater over her head and tugging her leggings back on. I go to put her shoes on but she swats my hand away, giggling.

"Beck, I can put my shoes on."

"Just let me do it, Little Dove. What did I say about doing as I say?"

Sloan huffs, "Fine, *boss.*"

I get her sneakers on and tied, giving her a little swat on her ass before I tell her, "Hop on!"

"You have got to be kidding!" Sloan's giggling now.

"Not kidding, get on, Little Dove, or else." I smirk.

"Or else what, Beckett?"

"Or else I'm going to tickle you!"

Sloan squeals and goes to run off, but I snag her by the waist and go to carry her bridal style out of the gym but she stops me.

"Fine, fine. Put me down. I'll climb on. You are not carrying me home like this, you caveman!" Sloan giggles.

"Good girl." I lean forward, as she hops on my back.

I grip her under her thighs, boosting her up. Her arms wrap around my neck and she leans forward, kissing me just below my ear.

As I lock up the gym, I realize this girl never fails to make me smile.

"Take me home, caveman." Sloan smacks my ass.

"Yes ma'am. Anything else?"

"Carbs! Please get us some carbs," Sloan begs dramatically.

"Carbs it is, Little Dove." I nibble the inside of her wrist around my neck.

As I carry Sloan to pick up pizza, she's giggling about my caveman antics almost the whole way home.

My heart feeling whole for the first time since Sutton left.

27
Sloan

I'm wiping down the counter of Wagging With Words. Every swipe of the cloth on the counter has my muscles screaming and my core clenching. I can't stop thinking about all of the positions Beck bent me in yesterday, which causes my skin to heat. I can still feel some of the bite marks and the scruff of his short beard between my thighs. I'm so distracted I think I've been cleaning the same spot for ten minutes.

Beck carries me the entire way back from the gym. Not even putting me down when we pick up the pizza from Zio's. I don't even bother fighting him. My entire body aching in the best way from the thorough fucking he gave me. I have never experienced anything like that in my entire life.

When we get back to the apartment, Beck fills the tub for me with Epsom salts and bubbles. Feeding me amazing pepperoni and banana pepper pizza as I soak.

After I finish eating and am almost completely pruned, Beck washes my hair like he promised he would. Massaging every inch of my scalp and shoulders. I almost fall asleep because it feels so good. When Beck is finished, he drains the tub and scoops me up and out, wrapping me in the fluffiest towel then carries me to my bedroom.

Sitting me on the edge of the bed I take in how gorgeous he is. Beck stands in front of me, taking his soft gray T-shirt off, and pulling it over my head. I slide my thumbs in the waistband of his shorts pulling him closer to me, tracing my fingers through the definition of his abs. The muscles in his neck flex, as if he's holding back restraint from touching me as he allows me to explore him on my own terms without saying a word.

Beck finally breaks the silence, pulling me to him. He cradles my face in his hands as he takes me in a burning kiss, biting my lower lip and tugging it between his teeth. Beck releases my face and lifts me, moving me up the bed. He begins to crawl over top of me, crushing his lips back down on mine.

"I need to stop, Little Dove. You're already going to be so sore tomorrow," Beck groans out.

"I'll be fine, Beck," I whimper, holding back a wince, lifting my arms to drape around his neck and pull him back down to me.

"You're already sore, baby. You can't hide from me," Beck says, getting up and pulling the covers down on the opposite side of the bed.

He crawls into the bed next to me. "Come here, Little Dove. Just let me hold you."

"What about Mayhem?" I question, as Mayhem pokes his head into the bedroom.

Beck taps the bed and Mayhem hops up. Laying down at the bottom of the bed, against his legs. A squeak leaves me, as Beck lifts me up from where I'm laying, setting me on top of him. Beck pulls back the covers where I was just laying and lifts me up and puts me back where I was.

"What are you doing?" I giggle.

"Get under the covers and get your fine ass over here, Little Dove. Don't make me ask again."

"Yes, boss." I pull the covers up over my legs and scoot over and rest my head on Beck's chest.

He grabs my face, tilting my head up so my lips can meet his.

It was so...perfect.

I don't think anyone's ever kissed me or taken care of me like that. Almost like I was this precious heirloom that needed to be handled with care.

But I know Beck doesn't think I'm fragile because he's training me to wield my own sword. Regardless, he still plans to be my backup shield and that does funny things to my heart.

I remember sitting in the nurses' station with the girls when they were interrogating me about James. They had asked if he set my soul on fire and I never even knew what that meant. More like James turned my life into a dumpster fire.

But kissing Beck... It's like sitting cozied up around a campfire eating s'mores with the perfect gooiest marshmallow. Warm, sweet with a little cinnamon spice and so comforting. My heart always turns to goo the second Beck cradles me to him and then is set ablaze the second his lips meet mine. My soul comes alive when he kisses me.

Maybe that's what they meant?

I never knew a kiss could feel so good. I never want to stop kissing him. Never want to leave his arms. And Beck always seems to kiss me like we have all the time in the world.

Snapping me out of my daydream, a familiar voice calls out, "Who put those hearts in my Sloan's eyes?"

When I look up, Sutton and August are strolling through the front door of WaggingWithWords with Khaos walking right between them.

"You're back," I squeak out, rushing Sutton and pulling her into a hug.

Khaos barks out a hello and I rub his big blond blockhead.

I have missed them so much.

"That proposal was pretty magical, August. 20/10! Engaged looks good on you." I smile, pulling August into a side hug.

"Sunshine's the real magic." August smiles, wrapping his arms around Sutton and tucking her into his chest.

"It was a good PR stunt." Sutton gently elbows him.

Chuckling, August says, "I tell you time and again, Sunshine. It was not a PR stunt. The world just needed to know you were mine and I was yours."

"Yeah, yeah." Sut giggles, her eyes so lit up.

Their love is contagious. Magnetic. You can't help but just be consumed with happiness for them.

"*How are my famous friends?*" Quinn shouts, running out of the kitchen, full force at Sutton, wrapping herself around her.

"I missed you too, Q." Sutton squeezes Quinn back just as hard.

"Dark and gloomy, you're looking a little less moody," Quinn jokes, pulling August into a side hug.

"It's kind of hard to be moody when your fiancée is made of fairy dust." August kisses Sutton in a chaste kiss.

"Ew. Didn't you kiss enough on stage? Get a room!" Quinn gags jokingly.

"Oh, Shoot. Speaking of rooms," I blurt out. "Beck is still staying in your room. His apartment won't be ready for another week."

"Beck can always sleep on the couch if he needs to," Sut says, glancing at August to make sure he wouldn't mind.

"Or..." Quinn smirks mischievously.

"Or?" Sutton questions her.

I immediately know what she's going to suggest. "No, Q."

"What am I missing?" August asks, eyeing all of us suspiciously.

Sutton and Quinn both smile deviously at each other.

"Or the bed in your room is a king. You and Beck have been a little cozy lately so you could share." Quinn grins almost maniacally.

"No, Q," I grumble, but secretly loving that idea.

"Ooooh, interesting. I can see it," August says, rubbing his jaw.

"See what?"

"I think what Auggie is trying to say is that we can see how you and Beck would actually be a perfect match," Sutton suggests.

"We're just friends, guys. Beck's been coaching me in the gym. I mean sure, we do have most meals together, watch movies sometimes, but that's because we've been staying under the same roof," I trip over my words.

"Okay, but you were daydreaming about someone

when I walked in." Sutton smirks.

"How could you possibly know that?"

"Because Sloan, you look different, but like good different. You look healthy. Less like a cornered animal. Lighter. Still jumpy, but lighter. And from what I've heard"—Sutton's eyes wander to Quinn—"you and Beck have been spending a lot of time together. So, it would make sense to maybe have a crush on him."

"I do not have a crush on…" I start to deny them.

Who am I kidding? I think it's more than a crush.

"Oh, hey. Welcome back," Beck says, walking through the door from the apartment into the café.

The air escapes my lungs at the sight of him.

He's dressed in a navy button-up with deep gray chinos that hug his thighs just right as he walks up to us.

"And where are you off to looking so spiffy?" Quinn quirks a brow at Beck.

"Always so nosey, Q. Hopefully my last neurology appointment. Crossing my fingers for clearance," Beck offers.

"I hope everything goes well." I smile at Beck, blushing slightly at the look in his eyes. Wondering if he's thinking about last night, like I have been all morning.

"Thank you, Little Dove. I'm sure it will, thanks to you keeping me in line." Beck kisses my cheek.

My cheeks must flush even more at his affection in front of everyone.

James always kept his arm on my lower waist to make sure everyone knew I was his at parties, but he was never openly affectionate. Never held my hand. Never kissed me. Mostly treated me as if I wasn't there.

"I moved my stuff out of your room into Sloan's room for now. Quinn said you guys were going to be back sometime this week. Is it cool if I crash on the couch?" Beck asks Sutton and August.

"Yeah, it's no problem," August replies, in solidarity with Sutton.

"Or..." I barely make out.

Quinn and Sutton gasp at the same time and their eyes light up.

"What?" Beck questions, eyeing all of us girls.

"Or...the bed is...big...um... I could share...but if you're not comfortable... Actually...I probably shouldn't be asking...you know, in front of everyone... I'm so sorry," I ramble off flustered. Opening the front door, I step outside, taking in a deep breath of fresh air.

My eyes meet the windowsill of WaggingWithWords closest to me and lying perfectly posed is a white rose with the smallest amount of red staining one of the petals.

Is that blood?

I feel hands on my shoulders. An ear-splitting scream leaves me and I rip away from the touch.

"Sloan, it's me. Don't run," Beck tries to soothe me.

"Beck..." My voice cracks, barely sounding like my own. I turn around to face Beck, throwing my arms around him as I tremble in fear.

"Hey, what's...?" Beck starts to ask but goes rigid. He must notice the rose on the windowsill too.

"What the fuck." Beck grits out, looking up and down the street. Keeping me tucked against his chest, he walks us over and picks it up where a Post-it note lies underneath. The note reads:

I'll never let you go.

XO, J

All of the blood must drain from my face because Beck lifts me up from the ground and carries me into the café, instantly locking the door behind us.

James. Found. Me.

"What is it?" August asks, concern in his eyes.

"Her ex... He found her," Beck grinds out.

"Fuck," Quinn curses.

"Sut, can you please call and reschedule my doctor's appointment?" Beck requests.

"No," I hiccup in between a sob. "Please go to your appointment. Your clearance is more important," I say, trying to calm myself.

"No, actually. Your well-being is more important," Beck says with so much conviction. Making my heart melt the slightest bit.

"Beck, please. At least go to your appointment. Please," I beg.

"We can stay here with her. James obviously hasn't tried to come inside. So, as long as Sloan doesn't go anywhere alone she should be fine," Quinn suggests.

"How about you come to my appointment with me? So I can keep an eye on you." Beck requests.

"Can you girls handle the café for a little?" I ask quietly.

"Yep. I've missed this place. Put me to work." Sutton tries to lighten the mood.

"Khaos and I will chill in the book room and keep an eye out," August offers.

"Mayhem's upstairs if you want to bring him down too," Beck suggests, nodding upstairs.

"I'll go grab my other handsome boy," Sutton squeals,

taking off for the stairwell to her apartment.

"Oh, and by the way..." Beck starts. Stopping everyone in their tracks.

All of our eyes are on Beck when he growls, "Yes, Little Dove, I will share that room with you. James will not get near you if I have anything to do with it."

"Okay," I whimper.

"I will keep you safe. Mayhem will keep you safe. You will keep you safe. You are safe," Beck says, gently stroking my cheeks with his thumbs, as tears run down my face.

"We will all do our absolute best to keep you safe. You're one of us now," Quinn says.

"Forever," Sutton offers from the stairs.

"Thank you," I cry.

"Come on, Little Dove. Let's get this appointment over with, so we can get back and have a nice night in. The lot of us," Beck suggests, lacing his fingers in mine.

"Movie night. I'll text Ash," Quinn shouts.

"You all will never know how truly grateful I am for you." I smile through my tears, squeezing Beck's hand tighter, leaning my head against his shoulder.

"We have you, Little Dove." Beck kisses the side of my head, keeping me tucked into his side. Where it feels like what I've always dreamed home would feel like.

28

Beck

When Sloan and I get back from my doctor's appointment, WaggingWithWords is closed. There is a sign up on the door that says, 'Closed early for the day. Will be open tomorrow for a welcome back concert from, *From Troy*.'

Sloan uses her key to get in while I stand behind her, caging her small frame in as I monitor the street for her ex. The second we get in, she turns around locking the door as quickly as she can, her fingers trembling.

"You're safe, Little Dove," I breathe into her ear from behind her. Gently squeezing her shoulders and brushing my lips just below her ear.

Goose bumps pepper her skin. Sloan drops her arms and leans back into me.

It's become so natural to touch her. To kiss her.

"James is here, Beck. He found me. Maybe I should try and leave tonight, before James can get to me," Sloan whispers, shoulders slumping.

"No. You aren't leaving, Sloan. That's not an option," I say fiercely, going rigid at Sloan even thinking of running.

Sloan whips around, facing me. "So, what? I just lie in wait. Wait for him to grab me? To attack me? Do you have any idea how terrifying that is?"

Grabbing her shoulders, I look into her gorgeous tear-filled eyes and I plead with her. "No, Sloan. I can't begin to imagine how afraid you are. But you're not alone anymore. You don't have to deal with this by yourself. If you run again, you have no one again. And you will still be lying in wait. You will always be waiting for him to find you. You'll have to go through this, all over again. Except, alone. We know he's found you. We will all do our best to make sure nothing happens to you. Please don't run."

"Beck, I'm so scared." Sloan breaks, crashing into my arms. Sobs racking her body. Holding her tight to my chest, I rub circles on her back. Just letting her cry. There's nothing I can say to make this better. All I can do is hold her and be here for her.

A loud thud has her yelping in my arms. I release her, pushing her behind me. Never letting my hand leave her hip, as we both turn and face the door. There's no one there. Walking closer to it, I look out the window while keeping Sloan tucked behind me. A dead cardinal lies on the sidewalk, just below the window. I turn to face her because she's gone silent, she's pale and trembling.

"That has to be a bad omen," Sloan whispers, her eyes wide.

"Hopefully, it's not. I think more birds fly into glass than we realize when they see their reflection, unfortunately. Are you ready to head upstairs now?" I ask. Wanting to get her away, just in case her ex is lurking somewhere we can't see.

"Yeah. Can you...umm...check the lock one more time, please?"

"Of course." I gently brush tears from her cheeks. Kissing her forehead.

Checking the lock and tugging on the door for good measure. "It's locked. You sure you're ready to go upstairs?"

Sloan nods.

"Your words, Little Dove."

"Yes, Beckett," Sloan sighs.

Scooping her up in my arms, Sloan wraps her legs around my waist, resting her head on my chest.

"A girl could get used to this kind of treatment, Beckett." I feel Sloan smile against my neck, as I carry her toward the doors leading to the apartment. Locking that behind us too—just in case.

"Good. Get used to it, Little Dove," I growl, carrying her up the steps to the apartment.

*O*pening the door, we're met with so much noise and chaos. I worry Sloan's going to shut down.

She surprises me though. When I set her down on her feet, there's a little light back in her eyes because of all the company in the apartment.

Quinn and Asher are finishing setting up silverware and plates in the kitchen. The island is covered in ingredients for a taco bar. Beef and shrimp tacos with all the fixin's. Nachos with queso, salsa, and guacamole; all made fresh by Quinn and Ash.

It looks unbelievable. My stomach growls at the smell.

It looks like Sutton may have premixed an entire pitcher of lavender margaritas for the girls. Sloan got them hooked on those before Sutton left for tour. I notice Sloan's smile grows when she sees it too. There's a vibrant, fresh fruit spread of berries and pineapple on the island.

"Isn't there a thing with pineapples?" Knox, From Troy's bassist, jokes, popping a piece in his mouth, while wiggling his eyebrows at Quinn.

"Something with swingers, right?" Sutton questions.

The same time that August responds from the living room, "Supposed to make cum taste better I think."

Knox bursts out laughing. "I was implying the cum, Sut, but the swinger thing is true too. I think it has to be upside down or something?"

"What do you think, Blondie?" Knox grabs her by the hip, pulling her to him. "Open." Knox pops a piece of pineapple in Quinn's mouth.

"I think it's if the guy eats the pineapple. But not interested in finding out, Knoxie." Quinn pats his cheek.

"Get the fuck out of my kitchen, unless you're going to be useful," Asher growls at Knox.

"Fine. Relax." Knox holds up his hands, walking into the living room to sit next to August.

Sloan and I both immediately make eye contact, having a silent conversation about their dynamic. Sloan's eyes lit up with humor, trying hard to fight back a laugh. But honestly so am I.

August and Knox are sprawled out on the floor in the living room. Both dogs lay on the throw rug near their feet.

Sloan's eyes fill with tears when she makes her way to

the tv. Her favorite movie, Ten Things I Hate About You, queued up and ready to go. I texted the girls when we were leaving the doctor's, suggesting that movie for Sloan.

"You guys..." Sloan whispers.

"We love you, Sloan." Quinn and Sutton come up and squeeze in on each side of her.

"I love you guys too. How did you know?" A lone tear streaks down Sloan's face.

"What's the verdict, man?" Ash questions, slapping me on the back.

I feel all three girls' sets of eyes on me, when I answer Ash.

"I'm good to start training again!" I grin.

"Is it time to eat yet? I'm fuckin' starved!" Knox groans, from the living room.

"Quit whining, Knoxie! Everything is finally ready," Quinn declares.

Sloan gets in line to make a plate. Eyeing everything on the counter, smiling. "This spread is incredible, Q, Ash. Thank you."

"It was nothing." Quinn kisses Sloan on the cheek.

Sutton passes out glasses of margaritas, filled to the brim, to everyone but Ash and I. Tossing bottles of water to us.

Sutton puts her glass in the air. "A toast... To love. To making our dreams come true. To friends becoming family. And to a home-cooked meal. Cheers!"

"To friends becoming family. Welcome back. Now everyone, dig in," Sloan and Quinn say in unison. Smiling at each other as Sutton walks over to them.

"I love that my besties have also become besties,"

Sutton expresses, pulling both girls in for a side hug.

Everyone plates their food and grabs their drinks. Heading to the living room to start the movie.

"You didn't want to invite Ty and Beau?" I ask August about the rest of the band members, trying to make polite conversation.

"Ty wanted to get back to Rachel. You know Beau, not much of a mingler," August replies, shrugging his shoulders.

"I missed my Blondie! That's why I came." Knox leans over, kissing Quinn on the cheek.

"Get out of here, Knoxie!" Quinn shoves his head away playfully.

Asher sits next to me, annoyance written all over his face. His posture rigid as he watches Quinn and Knox's interaction.

"So, you gonna be ready to start training again tomorrow?" Ash asks me, faking being amped up. My guess is he's trying to distract himself from Quinn and Knox.

"Yes. Little Dove and I will be there." I nudge my foot against hers.

"Actually, I saw the sign that you guys are putting on a show tomorrow night. Do you need me here? I can skip a day at the gym. I'm pretty sore from yesterday." I notice Sloan's cheeks flush.

I try to hide my smirk, biting into a shrimp taco. Groaning at how good all of the flavors pair well together. Pops of habanero, mango, and coconut light up my taste buds.

"It would actually be great if you could be here. If you don't mind. We could use an extra set of hands. It's going to be pretty busy," Sutton says.

"If I can make a suggestion." Asher clears his throat. "Not to dampen the mood, but Sloan, with your ex lurking and the show tomorrow, not to scare you, but it gives him a chance to sneak in with a large crowd potentially. I'd actually like for all three of you girls to let me run a couple knife training drills with you tomorrow before the café opens. Just in case, you know?"

"Ooooh, Sunshine's gonna be a grizzly tomorrow if you're waking her ass up early," August chuckles.

"You hush." Sut puts her hand over August's mouth. He laughs harder under her hand.

"You get one hour, Asher Ward," Quinn huffs in agreement.

"Got it, Sugar." Asher winks at Quinn.

"Only one, Ash," Sutton groans. "You know I need my eight hours of sleep."

"I will be there. Thanks, Ash," Sloan agrees, slightly tense.

"It would make me feel better. Thank you. We can man the doors like old times if you want, be on surveillance. I can see if a couple of the other guys from the gym wouldn't mind helping out too. Make sure there are a few of us and we're all vigilant," Ash offers.

"That would be really great actually. Thank you," Sutton says.

"All hands on deck. I imagine it's going to be crazy with you guys having gone viral," Quinn squeals.

"We got this. Like old times." I smile.

"Like old times," We all cheers.

"It's still so surreal," August says almost in awe.

Sutton leans her head against his shoulder. August wraps his arm around her, pulling her close to him, kissing the side of her head.

As I watch them, I don't feel anything. Not hurt, not mad, nothing. I'm happy for them.

"It really is," Knox sighs.

Tapping his stomach like he's full. "This was so good, Blondie. Can you cook for me all the time?" Knox questions with hearts in his eyes.

"What do I get out of it, Knoxie?" Quinn teases.

"Pineapples?" Knox jokes.

We all burst into laughter except for Asher, who's once again glaring daggers at Knox. Sloan and my eyes meet.

"Interesting," I mouth to her, raising my brows.

"I know, right," Sloan mouths back in agreement.

*T*he end credits of the movie are running. Everyone is fast asleep except for me.

I'm taking everything in. Sloan's tiny breaths tickling my neck, her body tucked tight against mine. Sutton is curled up against August on the other end of the couch with August's arm holding her tightly to him. Quinn is sandwiched between Asher and Knox on the floor. Quinn's left leg draped over Asher's; his hand firmly placed on her thigh while his head leans against the cushions of the couch. Quinn's head is on Knox's shoulder and Knox's head rests comfortably on top of Quinn's. Even the dogs are curled up together.

Safe. Everyone is safe.

When did we become a family? My friends have shown

so much love and affection toward me, even toward each other, more than my own parents ever have—ever had.

I haven't spoken to my father since he left when I was a teenager. But my mother and I keep in touch with each other a few times a year.

Sloan stretches out next to me on the couch, yawning, taking me out of my head.

"Ready for bed, Little Dove?" I whisper in her ear.

"Yes, please." Sloan smiles drowsily at me.

She's just so sweet...so beautiful. The way her dark lashes fan eyes like I've never seen before. They pierce my heart every time they connect with mine. How could anyone ever want to hurt her?

When did this girl steal my heart?

Scooping her onto my lap, I stand up with her in my arms, carrying her to the bathroom. Sitting her on the bathroom sink, I put toothpaste on her toothbrush and hand it to her as we brush our teeth in a comfortable silence. Taking a warm washcloth, I gently wash her face for her. Sloan sinks into my hand, just letting me gently trace her face with the warm cloth. Closing her eyes, she lets out a contented sigh. Handing her a towel, I let her dry her face herself.

"Ready?" I ask, before hanging the towel back on the rack and scooping her back into my arms.

"Mm-hmm," Sloan mumbles sleepily.

Sloan hits the light switch off, as I carry her out of the bathroom into the bedroom. Mayhem follows behind us, never letting Sloan out of his sight for long.

Pulling the covers back, I lay Sloan down. Mayhem hops up on the end, walking in circles before lying down against her legs. Sliding into the bed next to her, I turn the bedside lamp off, before holding her close and tucking us in.

A couple minutes pass before I break the silence. Allowing the dark to give me courage to ask her something that's been on my mind a lot the last couple of days.

"How come you never fight me?" I ask softly.

"What do you mean? I literally punched the hell out of you yesterday." I feel Sloan's head tilt up toward me. She chuckles quietly.

"Not like actually fight me. Sutton… Never mind…" I start. Changing my mind because I don't want to bring Sutton up and make Sloan uncomfortable.

"You can talk about Sut to me Beck. She was your friend before you guys tried to be something else. Sutton is still very much your friend, and now mine. We can talk about her. I didn't mean that we couldn't when I said I wasn't going to be your second choice," Sloan declares.

"If you're sure," I breathe into her hair.

"I'm sure. Talk to me." Sloan gently traces circles on my chest with her finger tips.

"It's just… Sutton used to fight me. She never wanted me to pick her up. Didn't really like when I did things to try and protect her or acted like a caveman as you call me. Sut is really independent. Not saying that you aren't because you are but you've never complained or told me to stop. You just sort of let me pick you up and carry you without saying a word. Let me wash your hair. Make you coffee. Things that I want to do to take care of you," I mutter.

"Beckett, I spent so much of my life doing everything I could to meet this goal and then once I met that goal, I set another one that I just needed to meet. I think I was running from myself. Plowing through life to become this independent woman that didn't need anyone but herself.

Do you know how exhausting that is? Why do I need to be that way? What am I even trying to prove? Who am I trying to prove it to? When is enough going to be enough? You know," Sloan says, sighing.

"I get it. To everyone that ever let you down, you want to shove it in their face how great you're doing without actually shoving it in their face," I reply to her rhetorical question.

"Yeah. You're probably right. When I met James, I think deep down I always knew he wasn't right for me. But everyone else thought James was so great, so perfect for me. It just felt like the next box to check off, and once I became his wife it got so bad, so fast. All I ever wanted to do was run away. I was constantly walking on eggshells, looking over my shoulder. I tried to be perfect but my perfect was never enough. His version of perfect changed every day and it was never me." Sloan shakes her head against my chest.

"I'm so sorry, Little Dove. Everything about you is perfect in my eyes." I kiss her forehead.

"So, to answer your question... Why don't I fight you? Honestly, it's just so nice to be able to just be with you. To just exist with you. To feel safe with you. I don't have to hide. When you say you have me, I can feel it in my soul that you do. I'm not sure when I found safety in you, but I did. And there is no part of me that wants to fight with you or run from you. I just want to exist in the safety of your arms. I just want to be free with you," Sloan almost whispers her last words.

"So, if that's accepting your caveman antics and just letting you carry me wherever your heart desires, then carry me, you shall," Sloan tries to make a joke to cover up her vulnerability. Placing a soft kiss on my chin.

"I will carry you, for as long as you'll let me, Little Dove."

Sloan's soft breaths brush my neck before I feel her lips kiss just under my ear.

"Thank you, Beckett. For always being an anchor for me. For being so kind," Sloan whispers before she's falling asleep in my arms.

Right where she belongs. I think before drifting off to sleep, wrapped around her like a cocoon.

29

Sloan

*B*eck and I are lying in my bed fast asleep when an alarm blaring has us both groaning and he reaches over to shut it off. Rolling on his side, Beck tugs me close to him, burying his face in my neck.

"If this knife training wasn't so important, I'd skip the gym and go back to sleep," I groan.

"Mmm… I have a knife for you to train with, Little Dove." Beck flexes his hips into my ass groaning.

"How much time do we have?" I flirt back, feeling bold.

Something I never would have asked James. I snuck out of bed before him every chance I got so he wouldn't touch me.

"Mmm… If you allow me to eat you for breakfast, we have fifteen minutes." Beck nips my neck with his teeth before he lifts up the blankets. Crawling down my body, he scoots down the bed.

"Yes or no, Little Dove?" Beck makes his way from my neck down to my inner thighs.

"Yes, please," I whimper.

"That's my good girl," Beck groans, sucking hard on my clit through my panties. "You taste so sweet this morning."

"Ahh..." I moan. "So, the pineapple...mmm"—his tongue traces me through my underwear—"actually works."

Beck growls, pulling my panties down with his teeth. "Fuck, yes. So fucking sweet, baby."

Fuck. Why is that so hot?

"Can I touch you please?"

"Yes, Little Dove," Beck assures me before swiping his tongue through my soaking wet folds.

I can't help but thrust my pelvis up and grind against his face because of how good it feels.

Beck's large hands spread me wider, digging his fingers into my thighs, holding me open for him, as he devours me.

Running my hands through his hair, I grip and tug on it, grinding into his face, as he eats me like I'm his breakfast, lunch and dinner.

"Ahh. Fuck. Beck, that's so..." I moan, my breath catching when Beck slides two fingers into my pussy, curling them upward and thrusts hard. I almost see stars.

Beck's mouth leaves my pussy, as he kisses his way up my stomach to my breasts. Taking one of my pert nipples into his mouth, sucking and then nipping it with his teeth, as he continues to thrust two fingers inside me.

He kisses his way up my neck, nibbling my ear with his teeth.

"Such a good fucking girl for me, Little Dove. Now come." Before he slams his lips on mine, hitting my G-spot just right with his fingers. He muffles my screams with his lips on mine, as my orgasm comes barreling out of me. Electricity shooting down my limbs. Lights flashing before my eyes.

Beck pulls away, staring in my eyes.

"You're so good. So responsive, baby." He kisses me softly.

"Mmm...your turn." I smile lazily up at him, reaching out for him.

"Later, baby. We have to get to the gym." Beck kisses me one last time, before he climbs out of bed.

His hard cock standing at attention in his boxers has my mouth salivating at the sight of it.

"Please?" I lick my lips eyeing his cock.

"Keep staring at him like that and you'll be choking on him, Little Dove."

My eyes go wide but I'm suddenly so turned on all over again. All the butterflies go straight to my pussy. Staring at Beck, in nothing but his boxers, is a religious experience.

The girls at work always joked and referred to James as a "Silver Daddy," but I never really saw it. Looking at Beck, it's evident the heavens took their time sculpting every inch of him. Beck's seriously the most divine of all daddies. I could stare at him for an eternity and never get tired.

"Baby," Beck rumbles.

"Okay, later. We don't have time to shower huh?" I ask still in a daze.

"No, but you already gave me a shower so I'm good. I'll get to smell you on me all day," Beck growls, licking his lips.

The way Beck's looking at me, has me clenching my thighs together.

Hopping out of bed, I scurry to the closet and pull out a sweatshirt and pair of leggings to throw on. Trying to hide just how much I still want Beck.

He watches my every move, but I'm watching him too, as he pulls on a pair of gray sweats that show the outline of his still hard cock. I pout when he pulls on a navy blue sweatshirt hiding his chiseled abs from me.

"Baby, eyes up here," Beck quips.

"I could say the same to you, Beckett. I see you staring at my ass," I tease back.

"It's a great ass, Little Dove." Beck winks, walking over giving my ass a little love tap.

"Are you ready? I don't think we have time for coffee," Beck says almost apologetically.

"Yep, I'll drink some when we get back." I smile at him, going up on my tippy toes giving him a chaste kiss.

Beck holds me to him, kissing me harder with more hunger. I groan into his mouth and he scoops me up by my thighs. I instinctively wrap my legs around his waist. Loving the feel of his arms flexing against my skin as he holds me close to him.

I pull away chuckling. "I thought we had to leave, Beckett."

"We do." He pulls the bedroom door open and everyone is sitting at the island waiting for us.

All eyes are on us. Devious smirks on Sutton and Quinn's faces, like they know what we were up to. Even Asher looks happy, maybe?

"Good morning, love birds," Quinn chirps.

Beck and I both chuckle. "Morning, Q. Are you guys ready?"

"Is anyone ever ready this early in the morning?"

Sutton groans.

"We were just waiting on you guys," Asher offers slyly. "Is Sloan injured?"

"What?" I ask, confused.

"Beck can't seem to keep your feet on the ground. Just wanted to make sure you weren't injured." Asher eyes Beck, smirking.

"I'm not injured. I like being carried. It's nice to be held and not weighed down for once," I respond to Ash, smiling at Beck.

"All right, let's get to it. We have a busy day," Sutton announces. She and Quinn smiles at me with so much love in their eyes.

30

Beck

Quinn, Sutton and Sloan are sitting against one of the padded walls in the gym.

Sutton looks annoyed to be awake. Quinn looks intrigued by our faux weapons. Sloan still looks a little flushed from being my breakfast in bed this morning, but I can tell she's a bit anxious by the way she wrings her hands in her sweatshirt.

Asher and I are in the middle of the mat getting out our resin knives—the size of pocket knives—we use to teach our classes.

"The best place to keep a knife is either attached to your waistband, in your boot, or on a necklace tucked under your shirt. Out of sight but easy to access," Asher explains.

"It's always important to remember all of the techniques we've taught you in the self defense classes. But having a knife to access, just in case things start to escalate too quickly is a great tool for you to carry," I add.

Asher tucks his faux knife into his waistband on his

right hip. "It's best to have the knife on the side of your dominant hand, but you should really learn to use it on either side."

I take this moment when he's slightly off guard to charge at Ash from behind, pinning his arms to his side, and start pulling him backwards, as if I'm trying to abduct him.

Asher immediately drops into a low squat, which allows him room to grab his knife from his waistband. He pulls it out and slices at my wrists to get me to release him and runs away.

"You always want to try to go for things that are going to debilitate the offender immediately. People always assume it's stabbing anywhere on the body that causes them to bleed, but it takes time to bleed out. Adrenaline buys the offender even more time to continue to attack you. So, go for the tendons or nerves in an arm or wrist that's wrapped around you. It forces them to let you go because those limbs functionally stop working. The tendon above the knee is also a place to go for. Their knee buckles and they can't run after you, giving you a chance to escape. Your goal is to get away, not to kill," Asher teaches us.

I lay on the ground with my knife tucked in my waistband getting into position for the next most common way to be attacked.

"Abusers..." I start meeting Sloan's eyes. Hoping I don't scare her. "I'm sorry, Little Dove. Abusers will try to get you on the ground, so they can have the upper hand. They might throw you, hit you, pin you, or choke you."

Asher climbs on top of me, sitting on my hips. Asher's body blocking the access to my knife. Asher reaches forward putting his hands around my neck like he's going to choke me.

I immediately thrust my hips upward, knocking Asher off balance, causing him to fall forward a little bit. I reach down to my knife and rip it out. I bring up the knife slashing at Asher's wrist and then slam my arms up and through Asher's. Completely knocking him off balance. I push myself up the mat still lying down, almost in a shrimp position and use my feet to push Asher away. Getting out from underneath him, I hop up and run off.

"You are going to want to thrust them up with your hips so you can get to your knife. Do anything to get them off of you. Get them off balance while they are on top. Try to get their elbow to bend so they release the tension around your throat. If you can get to your knife, your options are going to be to slash at their arms so they release your neck, or slash at their forehead or eyes," I continue, demonstrating the technique of how to hold the knife and how to slash the person or the air in this case.

"A scalp laceration bleeds like crazy. They won't be able to see anything, so you'll be able to get out and run," Asher offers.

"Are we going to get to practice or did you wake me up early for nothing?" Sutton sasses.

Asher chuckles, "Yes, you ladies can practice on each other. Take turns. We'll watch and make corrections as you go."

"Start with the ground exercise first, we only have about a half hour left," I instruct.

"Yes, boss." Sloan winks, getting up from the wall. She walks over and lays in the middle of the mat where I just was laying. Surprising all of us when she says, "I would feel more confident if you were the one pinning me and I was actually able to get out from underneath you, Beck."

Quinn whistles.

Sutton's eyes are like a pinball, bouncing back and forth between mine and Sloan's. Bugged out of her head like a cartoon character. She's holding her breath waiting for my answer.

Asher snaps his fingers at Quinn and Sutton. "You two. Get on the mat and start practicing."

"Not a chance. I need to watch this," Quinn sasses Asher.

"Sugar."

"You heard me, Asher."

Asher huffs out in annoyance but doesn't say another word.

"You're sure, Little Dove?" I ask Sloan quietly, almost like we're the only two in the room.

She looks me dead in the eyes. "Yes, Beckett. I'm sure. You're so much bigger. So much stronger than James. If I can get away from you..." She inhales and then exhales. Shaking her head, like she's trying to shake off a bad feeling. "Then I could get away from him..."

"Okay, Little Dove." Tucking my knife in the waistband of her leggings on her right side. I climb on top of her, pinning her pelvis down to the mat with my hips. Feeling the knife underneath me.

"Beckett?"

"Yeah?"

"Do not hold back on me. I need to prove to myself I can do this," Sloan declares, her eyes never leaving mine.

"I won't. But I will not bruise this body unless it's for pleasure, Little Dove. Our safe word still stands for this," I lean forward to whisper in her ear for only her to hear. Kissing her just below it.

"I'll say stop if it's too much for me."

"Ready?" I ask sitting upright on top of her. Reaching forward, I put my hands around her tiny neck.

"Ready," Sloan whispers, fear mixed with determination in her eyes.

The room is dead silent. You could hear a pin drop.

I sit my full weight down on Sloan's pelvis and start to apply pressure to her neck. Enough that she feels it, but not enough to actually harm her. No part of me wants to harm a hair on her head. I want to be a place for her to rest, not another war zone.

Sloan starts to thrust her hips up but she can barely move my weight.

"You just need to pop yourself up enough, to try to twist the littlest bit to your right side so you can get to your knife, Sloan," Asher instructs her. "Don't tire yourself too soon."

"You're too heavy," Sloan screams out, frustrated.

"Do not quit, Sloan. You're going to have more adrenaline if you're scared. Pretend I'm James. Use all of your might to get me up so you can get to your knife," I demand.

Sloan takes a deep breath and then yells out, thrusting up as hard as she can and twisting to the right a little bit. Sloan's able to wiggle just enough that she can reach for her knife.

I apply a little bit of pressure to Sloan's neck, just to remind her that I'm still choking her. That she only has so much time and needs to be efficient with it. Get her knife. Get out of there.

Sloan's hand holding her knife comes stretching up between us and she slices at both of my wrists. I pretend to drop forward on her, as if my wrists give out.

Sloan shoves me and starts scurrying back, tucking her

body and scooting up the mat, until she's free. Sloan uses her feet to shove my shoulders back to get further away from me and then jumps up, running toward the girls.

Tears are streaming down Sloan's face when Quinn and Sutton both wrap her tight in their arms.

Storming over to her, I rip her out of their arms. Spinning her around, I cradle her face in my hands and kiss her. Pouring into this kiss how fucking proud of her I am. For fighting. For not giving up.

When I pull away, Sloan's in a daze. "I'm so fucking proud of you. That was perfect." I drop another soul-searing kiss on her lips. Completely forgetting we have an audience.

When I look behind her, I see Sutton and Quinn are staring at me with shit-eating grins on their faces.

"OMG, I called this. Close proximity. One bed," Quinn squeals with glee, hopping up and down.

"All of our favorite tropes. You so called that." Sutton giggles.

"We are right here you guys." Sloan laughs.

"We know." Sutton and Quinn each drop a kiss on Sloan's cheeks.

"Your hour is up, ladies. Looks like you are free to go." Asher shakes his head at their shenanigans.

"We will walk you back to the café," I suggest.

"We still need to work out, man." Asher slaps my back.

"I know. We will. After we walk them back."

"Always so damn protective. Shit," Asher rags but throws his arm around Quinn's shoulders, pulling her close to him, as the five of us walk out of the gym.

My Little Dove tucked in close to my side too.

I guess I don't have to carry her everywhere.

31
Sloan

Quinn, Sutton, and I are standing around the counter sipping on our second iced toffee lattes of the day, taking a breather. We have been prepping the café for the show tonight since we left the gym this morning, while still serving customers.

We only opened from eight to noon today so we'd have time to get everything set up and stored away.

Sutton and the guys also needed some time to practice a little bit before the show.

We moved some of the tables and chairs back into the kitchen to give us a little more space than we usually have for shows.

With From Troy being back in their hometown and putting on a free show to celebrate how successful their first tour has been, we're expecting to be pushing max capacity tonight.

We honestly should have hired actual security but Beck

and Asher will be here along with four other guys from the gym, so hopefully things will run as smoothly as they can.

From Troy has been setting up special effects lighting around the stage, along with a smaller smoke machine. Their surround sound and microphones have been upgraded since they performed here last. They're using a more condensed version of their tour set tonight since everything they've accrued on tour won't fit in here.

A large speaker sits on either end of the stage. Beau's drum set, along with Knox and Ty's guitar and bass are leaning against the walls, tuned and ready to go.

Lights were installed in the ceiling before you enter our book room that drop down and project like strobe lights onto the stage.

They will be illuminating Sutton and August's every move on stage tonight.

I can already feel the excitement of From Troy being back and the show hasn't even started yet.

"It looks perfect, Sunshine." August comes up, grabbing Sutton gently by the throat. Pulling her to him and pressing his lips to hers.

She's blushing when August pulls away. "Thank you, Auggie."

"Your room is literally upstairs. Use it." Quinn dramatically pretends to dry heave.

"You're just jealous, Blondie," Knox quips, crushing his lips down onto Quinn's.

Quinn definitely kisses Knox back, but she shoves him off of her as fast as Knox's lips were on Quinn's. "You have three seconds to get out of my face before I slap you, Knoxie!"

Sutton, August, and I are dead silent. Just watching the

exchange between the two of them.

"Oooh, please slap me, baby." Knox drops a quick kiss on Quinn's lips again before he's jogging backwards toward the door.

"Bro, where are you going?" August asks.

"I don't live here like the lot of you. I'm gonna run home and change. I'll be back in an hour," Knox replies. Blowing one last kiss to Quinn before he's out the door.

Sutton and I burst out in laughter at the look on Quinn's face.

Quinn looks equal parts flushed and disgusted.

"I'm going upstairs to change," Quinn huffs. "Who's coming with me?"

"I could use a quick shower. I'll be right up," I say, before grabbing our coffee cups and running them back to the kitchen to wash and put away.

"We need to get ready too," Sutton says, smiling at August.

August walks over to the door that heads up to the apartment.

Opening the door, he puts his arm out. "After you ladies."

After I finished showering, I let Quinn and Sutton dress me in their concert attire.

Quinn gave me a pair of her black ripped skinny jeans

to wear and a pair of black platform Converse boots. I already had a light blue long sleeve cropped top. The girls approved so I went with it.

Quinn put my hair in half up, half down space buns. Sutton gave me the perfect winged eyeliner. And when Sutton handed me her cherry red lipstick, I paused for just a second, before swiping it on my lips and sending a giant 'fuck you' to James.

I haven't worn anything like this since college. But honestly, I'm not sure I've ever worn anything quite this tight or revealing. My parents would have never approved and James... He would probably lose his mind in the worst way if he saw me in this.

Which is why it felt that much better to wear a bold red lip.

There were no roses or concerning notes left anywhere today. So, I'm a little less weary that James will show up tonight.

I head downstairs to do one last sweep of the floor, while Sutton and August do their vocal warm-ups upstairs.

I still check to make sure the door's locked before wandering around to make sure everything is set up exactly as planned.

The bookstore and kitchen are closed and locked for the night, so nothing can be tampered with.

The fairy lights are lit on the back patio giving it a soft ambient glow.

It's a perfect, cool fall night. Having these doors open is going to feel amazing once the café is packed.

The stage lights are set to a dimmed blue, softly illuminating the stage.

Stealing a peek out the glass windows, it looks like a

whole hoard of people are waiting outside the door.

Beck must see me through the window. He knocks on the glass door before using his key to get in. Letting in Asher and a few of the other guys who look familiar from the gym, before Beck locks the door behind them. Tugging on the door for good measure without me even having to ask.

My heart swoons at his thoughtful actions.

"That line wraps all the way down the block and around the bend," Asher exclaims.

"Fuck me. Are you trying to kill me, Little Dove?" Beck growls when he finally gets a good look at me. "Come here."

I stare at him with fire in my eyes but I don't move.

"Come. Here. Now." Beck rasps. "Please."

Slowly strutting over to him, sashaying my hips the slightest bit, my eyes never leaving his, I make my way to him. Stopping as soon as I'm directly in front of him. "Beckett."

"Little Dove." Beck swallows.

"Would you two just fuck already?" One of the guys from the gym says.

He barely makes out a chuckle before Beck is grabbing him by the throat and shoving him into one of the glass windows. "Watch your fucking mouth around her, Sullivan or you'll be swallowing your teeth," Beck snarls.

"Beck!" I gasp, trying to pull Beck's arm to make him let go of Sullivan.

Beck let's him go, turning to me. "I'm sorry, Little Dove. But no one fucking talks to you or about you like that."

"Okay. Just as Sullivan should watch what he says, you should watch putting your hands on people, Beckett," I scold them both.

"I'm sorry, baby," Beck apologizes.

"I'm sorry too, Sloan," Sullivan offers.

"Thank you." I nod at him, before turning to Asher and Beck.

"Any who, Sutton and Quinn would like you to set up like actual security. I'm not sure if you can start a group text just in case. They want at least one guy out back on the patio for the show. Two at the door. Two at the front of the stage and maybe one just sort of floating, walking around like a normal guy, but available," I explain to the guys.

"Sounds good. Beck and I can watch the door. Luca and Sullivan can be up at the stage. John can stand out on the patio. Bigs you can mingle in the crowd and keep an eye from the middle," Asher instructs.

"Got it," they all say in unison.

"Little Dove, promise me you'll stay close to Q all night?" Beck asks sweetly, cradling my face in his hands.

"I promise. I don't plan to leave her side."

"Good. If you need me, you know where to find me. If it's too crowded and you can't get to me, don't hesitate to text. I'll keep my phone on vibrate. I will move heaven and earth to get to you." Beck presses a soft kiss to my lips.

"Okay." Grateful to know Beck has my back.

"Baby, one last thing." Beck pulls away looking into my eyes.

"Yeah?"

Beck pulls out a pocket knife attached to a small silver chain. "Do not take this off, unless you need to use it."

Beck moves behind me, gently moving my hair to the side, before placing the pocket knife necklace around my neck and clasping it in the back.

Beck's fingertips gently trace my clavicle before he tucks the knife under my shirt. Making it look like I'm just wearing a dainty silver chain.

I graze my fingers over the little knife. "Thank you."

"All you have to do is tug down on it with a little bit of force and it'll break the chain free so you can use it," Beck explains.

Stretching up on my toes, I plant a soft kiss on his lips. Telling him thank you with my kiss.

Beck pulls me closer to him, deepening the kiss. "Be safe, baby. We'll finish what we started this morning later tonight."

Asher clears his throat, stating, "Doors open in 2 minutes, we gotta get in position."

My skin feels flushed as I pull away from Beck.

Quinn comes running down the stairs, dressed in a black sequined bodysuit and hot pink leather pants. "Sorry I'm late. Is everybody ready?"

"You look..." Asher swallows. "Wow." His eyes light up at the sight of Q.

"Thank you, Ash." Quinn kisses his cheek, leaving a hot pink lip print behind.

"Oops, sorry." Quinn goes to wipe Asher's cheek off with her thumb, but he gently grips her wrist, stopping her.

"Leave it," Asher commands.

"Ooh...um...okay," Quinn fumbles her words, a bit surprised.

"Q, please don't get separated from Sloan tonight," Beck pleads.

"Scouts honor." Quinn salutes Beck. "Now go man your stations, boys!"

"Yes ma'am!" The guys all salute and disperse.

Quinn and I are sitting on the counter trying to get some air.

I have the best view in the house of Beck from here.

Beck and Ash check attendees for weapons before letting them in.

Beck's dark gray T-shirt stretches across every inch of his defined back. His sculpted biceps flex every time he pats someone down.

I catch myself fidgeting sitting next to Quinn.

When did I become such a hussy for this man?

"This place is packed like a can of sardines! I'm pretty sure we are breaking more than one fire code violation," Quinn says almost in awe, snapping me out of my daydream of Beck. The vision of his biceps flexing while he held my legs open devouring me this morning.

"It's pretty incredible being a part of this. Seeing how far they've come in such a short period of time." I smile at Quinn.

"They definitely deserve it. Sutton knew that from the moment she heard August sing," Quinn offers with pride.

The lights in the café flicker on and off a few times to get everyone's attention.

Sutton and August appear behind us out of nowhere. They both have black hoodies on, remaining discreet from the crowd.

"We're behind you, Sloan. Don't want to startle you," Sutton says before getting too close.

"What are you guys doing over here?" I ask.

"We could ask you the same question," August chuckles.

"We needed air. It's already a sauna in here," Quinn replies.

"We just wanted to take it all in for a minute from this angle, without anyone recognizing us." Sutton smiles, leaning her head on my shoulder.

"It's pretty fucking amazing!" August's eyes light up, as his eyes scour the room.

"You guys really did it!" Quinn squeals. "I'm so fucking proud of you!"

"You're both such an inspiration, truly. Thank you for allowing me to be a part of your world." I lean my head down on Sutton's.

"We wouldn't want it any other way, Sloan." Sutton smiles, kissing me on the cheek.

My heart relaxes in the presence of these girls and their open affection.

The lights overhead flicker one last time.

I watch as Beck and Asher have to turn away a line of people as they shut the doors and lock them.

A whole slew of people just stand outside staring through the windows. Not making a single move, in hopes to see the show from the sidewalk.

"Want to watch the show from here or try to get to the stage?" Quinn asks.

"Wait, where did Sut and August go?" I ask, looking everywhere.

"They're ninjas! They wanted to sneak up toward the stage when the lights flickered and people were distracted," Quinn quips.

I catch Beck's eyes from across the room as he casually leans against the doors facing the stage.

He winks at me. Making me giggle.

And then…the lights go out.

Concerned that something went wrong, I reach out for Quinn's hand.

"Quinn…" I start, worry laced in my voice.

Quinn gives my hand a reassuring squeeze before, "*You'll be my demise,*" is screamed in a harsh raspy vocal by… Holy shit, Sutton.

Quinn and my head immediately swivel toward each other, in complete confusion and awe.

Our eyes going instantly back to the stage when blue stage lights start flickering above Sutton's head immediately after that sound just left her body. The lights illuminate the band standing behind her and August. While August stands right next to her, beaming with so much pride on his face.

My jaw drops. I knew Sutton could sing, but scream? Like August?

Beau's drums start out playing softly, so Sutton can own the stage before Knox and Ty start strumming their guitars in a heavy hitting melody, mixed with some electronic sounds.

In a few seconds, August starts screaming in his deep growly vocals. "So, break my ribs. Drive in your knife. Rip my heart open. With every word left unspoken." As Beau beats the bass of the drum even heavier.

"Every time I die. Everything inside me just screams.

With you I feel alive. In your hands, I just bleed," Sutton screams in this hauntingly ethereal voice, staring longingly in August's eyes.

Knox and Ty intricately play riffs on their guitar while incorporating some pick scrape techniques to give them a newer sound.

I'm almost hypnotized by the sounds of their voices. By the atmosphere they've created of this heavy yet ethereal scene for us. I can feel every bit of longing in their words. The pain they must have each felt in their time apart.

My heart breaks at the thought that they must have written this about that time but over the moon they found their way back to each other to create something as beautiful as this.

"*Another hour passes. Another day gone. Cardiac arrest she crashes. Her love for him lives on,*" Sutton wails with such an ache in her haunting melodic tone. A lone tear streaming down Sutton's face.

My heart is aching for her.

August screams in such a painful, rasped voice about wanting to just crawl into her, breathe her back to life.

Sutton and August sing their chorus together before an earth shattering break down about them either going up in flames or coming out on the other side. In such a heavy hitting moment.

Which has the crowd going completely nuts after their recent engagement news.

"*So, keep me tethered to you,*" August growls, getting in Sutton's face.

"*Ruin me, unravel me, I only bleed for you,*" Sutton shrieks, shoving August's chest. Almost like she's demanding him with her words.

"*Just keep me tethered to you,*" they sing together in such a soul crushing sound. As if they're begging each other to hold on for dear life. As August reaches for Sutton's hand. Their fingertips touching from a distance.

"*Ruin me, unravel me, I only bleed for you,*" August rasps. Slowly walking closer to Sutton, their fingers never leaving the other's.

"*You'll be my demise,*" Sutton sings barely above a whisper, as her and August meet in the middle of the stage again.

"*You'll be my salvation,*" Sutton and August harmonize together, in one microphone in the middle of the stage. Kissing each other softly, as Knox and Ty strum out the last few chords of the song on their guitars.

The crowd roars! They're clapping and whistling.

Quinn lets out a whoop next to me.

I'm beaming with excitement, screaming for them, tears streaming down my face.

Quinn faces me to wipe my tears, but tears are streaming down her face too. "I'm so fucking proud of them! Goddammit!" Quinn swipes her tears again.

"Me too." I rest my head on her shoulder, squeezing her hand in mine.

"Give it up for my girl! Sut's been working on those screams for weeks! I think she nailed it. What do you all think?" August gets the crowd amped up.

Whoops and whistles go off throughout the crowd again.

"Thank you all so much for coming tonight! We are From Troy! That was one of our newest songs called *Bleed* that we've been in the studio recording since we've been back. Tonight, we have about fifteen songs to play for you all. I'm not sure if there's much room to open up a pit but I want to see you head banging and hear you singing along," August yells in the microphone.

The crowd starts to cheer but then immediately goes silent when August squats at the front of the stage and growls, "Lets. Fucking. Go!" into the microphone before he starts growling and singing one of their most popular songs.

August really knows how to work the stage and the crowd. August becomes a puppet master the second he gets on stage and we are all just his marionettes.

Sutton also is such a light on stage. Working every angle, so in tune with August, like they're just on the same wavelength all the time. Sometimes Sut does these cute little dancey dances right after she sounds like a feral animal screaming. It is impossible not to have a girl crush on her.

They weave through their set list from heavier songs to their most famous song *Chokehold*, where August and Sutton duet beautifully. I swear half the crowd had tears in their eyes along with August and Sutton.

"Hey, I've been trying to hold it but those coffees are finally catching up to me. I'm going to run to the bathroom, do you want to come with?" Quinn asks before hopping down from the counter.

"I'm good. I'll just stay right here. I kind of don't want to miss anything." I smile at Quinn.

I'm loving every second of this show. I haven't really been to many shows in my life. It's still mind-blowing that I ended up friends with this incredibly talented group.

"Okay. Promise not to go anywhere? I don't want Beck putting me in a choke hold later for not 'obeying' him." Quinn rolls her eyes.

"I promise, I won't move. And don't worry, I'll deal with Beck later if he finds out." I wink at Quinn.

"Okurrrr, Sloan. I see you. I see you." Quinn giggles, making her way to the bathroom.

Quinn isn't even gone five minutes when I feel a presence lurking next to me.

A man of average height and average build walks over and leans against the counter, about five feet away from me.

At first, I wonder if he's lost and looking for someone.

I watch out of my periphery, avoiding making eye contact, as his head swivels, like he's trying to look for someone in the crowd.

Slowly, the man shuffles closer to me, as he continues to keep his eyes on the crowd.

I'm not sure if I'm praying more for Quinn to get back or for him to find whoever he's looking for and walk away.

Alarms start blaring in my head, when the man scoots so close to me. His arm is almost brushing my leg, that's hanging off the side of the counter.

It takes everything in me, not to immediately throw hands. Not to break his fingers that are now almost nonchalantly resting on the side of my thigh. Especially 'cause my body is screaming at me, to do so.

"Hi gorgeous, I'm Greg, what's your name?" He scoots in close to me.

"Um... Hi. I'm Sloan." I try to brush him off. Turning my head back toward the stage to watch the show.

He's even closer now. If that's even possible. He probes, "Why are you sitting up here all alone? How are you even allowed to sit up there?"

"Greg, I'm not trying to be rude, but could you take a

few steps back please. I don't really like people in my space. That's why I'm sitting up here. I wanted to watch the show, but I'm not all that comfortable in large crowds," I offer, trying to be polite-ish.

"Well, if you can sit up here, so can I," he snarks, trying to hop up next to me.

"No, actually you can't," I almost growl. "My friend is part owner of this café and she just stepped away to use the restroom and will be back any minute. We can sit here. You cannot. Please just go watch the show elsewhere."

"What's the issue really, gorgeous? You think you're too good for me or something?" He runs his fingers down my thigh. "Can't come down off your high horse?"

"Enough, Greg," I snap, going to slap him across the face, but he catches my wrist in the air, halting me from slapping him.

"I know women like you. I also know how to break them in real good. Take you home and put that mouth to use," he growls.

"Listen, Greg. That's enough!"

Grabbing me by the neck, he pulls me off the counter onto the floor. "No, you listen, you little bitch!"

I have to catch myself by gripping onto the counter so I don't fall.

With his face entirely too close to mine though, that's when I immediately smell alcohol on his breath. The smell makes me want to dry heave. It has my mind spiraling back to all of the times James grabbed me by the neck or by the hair when he was drunk.

"Don't you fucking disrespect me. You aren't better than me," Greg spews venom.

"You have two seconds to get your hand off of me or

I'm breaking your fucking fingers!" I scream in his face.

A snarl forms on his lips, as I count to two in my head.

"*Two*," I think to myself before I'm slamming my knee into his dick. Ripping his pinky out to the side as far as I can, of the hand that's wrapped around my neck, before he yells out in pain, buckling over.

"You bitch!" Greg barely grits out before I see Beck by the door.

We make eye contact and he goes on alert.

"Help, please," I mouth to him. Taking several steps back away from Greg, as he lays crumpled over on the floor.

I watch him have a short conversation with Asher before he's charging through the crowd toward me.

In seconds, Beck's in front of me scooping me up in his arms. Checking over every inch of me.

"What the fuck did you do to my girl?" Beck growls at him, still holding me in his arms. My legs wrapped around his waist.

"She never said she was your girl!" he barks back.

"You never asked before you put your disgusting hands on me," I snap at Greg.

"The stupid bitch is all yours!" he curses, slowly trying to get up off of the ground.

"What the fuck did you just say?" Beck demands.

Setting me down on the counter. Beck stands in front of Greg, stepping on his very obviously broken hand, making him cry out. Gripping him by the shirt, Beck starts to lift him up, as he continues to stand on his hand, making him yell out in pain.

"I said. What. The. Fuck. Did. You. Say?" Beck snarls in Greg's pained face.

"I can have you both arrested for assault!" he cries out.

"The fuck you can. As far as I see it, you assaulted my girl and we have at least ten friends here as witnesses to back that up. On top of that, my buddy Ash, over there by the door, is security tonight and so am I, so good luck, asshole," Beck says menacingly.

"What the fuck happened?" Quinn screeches when she returns from the bathroom.

"This asshole put his hands on, Sloan. He was just getting ready to leave," Beck offers.

"You did what!" she shrieks, gripping Greg by the hair and tugging his head up.

"I watch enough true crime to make your body disappear. Not a soul would ever find you. Touch one of my friends again and you're dead! Touch another woman again and I find out, you're dead! Now get the fuck out of my café!" Quinn rears back kicking Greg in the dick herself.

"Let me help escort you out, asshole." Beck manhandles Greg's hunched over form.

Poor guy looks like he's trying to fight back tears.

"I'll be right back, baby." Beck kisses my cheek softly.

I sit on the counter top as the show continues. Not many people noticing the slight interruption in our corner thankfully. I watch him haul Greg by his shirt to the front door.

As Beck reaches the exit, Asher opens it, both looking furious. "Don't ever come back here again!" I watch Asher yell as Beck shoves Greg out the open door, hitting the cement outside. Asher slamming it shut.

Beck immediately makes his way back over to me, pulling me off the counter into his arms.

"Please tell me you're okay, Little Dove." Beck cradles

my face in his hands, kissing my forehead, nose and then my lips so gently.

"I'm okay. Thank you for coming when I needed you." I sigh. Kissing him back and wrapping my arms around his waist.

"You really fucked up his finger." Beck chuckles. Leaning his forehead against mine. "Nice work, baby!"

I giggle back. "Some guy taught me how to do that. It stuck with me."

When we pull away, Beck turns me around so I face the stage, but tucks me against his chest.

"I'm not letting you out of my sight the rest of the night."

"You were in my line of sight all night, babe."

"Have you been watching me, Little Dove?"

"I don't know? Have I been?"

Quinn sits on the ledge of the counter just watching us with a knowing look in her eye and the widest grin on her face.

"Ahhhh! I fuckin knew you two were gonna be endgame!" Quinn squeals.

I twist my head to look up at Beck, our eyes meet, and we both start laughing.

He leans down and kisses me softly. "I'm really glad you're okay, Little Dove."

"I'm really glad I met you, Beck. Thank you." I kiss his chin and then nestle back into his arms, to watch the rest of the show.

"What are you thanking me for, baby?" he whispers in my ear, as he holds me tucked into his chest.

"For being you. Just for being you, Beckett Scott."

32

Beck

Waking up next to Sloan in my bed feels different today than it did waking up yesterday in her bed at Sutton's.

Sloan's curled up in the tiniest ball on her side facing the window in my apartment bedroom. Her hands tucked under her head like in prayer as she sleeps peacefully.

I can't help but stare at her.

Her slender leg pokes out of the covers at the end of the bed.

Long black hair fanned out around her head like a halo, on the pillow we share together. Porcelain skin, not a tattoo in sight. So different from Sutton, yet it doesn't cause an ache in my chest to think that anymore.

Sloan's blonde lashes flutter softly against her closed eyes as if she's in a deep sleep dreaming. It's always been a conundrum to me that her eyes are such a unique light purple and surrounded by light blonde lashes, when her hair is jet black.

Tucking my left arm under my head on the pillow, I

continue to watch Sloan sleep, as I draw small circles on her hip with my right hand. I trace my fingers along her soft skin, slowly rousing her from sleep.

Sloan lets out the tiniest little groan before rolling toward me.

"Hi." Sloan smiles sweetly at me. Her eyes still slightly closed.

"Hi, baby," I lean down and press my lips gently to hers, continuing to run my fingers along her skin. I gently trail my fingers on her toned stomach, where my shirt rides up on her.

"Mmm...that feels so good."

"How do you feel about staying in bed all day, Little Dove?" I ask, nipping her ear with my teeth.

"I like that idea."

"I want to taste you. I want to fuck you on every surface of this apartment. I want you naked and mine to pleasure, Little Dove. All. Fucking. Day," I growl, crawling over top of Sloan.

Sloan's eyes finally pop open and she smirks at me.

She must see the confusion on my face at her smirk because she wiggles below me just the slightest bit. Pulling my shirt over her head and tossing it to the floor. "Yes, boss."

"Fuck, baby," I rasp before slamming my mouth down on hers. Biting her lip, Sloan moans in my mouth, giving me access to slide my tongue into hers. Swirling my tongue with hers. Giving her a preview of how I'm going to make her my breakfast, lunch, and dinner today.

Pulling away, I sit back on my feet. "I want to try something. Do you trust me, Sloan?"

Sloan gives me doe eyes and the sweetest smile. Not

even a trace of fear. "Yes."

That one word has my heart soaring.

"Will you touch yourself for me?" I ask, my eyes never leaving hers. "I want to see how you like to be touched."

Sloan sits up beside me. Reaching her arms up over head stretching. The sheets falling, giving me the perfect view of her tits. She kicks the blankets down the bed over my legs. Leaving herself completely exposed for me.

I barely hold back a groan at how sinful her body is.

"Only if you stroke yourself for me. Show me how you like to be touched, Beckett." Sloan licks her lips.

Fuck me. Little minx.

Standing up from the bed, I pull my boxer briefs down my legs. I watch as Sloan's eyes map every inch of my body, setting my skin on fire with one single look.

Gripping the sheets, I throw them on the floor and sit back on the edge of the bed facing Sloan. She scoots back against my headboard.

Our eyes meet and hold for just a couple seconds before Sloan drops her knees open, running her fingers over her collarbones. She gently traces them down over her nipples, then her stomach, halting right before she grazes her pussy.

Leaning back on the bed, I tell her, "Eyes on me, Little Dove." I grip my cock in my hand and start stroking it.

Sloan takes the encouragement, rubbing small circles on her clit. Her eyes never leaving mine.

"Mmm. Such a good girl. How wet are you for me baby?" I ask, stroking myself.

Sloan runs her fingers through her folds, pressing two fingers inside of herself. She lets out the smallest whimper.

"I need to hear you, baby," I encourage, groaning as I

clutch the tip of my cock.

Sloan pulls her fingers out of herself, stroking her clit again. Then places each one into her mouth, slowly running her tongue around them. Tasting how delectable she is, never breaking eye contact with me, before diving her fingers back into her pussy.

"Such a good fucking girl. My good girl."

I'm so fucking turned on.

Her eyes flutter closed as she uses her other hand to tug on her nipples. She moans and I watch as the muscles in her thighs flex.

"Give me those eyes, baby," I demand.

"Mmm. Yes, Daddy," Sloan moans. Her eyes open wide at her slip-up as she covers her mouth with her hand, staring at me completely frozen.

Fuuuck.

"Don't fucking stop. Come for Daddy," I growl while pulling and tugging on my cock harder. I'm so close to coming myself. I refuse to come before my girl though.

She starts to rub her clit even harder. Sliding two fingers into her pussy with her other hand. Sloan's body bucks as her orgasm crashes into her.

"Where do you want Daddy's cum, baby?" I ask, stroking myself as I get up and walk over to her.

"Mmm... Paint me with it, please," Sloan mewls.

Doing as my girl asks, I paint her tits and stomach with my cum. Groaning at how good it feels to mark her perfect skin.

Sloan runs her fingers through it.

Smirking up at me.

Fuuuck... So fucking sexy.

"I'll be right back, baby," I groan, biting my fist at the sight of her. A perfect canvas painted with my cum. I reluctantly walk out of the bedroom, to go grab a warm washcloth.

I come back in to Sloan's lying sprawled out on my bedsheets, looking like a fucking angel.

I gently wipe my cum off of her. Grabbing the sheets off of the floor, I crawl back into bed next to her and pull her close to me. I cover us up as she rests her head on my chest.

"You did so good, baby." I kiss her head.

Sloan's so quiet for a few minutes. Not saying a word. I'm worried I pushed her too far.

"Baby…"

"I'm okay," she whispers.

"You're being too quiet. If I did something… Please tell me. I can't fix it if I don't know what I did."

"You didn't do anything, Beck. I-I can't believe I called you Daddy. I have no idea where that came from. I'm just embarrassed." Sloan tucks her head, refusing to meet my eyes.

Tilting her chin up so she has to look in my eyes, I tell her, "You have nothing to be embarrassed of, Little Dove. When you say boss it's cute, a little bratty but still obedient. But Daddy was fucking hot," I admit.

"You swear?" Sloan asks shyly.

"I promise, baby." I press my lips gently to hers, giving her a chaste kiss.

Pulling away, I roll over lying flat on my back. "Come here, Little Dove."

"I am here." Sloan looks confused.

"No. Come here," I growl, pointing at my face.

"Pardon?"

"I still haven't gotten to eat my breakfast yet. Be a good girl and come sit on my face. Now, Little Dove. Don't make me ask again."

Sloan sits up and leans forward on all fours and literally crawls her way over top of me. Her hair falls around us, sheathing us in our own little bubble. She sits her naked pussy on my abs just above my cock. I'm not even inside her and I could erupt again. I try to think of anything but how fucking beautiful she is, but I'm enamored.

"That's not my face, baby." I grab by the waist and drag her up my body until her perfect little pussy is just hovering over my mouth. "Sit." I lift my head up, nipping at her inner thigh.

Sloan lets out a little squeal before she sits her sweet ass down on my face. Diving in, I swipe my tongue through her folds, pulling her clit in my mouth with my teeth, sucking on it hard.

Sloan lets out the sweetest little mewls and whimpers as I can continue to devour her. She reaches for the headboard to hold herself upright, panting hard above me.

I grip and knead her ass, spreading her wider for me. I can feel her legs starting to tremble around my head.

"Come for me, Little Dove," I groan before sucking on her clit hard.

Sloan's legs tremble as she squeezes my head with her thighs, screaming, "Beck."

I lick her mess clean with my tongue, making sure I don't miss a drop of her. I scoot back, positioning myself so my back and head are slightly at an angle.

"Will you...?" I start to ask but Sloan knows what I

want.

Sloan wraps her hand around my cock, pumping me a few times. I'm throbbing in her hand when she lines it up with her pussy.

She's soaked. I groan at the feel of her dripping down on my cock before she slides down and grips me so fucking tight.

Sloan starts to ride me. My face at perfect eye level with her tits as they bounce with every move. I thrust up as she bottoms out, holding her there for a second. I want her to feel full of me. Releasing her, Sloan clenches and continues to ride my cock, taking me deep.

The slightest bit of sweat coats her skin and I want to lick off every drop with my tongue. I grip her tits, pulling and tweaking on her nipples. Sloan groans and I feel her pussy flutter around me. Running my fingers up to her neck, I gently wrap my hand around her throat. Sloan's movements falter.

"I got you, baby. I promise not to hurt you."

I continue to gently squeeze Sloan's throat, her eyes meet mine again. Trust mixed with the slightest hesitation before her movements pick up again. The way she's trusting me, makes me that much fucking harder for her. I can feel my cock pulsing inside of her. Pulling her toward me by the neck, I swipe my tongue over her lips, coaxing her to open for me. I take her in a deep kiss, rubbing her clit, as she's chasing her release.

"Baby I'm gonna come. Come for me." I thrust upward, meeting her hard and deep with every movement, before we're both falling over the edge.

Sloan's body slumps forward with my cock still semi hard inside of her. We just lay there, coming down from the high.

Moving Sloan's hair to the side, I press gentle kisses to her shoulder. Rubbing small circles on her lower back as I hold her against me. "Such a good girl for me."

Her breathing evens out and I think she's fallen asleep that is until her stomach makes a sound so loud causing her to giggle.

"Looks like my baby needs some food. What shall we order? 'Cause we aren't leaving this bed for anything but a shower today." I kiss her hair.

"Tacos!"

"Tacos it is, Little Dove."

Anything for my girl.

33

Sloan

I'm sitting on a stool behind the register sipping my second iced toffee latte of the day, writing in my journal.

Quinn left around lunch time to go run some errands because it's been such a slow day today.

It's been nice though.

It's allowed me to sit with my thoughts and reflect on how different I am around Beck. Different in a way that I've grown to love myself.

There may be times when we unintentionally do something that causes the other to pause briefly, but we're both learning how to communicate in ways we were never able to with others before.

Beck provides me with a sense of fierce protection to just exist in his presence, while also allowing me to work through my own hurts and fears. Giving me a safe space to figure out who I actually want to be. Teaching me to use my voice and express my needs to him. Something I would have been terrified to do with James, and even my own father. Beck holds my hand and shows me just how capable I am on my own but offers his silent support always.

I never saw the value in a man this way. Because I had never encountered one this grounded and self-assured. This must be the balance the girls were talking about when I lived in Boston.

Beck and I spent the day at his apartment yesterday and I couldn't help daydreaming about what it would be like to wake up to him every day.

The perfect lazy Sunday, the only time we moved from the bed was to shower together. Beck took me in positions I never knew my body could bend, bringing me pleasure, I never even knew existed. Allowing me freedom to express my desires. Some I didn't even know I had.

Feeding me tacos while I was wrapped in his sheets.

Belly-laughing at the most ridiculous things.

One of which was waking up this morning thinking Beck was sprawled out on top of me. Only to find Mayhem stretched out like Superman across my entire body sleeping peacefully.

"Mayhem might actually be as tall as you, Little Dove." Beck lets out a deep chuckle. That sends instant shivers down my spine.

"Oh, he definitely is. Who's my handsome boy." I giggle, wrapping my arms around Mayhem, giving him kisses all over his face.

"I thought I was," Beck growls, nuzzling his face in my neck.

"You are. You are!" I let out a deep belly-laugh, at Beck's short beard tickling my neck.

Mayhem hops up, barking, joining in on the fun.

Beck immediately crawls over top of me and takes over Mayhem's spot. Tickling me to death.

I let out a yelp and can't catch my breath. I'm laughing so hard.

Beck stops tickling me. Leaning down to kiss me. "I love your laugh, Little Dove. It's become my new favorite sound."

You've become my new favorite person, Beckett Scott.

A girl could rise in love with a man like you.

*T*he last customer of the day finally closes her book and heads toward the door.

"Have a nice evening, Sloan." Lucy waves goodbye on her way out.

"You too, Lucy." I wave back, following her toward the door to lock it.

The sun is setting. The sky is painted like a canvas of cotton candy, pastel pinks and baby blues mixing into a perfect fluffy texture. Like you could reach up and grab it and it would be the perfect sugary concoction.

It's such a beautiful, balmy evening. Closing my eyes I take a deep breath and just enjoy the moment before locking up WaggingWithWords.

My phone chimes with a text from Beck, that has me smiling even harder to myself.

Him and Mayhem are on their way over from the gym and are grabbing dinner for a movie night in. Falling into a routine with Beck and Mayhem has become natural. Like we were always meant to be doing this. I've grown to really love spending the evenings with them.

August and Sutton have been spending late nights at the recording studio, so I don't expect they'll be back anytime soon.

Heading toward our apartment stairs, I rush up the steps to the door so I can freshen up really quickly before Beck and Mayhem get here.

The door's unlocked when I twist the handle which makes me pause for just a second.

I shake off the discomfort. Figuring Sutton, August or Beck must've accidentally forgot to lock it this morning.

When I turn around to lock the door, my hair stands up on the back of my neck.

My senses are on high alert.

Something feels off.

Whipping around, a dozen white roses stand at attention in a vase on the island.

Beck knows I hate white roses.

August only ever gets Sutton purple flowers.

I turn around and go to rip the door open to run. But my feet become paralyzed at the sound of his voice, as my hand grips the doorknob.

"Take one more step, Reesey and the blonde girl gets hurt."

A whoosh of air leaves my lungs. "No."

Not Quinn. James better not lay a single finger on her.

"Yes." His single confirmation causing bile to rise in the back of my throat.

"Don't make another move. Don't say a fucking word or I will kill you both," James rasps in my ear, sneaking up on me.

"Where is Quinn? What did you do to her?"

"I'm sure you'd like to know where I took your little friend when she left work earlier today," James mocks.

He presses his body so close to the back of mine. Almost pinning me against the door.

My body is screaming at me to get the fuck out of here.

It takes everything in me not to recoil. Not to figure out how to rip this door open while he has me cornered like this and run.

But Quinn. I need to know she's safe.

I'm completely frozen on the spot as James stands even closer behind me with his arms wrapped around my chest. Pinning my arms to my sides. The door directly in front of my sight.

My heart is beating so hard I can feel it thumping in my ears.

Do not panic, Sloan. Do not fucking panic.

"It took almost an entire fucking year for the idiot private investigator to track you down and then another few days to figure out how to get in here and get you alone, Reesey. But here we finally are. You're never fucking alone here!" James slams his hand hard against the door, next to my head, causing me to flinch.

"How dare you fucking run from me! No one leaves me, Reese!" James booms. Squeezing my arms to my body so hard, I feel like I could pop.

"All the roses... It wasn't all in my head." I can barely speak.

"Hmm...I don't know? Was it all in your head? What roses are you talking about exactly? The ones on your island? I brought those just for you. I know how much you love them," James remarks.

His hand slides up into my hair, gripping it hard and yanking my head back. Tears prick my eyes at how hard he's pulling my hair. I can barely move. James has me trapped.

My vision starts to go blurry. I feel like I can't breathe.

No. Do not fucking panic, Sloan.

"You really thought you could leave me, Reese's Pieces? I always fucking hated that nickname the girls gave you. Thought you could just disappear without a trace? Stop showing up to work without turning in a notice? Humiliating *me*? Embarrassing *me*? Making me look stupid because I have to make up lies for my wife?" James bites out.

"I...I'm sorry James," I start to cry. Hoping if I show signs of regret that it'll buy me time to form a plan to get me the hell out of here. To make sure Quinn is safe.

James pulls my hair back even harder causing me to wince.

A lone tear streams down my face from the pain.

An evil grin splits his face.

"A sheriff came to our home and delivered me divorce papers, Reesey...and you know what else? A restraining order," James scoffs.

"What do you need that for? I gave you the perfect life. Everything you could possibly fucking need and you have the nerve to be an ungrateful little bitch. You have a man come to my home and serve me papers?" James snarls disgusted.

"I'm s-s-sorry, James. I w-w-was just scared." I stutter, tears running down my face.

"You think a measly little piece of paper can keep me

from my wife?" James chuckles. "I threw those papers in the shredder. They're null and void, Reesey. You are mine. You became mine the second you signed your life to me at our wedding."

"Okay." I try to nod my head, hoping he'll release my hair some.

"You humiliated me. Those two little bitches at the hospital you spent too much time with said you probably left me. Started rumors, saying you probably couldn't stand me anymore. That you had no other choice. I made sure they were fired for disrespecting me. Made sure the hospital knew you were on medical leave. Suffering from a depressive episode. Had a psychotic break and I had to institutionalize you for your safety," James growls.

No. No. No. Not Kailey and Maria. He couldn't have... But he could... James has so much pull at the hospital, almost like he's royalty that they would do anything he asks to make sure they can keep him.

"Even here, you are still humiliating me. I saw you fucking that meathead in the window of that gym! You are a filthy fucking whore. Spending too much time gallivanting around here with other men. Acting like a whore. Serving fucking coffee. You were a nurse for fuck's sake. You serve nobody except for me. Do you hear me, Reesey?"

"I... Yes, I hear you. I'm so sorry, James. Please let me go. Can we please sit and talk about this?" I beg.

"You see, the way I see it Reesey is you have two choices. So, choose wisely—" he starts talking over me.

"Please let me go, James. We can talk about this in the living room," I suggest softly. Trying to make him think I'm being compliant.

"You don't get to speak or tell me where to have this conversation. You lost that privilege. Now listen to me,

Reese. Your two options are," he growls. Yanking my head back, almost knocking me off balance.

"One, you quietly disappear from your pathetic life here. Never see or speak to that numbskull again and come back to Boston with me. You come back to the hospital and tell everyone you spent time in another state institution for your mental health, but you are back and doing much better. You should be able to get your job back with my help."

"I'm not—" I start, trying to reach under my shirt for my knife without him noticing.

"Or you end up like Jessica," James snarls.

"Jessica?" I question. Completely caught off guard that he's bringing up his ex-wife—his dead ex-wife.

I buy myself some time, while gripping my knife under my shirt, I try to brush my ass against his bulge to distract him, so he doesn't notice I'm popping it from the holster. I retch at just barely grazing his dick.

James groans, "Is that a yes to coming home then, baby?"

"What do you mean about Jessica, James?" I question again. Genuinely curious if he's admitting to something or not.

Spinning me around, James grabs my face forcefully like he's going to kiss me except he holds my cheeks. James squeezes so hard, it feels like he could crack my jaw.

I try to fight back a wince. I stiffen slightly, but try to coax my body into relaxing as much as I can. My knife is in the perfect position if I need to use it.

Focus Sloan.

"Option two is die, Reese, like Jessica. You don't want to end up dead like she did, do you?" James questions, venom laced in his words.

I fucking knew it!

"I thought that was an accident." I play stupid, looking up at him with doe eyes.

"No one leaves me, Reesey. A little brake malfunction goes unnoticed. A car accident is an accident." He brushes my hair behind my ear, leaning in for a chaste kiss. That immediately has bile rising in the back of my throat.

I squeeze my eyes shut as hard as I can to block out having to watch his lips come near me.

"You cut Jessica's brakes?" I gasp. Going completely still.

Every inch of my body is screaming for me to run.

"Mmm... She was planning to leave me. I found a bag she had stowed away in our spare bedroom closet. Jessica was going to steal my money and run." James looks disgusted.

I use my other hand, not holding the knife, to graze the bulge in his pants, to see if I can divert his attention while he's thinking about Jessica.

I need to get free even if touching him makes me ill. Do it to save your life, Sloan!

James lets out a groan and the second I notice his eyes fluttering closed in pleasure; I bring my knife up swiping at his right wrist.

Blood sprays across my face but I couldn't care less.

James swings his left hand so hard at my face, he knocks me to the ground. My knife tumbles out of my grip, several feet away from me on the floor.

My cheek is throbbing. My vision blurring slightly at the impact.

I have to make a quick decision to crawl for the knife or make a run for it.

Then it dawns on me. There's a fire escape in Sutton's room.

I need to get to the fire escape. I need to get out of here.

James will kill me. He could kill Quinn. What if he did already?

I feel myself almost starting to panic at the thought.

I close my eyes and take a deep breath through my nose. Trying to center myself. I run through all of the training Beck has taught me over the last several months and will the panic at bay. I feel my heartbeat starting to pick up but try to take a few more breaths to keep my mind clear.

I take the opportunity while he's holding his right wrist with his left hand to make a run up the stairs to Sutton's room. James is cursing from a distance but I can't hear what he's saying.

My mind is set on getting the fuck out of there. Slamming her door and locking it and heading for the fire escape.

As I slide the window up and crawl out of the window, I hear James kicking at the door and screaming at me.

My feet just barely touch the landing, but then I'm rushing down the stairs. I almost trip closer to the bottom, but catch myself on the railing. I'm hopping off of the last step in the alleyway when James steps on the landing of the fire escape. It's gotten fairly dark. A small street light barely illuminates a path for me to see to the street.

"No one fucking leaves me and lives, Reese! Get fucking back here you, whore!" James hollers out with my knife in his hand.

Screaming for help at the top of my lungs, James

catches up to me. Gripping me by the hair and wrenching it. "Shut the fuck up, you little bitch!"

"James don't. I have a restraining order. You could get arrested. It will ruin your career. Just let me go. Please."

"You stupid, stupid girl. You really think you could just leave me? Think a restraining order would keep me away? I told you. I ripped that up. It isn't even valid," James scoffs, rearing the knife back, like he's going to plunge it in my abdomen.

"James, please. Just let me go."

My tears are mixing with his blood on my face. My cheek throbs where he hit me.

James tugs my hair so hard it whips my head back and it throws me off balance, causing me to topple backwards and hit the ground hard. I feel the back of my skull crack off of the pavement.

I hear the thud in my ears. As the air whooshes out of my lungs.

James climbs on top of me, wrapping both hands around my throat and starts squeezing. Harder and harder. *His grip a little weaker on the right, but still too hard.*

My visions already blurry from hitting my head and now little black spots are dancing behind my eyes.

Don't panic Sloan. What did Beck teach you? Think.

Inhaling one more deep breath through my nose, I reach up and pull as hard as I can on both of his small fingers, bending them out to the side as far as they go until I hear... *Snap.*

"You fucking bitch!" James rears back. Letting my throat go, trying to reach for his now broken little fingers. Giving me just enough time to try to scoot back a bit.

As I'm crawling backwards away from James, my right

hand grazes a piece of glass from a broken beer bottle. Gripping the broken glass into my palm, I feel it slice my flesh but I welcome the pain. The pain clears some of the fogginess in my head.

So, I lie in wait, waiting for him to attack again.

A few seconds later, James is lunging on top of me. The second his face is near mine; I don't even give him a chance to get his hands on me again. I just strike.

I swipe the air with the broken glass over and over again to try to keep him out of my face. To get him to back up away from me.

"What the fuck are you doing? Fucking stop!" He lets out a blood curdling scream.

Blood is dripping everywhere I can feel it on my skin. Smell the iron in the air. The metallic taste of it on my lips, mixing with the salt of my tears.

But I keep my eyes squeezed tightly shut and keep swinging. Letting the cold ground seep into my bones.

James is snarling and yelling for me to stop.

"My eyes! My eyes! You fucking bitch!"

A ferocious bark has me snapping my eyes open.

My vision's a little blurry and my head is pounding.

Blood is dripping everywhere. It looks like a murder scene.

Ash wasn't wrong. Scalp lacs really do bleed a lot. I think I chuckle before I drift off.

34
Beck

"Fuck! Stop!" I hear James yelling again.

Mayhem is lunging toward James, snarling and snapping his teeth.

"Sloan. Little Dove. It's me. Open your eyes!"

"Ha. Sloan. She's a whore and a liar!" James barely gets out in between screams as Mayhem continues to bark and growl in James' face. Never biting him, but keeping him down and away from Sloan.

I imagine he can't see him through all of the blood.

"Shut the fuck up you whiney piece of shit! Before I bloody your mouth too," I growl at James.

Trying to assess Sloan and get her to open her eyes. Sloan's covered in so much fucking blood but so is James. I can't tell if it's hers or his.

"Are you the fuckwit who fucked my whore of a wife?"

"I said shut your fucking mouth!" Turning around I lunge toward James throwing two jabs and a cross straight into his face until he's unconscious.

Rushing back to Sloan, I gently caress her cheek with my fingers. "Little Dove, are you hurt? Please open your eyes."

Sliding my arms under Sloan's waist. I lift her off the ground, cradling her into my chest. She's shivering in my arms.

I lie her down on the ground, removing my sweatshirt, placing it over her, before holding her again in my arms. Gently rubbing her arms for some friction to try to warm her up.

Sloan still won't open her eyes but I feel her burrow deeper into my chest.

"Don't worry, Little Dove. The police should be here any minute. I'm so proud of you. You're safe, baby. I got you." I kiss her head, soothing her.

Sloan's eyes flutter open, but she's shaking violently in my arms. Her teeth are chattering. Sloan is groaning like she's in pain.

"I got you. You're in shock." I try to calm her.

Mayhem is pacing and barking in James' face, but he still remains unconscious.

"Gut. Sitz. Bleib," I command and Mayhem goes silent. Immediately sitting near James' head.

Mayhem scoots the smallest bit closer, as if he's ready to go back into attack mode at the first command given.

James lies on the ground groaning, his hands covering his eyes that are covered in blood.

Sloan slowly rouses and starts mumbling. "He...he... killed his last wife. James said he killed her. I always wondered if he did but he always said it was an accident." She starts to sob. "I knew he would've killed me if I stayed.

I knew it in my bones. That's why I ran. That was the only way I knew I could stay safe."

I pull her in closer to my chest. Holding Sloan tight to me. Handling her with care, my precious Little Dove.

She wraps her legs around me. Letting me soothe her. I cradle her to my chest.

"You are so brave, baby. You did what you had to do to protect yourself. You're a survivor. I'm so proud of you," I kiss the side of her head as it's buried in the crook of my neck.

Sirens are nearing closer to us.

"Beck, I have to be honest with you before the police get here. My first name is Reese. My middle name is Sloan. That's why he called me a liar. I've been going by Sloan to keep myself and all of you safe. I never meant to lie to you. I just wanted you to know before the police start questioning us," Sloan rambles.

"Don't worry, I know you had to do what made you feel safest. Sloan or Reese... You are still my, Little Dove," I declare, rubbing small circles on her back as she continues to cry into my chest.

"Put your hands where I can see them!" the police officers yell.

I gently put Sloan down and we step apart with our hands above our head.

James groans out, "Officers, they tried to kill me. Arrest them!"

Mayhem growls and barks at him and James immediately goes quiet. Not moving an inch.

"Gut." Mayhem sits at attention.

"That's not true. My name is Reese Sloan McAllister. I have a restraining order against James McAllister that I filed in Boston. I was, am, his wife. Hopefully soon to be ex-wife. I have been living here in hiding, going by Sloan Archer, my maiden name for almost a year. James tried to attack and kill me in my home today. I tried to get away by taking the fire escape but James chased me into this alley," Sloan says, her voice starting to crack.

"Hey, you're Beckett Scott," one of the police officers says.

"Yes, I am, sir."

James starts groaning behind us. "I need medical attention immediately, officer. I'm going to lose my eyes. I'm a fucking surgeon. A world-renowned surgeon."

Every time he tries to move, Mayhem growls at him.

"I'm Officer Tony. What is your involvement in this situation, Mr. Scott?" he asks, ignoring James.

"Sloan and I are great friends. I've been teaching her self-defense in my women's class. She and I both have been staying here. My apartment had some water damage that has been getting repaired and we were sort of house sitting for Sutton and August until they got back from tour," I point to WaggingWithWords.

We're so much more than friends, but I can't give the officers a reason to blame Sloan for this.

"Oh my gosh! Quinn!" Sloan gasps and bursts into tears.

"What happened? What about Quinn?"

"Who is Quinn?" Officer Tony questions.

"James said he would hurt my friend if I ran when I found him in the apartment. I assumed..." Sloan is crying even harder now. I can barely make out what she's saying.

"Officer, may I please use my phone to call our friend? I will put it on speakerphone."

"Yes, go ahead, Mr. Scott," Officer Tony replies.

The phone rings for what feels like an eternity before Quinn finally answers.

"Hey Q, it's Beck, where are you?"

"Why's it any of your business, Beckett?" Quinn sasses.

I clear my throat, "It's not but uhh…Sloan was attacked and her ex said he would hurt you if she didn't comply so we were just making sure…"

"Holy fuck! Where are you? Is she okay? I'm okay," Quinn screeches. Immediately changing her tune.

"I think Sloan's in shock." I eye her up and down. "But we're in the alley next to the café."

"I'll be right there." Quinn hangs up.

"Can you…um…can you put James in your police car please?" Sloan asks, barely able to get out the words.

"I… I don't feel safe." Sloan's voice cracks. She wraps her arms around herself, trying to hold herself together.

The adrenaline wearing off, the exhaustion and fear seeping in.

"I do have confirmation that she has a restraining order on Dr. James McAllister. The names she has given you for herself are also valid," another police officer walks up to us and states.

"Can our EMTs take a look at you?" Officer Tony asks.

"Can you put him in your car first?" Sloan requests.

"Yes, Travis put him in the car until the EMT checks over Ms. Archer, and then you can ride with Mr. McAllister in the ambulance to the hospital," Officer Tony instructs Officer Travis.

"Yes, sir," Officer Travis agrees.

"It's Dr. McAllister. My eyes. What about my eyes!"

James yells out, as Officer Travis starts to pull James up from the ground with his arms behind his back.

"Thank... Thank you," Sloan whispers.

Reaching for Sloan, I scoop her up under her legs.

"Mr. Scott, I have a few more questions," Officer Tony states.

"You can ask me anything you want, officer, but I am not letting Sloan out of my sight," I affirm.

"Very well," Officer Tony sighs.

I carry Sloan over to the ambulance; I take a seat on the edge and gently pull her onto my lap. I wrap my arms around her, holding her upright but not squeezing too tightly.

"Hi, Miss Archer, I'm Leo, is it okay if I check your vitals?" Leo, one of the EMTs, asks.

"Yes, it's okay. Thank you," Sloan confirms. Nestling a little deeper into me. Her shaking easing up slightly.

Leo hands me a blanket to wrap around Sloan, as I continue to hold her.

Once Sloan appears comfortable, Leo places a pulse ox on her finger and a blood pressure cuff on her arm. Leo makes note of the bruise starting on Sloan's upper arm and the bruises on her neck.

Apparently, the back of Sloan's head has a gash, likely from where she hit it off the pavement. Some gravel is embedded in her hands and Sloan may have a mild concussion but her pupils are reacting okay and her vitals are stable.

Thank fuck. Seeing her covered in all of that blood, almost had my heart stopping.

"Everything is stable. You may still want to go to the hospital to be looked over and get this incident documented so you have this information for your case." Leo suggests kindly.

"I can take her."

"We can be twinsies. Have concussions together." Sloan tries to make a joke.

"Baby, I never wanted you to have a concussion and I never want you to have a concussion again. So, let's not joke about that, please?" I grit out.

I'm trying to stay calm for her, even though I would love to crush James' windpipe with my bare hands for laying his grimy fucking hands on my girl. That would only make this situation worse for Sloan though.

"Most of the city streets have video surveillance, so we should be able to pull footage for evidence if you are pressing charges, ma'am," Officer Tony says when he walks up to us.

"I am," Sloan states firmly.

"I also agree with Leo, Ms. Archer. For documentation purposes in a trial, I would recommend having this incident documented by someone at the hospital. Unfortunately, with someone of Dr. McAllister's pedigree, you will need all the evidence of your attack documented so there is no doubt that he will be found guilty," Officer Tony says looking disgusted.

"Okay, sir," Sloan agrees.

"Can I ask again, Mr. Scott, if you and Ms. Archer have been house sitting together why you were here in the alley but not here for the home invasion?" Officer Tony asks suspiciously.

"Excuse me, officer. I don't mean to be rude, but you are questioning the wrong person. While Beck and I have been house sitting together, Beck works full time at his gym. Mayhem is where Beck is, always. He was on his way home from the gym and was bringing us dinner. I had just closed the café and was going upstairs. Beck had just texted me that he was on his way.

"James was hiding somewhere in the apartment and had placed a vase of roses on the countertop. My guess is that he was trying to throw me off before attacking me. I have no idea how he got in, but he's charming, so who knows. James threatened me by saying he was going to hurt our friend Quinn if I ran. James admitted to killing his ex-wife Jessica and told me if I didn't come back home to Boston, he would kill me too.

"I ran down the fire escape. Found a broken bottle in the alley and used that to protect myself until I felt the threat was no longer a threat. That's when Beck and Mayhem showed up. Neither one of them touched James. That's the whole story. There's no need to question, Beck! And as you said, you can obtain the video surveillance," Sloan declares confidently.

"Is that your statement?" Officer Tony questions.

"Yes. It is," Sloan confirms, looking Officer Tony dead in the eye.

Sloan and I stand up and make our way toward the café door, so they can move James from the police car to the ambulance. I know Sloan doesn't want to be anywhere near him.

"Okay, Ms. Archer. They will be taking Mr. McAllister to the hospital to be evaluated. A police officer will be outside of his room. I advise you to get checked over again, as well. We will keep you updated," Officer Tony assures Sloan, walking past us.

"Sut is calling because Quinn called her. Is it okay if I tell her what happened?"

"Yeah. It's okay. I probably should tell you guys the whole story," Sloan offers ashamed.

"The apartment is a crime scene until we get permission to sweep it and clear it. Are you able to stay somewhere else?" Officer Tony asks.

"Yeah, we can go to my place. I just got the green light to move back in a few days ago," I offer before stepping away and answering the phone.

"Hey, Sut, Sloan was attacked—" I start, the second I answer the phone.

"Quinn told me! Is she okay? Let me talk to her. Where are you? I'm coming right now," Sutton screeches in the phone.

"Sut, breathe. We're in the alley. The police are here. We aren't allowed in the apartment until they document it, so we are going to my place. Sloan's okay just shaken up," I continue.

"August and I are almost there." Sut hangs up.

Next thing you know, August, Khaos and Sutton round the corner.

Sutton rushes Sloan and is pulling her into her arms in seconds.

August comes up behind Sloan and looks at her with pain in his eyes and then relief after gently assessing her.

"Oh my Gods. Let me look at you. Where is that motherfucker? Is he dead? Did he put his hands on you? Your neck is bruised. He better be dead," Sutton is yelling now.

"Sunshine. The police... You can't say..." August starts to say.

"Hush you! I'm just being dramatic. Kind of." Sutton points at August.

"But really, his ass better be going to prison. For. Life." Sutton turns around pointing at Officer Tony.

Officer Tony tries to remain stoned face but there is the tiniest glint in his eye and a hint of a grin on his face.

There isn't a single person on this planet that isn't the slightest bit affected by Sut. I'm pretty sure she'd make a robot smile.

"Do a thorough search. Find out how he broke in. Take whatever you need but please don't tamper with anything unrelated to the attack. His ass belongs in prison away from my best friend," Sutton barks at Officer Tony.

"Babe, can you show them to the apartment, please?" Sut asks August so sweetly.

"Yes, Sunshine. Behave. You're acting scarier than Quinn," August chuckles, kissing her cheek. August guides the police officers to the door of the apartment inside WaggingWithWords.

The ambulance takes off with James inside handcuffed to the gurney.

Sloan lets out a deep sigh of relief.

"I know you aren't okay. You've gotta be terrified. But physically, are you okay? Did he hurt you?" Sutton asks Sloan, her eyes pained, looking over every inch of her.

"My head's sort of throbbing and my throat's a little sore from him choking me, but I think he's in worse shape than I am," Sloan offers, still shaken up.

"Thankfully Beck got here when he did." She smiles sweetly at me.

"I'm not the one who broke his finger and ruined his face. That was all you, Little Dove. Smart and fast thinking. I'm proud of you." I squeeze Sloan close to me.

Not even twenty minutes later, one of the officers

approaches us to let us know they pulled footage from the alley that shows James grabbing Sloan, pinning her and choking her. They also mention that they saw him with her knife in the beginning of the footage as well.

It also shows Sloan slashing the hell out of the air and his face.

So fucking proud of her.

They can't find any areas of forced entry into the apartment, other than Sloan and James going through the fire escape. They aren't sure if he somehow snuck in through the café and just lingered somewhere without Sloan knowing.

"With him going against the restraining order, the breaking and entering, and the battery charges, he should be spending quite some time in jail," Officer Tony states. "Would you all mind sticking around town just in case we have any further questions? I think it should be a fairly cut and dry case though."

"Of course," we all say in unison.

"You are all free to stay here tonight. We got everything we need," Officer Tony encourages.

My girl can finally be free.

35

Beck

Sloan, Sutton, August and I are sitting in their living room together in comfortable silence.

Looking at the two of them curled up on the couch, I feel nothing but happiness for them.

The apartment was cleared by the police fairly swiftly since Sutton gave them the green light. The roses were really the only evidence in the apartment to report. Sloan was more than happy to see those roses being taken away.

Note to self, literally never bring a white flower home to Sloan, ever.

The alley video footage was the most important. The footage was fairly dark but they thankfully obtained that quickly and they could see what they needed to, to let Sloan and me off the hook.

Mayhem lays at Sloan's feet, while Khaos lays at Sutton's.

When did Sloan become his to protect?

Sutton wrapped Sloan in three blankets and made her

the largest cup of tea I've ever seen the second we got in the door.

I asked Sloan to let me take her to the hospital but she declined. I also asked her to come back to my place with me but she said she'd rather stay here tonight which I was surprised about given the attack.

After what Sloan went through, I don't want to be away from her.

The sight of her pale skin, her covered in blood, and her going in and out of consciousness, nearly had my heart stopping.

Thankfully Mayhem reacted to James getting near Sloan as quickly as he did, snapping me out of my own fear of her possibly being hurt.

The front door bursting open startles all of us. When Quinn rushes over to Sloan, shoving me aside and squeezing Sloan to her.

"Oh my gosh! Let me look at you. I got here as fast as I could. I hope that piece of shit rots in prison!" Quinn yells, holding Sloan slightly away from her as she looks her over, before pulling her back into a tight hug.

"Blondie, let the girl breathe," Knox chastises Quinn as he walks in behind her, taking a seat on the floor near August. I didn't even notice him coming in.

Ash follows in last, closing the front door and locking it behind him. Ash pulls up one of the barstools from the kitchen. Pulling it into the living room and closing out our little circle.

When did we become a circle?

Wait. Why did Knox come with Ash and Q?

"How are you holding up, Sloan?" Asher asks her quietly.

"I'm... I'm okay. Shaken up. But it's almost like I feel free," Sloan whispers so softly.

"Could you... Would you tell us what happened?" Sutton asks cautiously, lacing her fingers with Sloan's.

Quinn laces hers through her other hand, squeezing gently.

"Do you promise you won't hate me for keeping so many secrets?" Sloan asks, eyes cast down to the floor.

I reach across Quinn, placing my fingers gently on Sloan's chin, tilting her head up, so her eye's meet mine. "We could never hate you, Little Dove."

"We promise," we all say in unison.

I hold my breath and brace myself to hear all that my baby has endured.

Present

We're sitting in a circle, squeezed into Sutton's living room.

I should be filled with anxiety at the thought of pouring all of my secrets out to this little family I've grown to love, but all I am is exhausted. I'm so ready to get everything off of my chest. To set my past free.

Taking a deep breath and blowing it out. I start from the beginning.

"Almost two years ago I was working as a nurse at Harvard in Boston under my real name Reese Archer. Sloan is my middle name. I was on track to become a nurse practitioner. Just three months away from getting my master's degree," I sigh.

My heart breaks at just how close I was to touching my

dream, but it was just out of reach.

"James was one of the best surgeons in his field and Harvard recruited him. Several months after he had been working there, he had asked me out on a date. I said no initially, but long story short, he continued to ask. Started leaving me notes. Leaving me flowers on my desk, specifically white roses.

"So, my two best friends that I worked with told me just to give him a chance and to stop being so stubborn. That I could find balance in my career and a relationship. Mind you, I had never really been in many relationships, not really any that mattered, prior to him. Just a few dates here and there, a couple short-term flings," I continue.

"Anyways, flash forward six months later, James proposes to me at my favorite restaurant with a very uncomfortably large, gaudy diamond ring. With my parents there, I felt pressured to say yes, so I did. Even though I had been hesitant. My friends and family adored him though, so I thought maybe it was just me. That maybe I still hadn't found the balance within myself."

Mayhem curls up into a ball against my legs and rests his head on my feet, offering his own support.

"We had an extravagant wedding. James invited everyone from the hospital and my family. James didn't have any family. His parents were killed in a skiing accident when he was in medical school. No siblings. His ex-wife, Jessica was in a car accident five years after they were married. Which I found out today was not an accident," I shudder.

Quinn and Sutton both rub small circles on both of my palms. Sitting so calmly and openly with so much love on their faces, it makes me want to burst into tears.

The guys all listen intently, not saying a word.

You could hear a pin drop in here.

My chest aches for how much I love these wonderful humans.

I swallow a few times before continuing.

"We weren't married very long when he...he started commenting on my weight, the clothes I wore, the way I did my hair, my makeup. Constantly calling me names and putting me down, but then parading me around at his dinner parties like I was his prized possession." I take a deep breath.

"James also was a borderline alcoholic. The drunker he got, the meaner he got. He started getting really rough with me, but never did anything that could injure those precious hands though. Only leaving marks where no one could see. Gripping me by the hair too hard. By the arms. Threatening to kill himself or kill me if I even mentioned needing space from him. He'd even wave his gun around to prove his point. If I upset him during dinner parties or before them, James would lock me in his basement."

"Oh, Sloan," Sutton murmurs.

Looking down at my hands, I notice out of my periphery that Beck has his hands clenched in fists. I don't even chance a look at his face.

"No man should *ever* lay their hands on a woman," August says so fiercely, lacing his fingers with Sutton's other hand, bringing it to his lips and gently kissing her palm.

"No, they shouldn't," Beck grits out.

"So how did you end up here? All the way from Boston?" Quinn asks gently.

"A month before I ran, James told me we were hosting a dinner party for his coworkers. We lived on a ten-acre property. One day while he was at work, I hid a bag filled with money, a fake ID I got from an undergraduate student, some black hair dye, and a few pairs of comfortable clothes inside of a bush in the woods and counted how many steps it took me to get to and from it from the basement door." I close my eyes, remembering that night.

"The night of the dinner party, I intentionally upset him hoping he would lock me in the basement, and he did. I had been able to finally make a copy of the key to the door. I counted and waited a half hour and snuck out, making a run for the woods. There was a motel about a quarter of a mile from the courthouse and I stayed there for a week. I had filed for a divorce and a restraining order against him the day before the party. I arranged it so he would get them the day after I left. James never showed up for the court hearing, so the restraining order was granted. I dyed my hair black from ice blonde. I fled and found a train to New York and then a train from New York to Pittsburgh. Paid in cash and only planned to stay a month or so but then I met you all," I say, finally genuinely smiling through my tears.

"I never really had a plan of where to go. Never really planned to stay anywhere. Sutton and Quinn, you both just welcomed me with open arms. Offering me a place to work and a place to sleep without even doing a background check. You both gave me a safe place when I needed it most and I will be forever grateful. I'm so sorry I lied to all of you." After all of the anxiety from the day and from secrets from these beautiful humans, I finally break down into a soul wrenching cry.

"We love you, Reese or Sloan, whichever you want to be called. We love you. Thank you for allowing us to become a safe space for you," Sutton says, squeezing my hand.

"Thank you for trusting us with your story. You are so brave, sweet girl. None of us could say what we would have done in your situation. You did what you had to do to survive. It's admirable. Don't think for one second that we love you any less," Quinn declares.

"You are safe now, Little Dove. You will always have our love and support. You are family," Beck offers.

"That prick better be going to jail for life," Knox says, breaking the tension in the room.

"Way to ruin the moment, Knoxie." Quinn throws a pillow at him.

Knox reaches up grabbing Quinn from the couch, throwing her over his shoulder. "What did I tell you about that nickname, Blondie!"

"Put me down you Neanderthal," Quinn squeals.

"I say we have a sleepover," Sutton suggests.

"The only place you are sleeping is in bed with me tonight, Sunshine," August says, pulling Sutton down onto his lap.

Beck scoots closer to me, pulling me into his side. "Is it okay if I stay here with you tonight? I just can't get the fear in your eyes out of my head. I'd just be more comfortable if—"

"It's fine, Beck. You can stay." I give his thigh a gentle squeeze. Still a little hurt by the fact that he told the officer we were just friends, but I want him close, especially after today.

37

Beck

The lights in the bathroom are off. Two candles flicker in the dark from the vanity. Sloan rests quietly in my arms in the bathtub. The lavender scented bubbles almost flow over the edge of the tub.

I'm entirely too big for this thing but I wasn't letting Sloan out of my sight.

Sloan's been so quiet since I slipped in behind her.

"Is it weird being in here with me?" Sloan whispers, breaking the silence.

"No. Why would it be weird?" I ask confused.

"Because it's Sutton's place, Sutton's tub. I…" Sloan shakes her head, not finishing her sentence.

"You what, Little Dove?" I pry, tracing my fingers gently up and down her arms.

"I can't help but wonder if you've been in here with her."

Reaching for her face, I gently tilt her chin up, so Sloan

has to look in my eyes.

"Little Dove, Sutton and I were only intimate a few times. None of those times were in this apartment. I promise you."

"Okay," Sloan says softly, twisting her face to stare straight ahead at the wall.

"Can I ask where this is coming from?" I question, keeping my voice steady.

"You... I was so scared earlier and the only thing that kept me fighting was that I wanted to get back to you. Wanted to fight for us. But then you told the cop we were just great friends and I couldn't help but think if I had been Sutton, you may have told him something different," Sloan says, avoiding my eyes.

"Sloan, the moment I saw you covered in blood, my heart was in my throat and I couldn't breathe. I kept encouraging you not to freeze in our training but I froze at the sight of you. If Mayhem hadn't..." My voice breaks. I squeeze my eyes shut at the thought of not getting to Sloan in time.

Sloan turns to face me again, reaching her hand up to cup my face. Tears line the rim of her eyes and they almost sparkle, as the candlelight flickers in them.

"The only thing I cared about was getting to you and making sure you were okay. I'm so fuckin' grateful Mayhem is as protective of you as he is." I shake off the uneasiness from earlier.

"Me too," Sloan whispers. A lone tear running down her cheek.

"I told the cops we were great friends to protect you, not hurt you, Little Dove Your ex could've twisted the scenario to make it look like you were cheating on him with me. That you left him for me. It could've completely ruined your case and James deserves to be behind bars. Nothing and nobody should point a finger at you for this. I tried to think of what the cops would want to hear because all I want is your safety. I want you to know that Sutton is just my friend. You have meant more to me than just my friend for quite some time, Little Dove. I care for you so much, Sloan," I promise her.

"Thank you," Sloan whispers, kissing my chin and tucking herself back into my arms.

"No need to thank me for being honest with you, baby." I kiss her hair.

"It's so much more than that, Beckett Scott. So much more."

38
Sloan

I'm asleep in bed in the warmest cocoon between Beck and Mayhem. The sound of my phone ringing wakes me up from a deep sleep. The deepest I've had in a while.

My head still aches and my neck is sore from where James was gripping it.

Beck curls closer around me as I answer the phone.

"This is Sloan…I mean Reese."

"Hi, Mrs. McAllister?" the woman on the phone questions.

"Yes, this is she," I offer, confusion in my voice.

I push myself up to sit up in bed, holding in a groan from just how bad my body aches.

"This is Dr. Huxley, your husband, Mr. McAllister, is out of surgery now. Unfortunately, we did everything we could—"

"Is James dead?" I question, almost hopeful.

"No, ma'am, what I'm trying to say is we did everything we could, but unfortunately, we were not able to save his eyesight. The damage from the glass was severe. Mr. McAllister is blind in both eyes and it's permanent," she confirms.

I pause briefly before asking, "Is James aware he's blind?"

Dr. Huxley clears her throat and a bit uncomfortably, "Mr. McAllister is… He had some choice words for me, I'd like to avoid repeating. He says I ruined his career."

"I'm so sorry if James was incredibly offensive to you," I apologize to her knowing damn well James never will.

"You have nothing to apologize for. None of us know how we would react if we were met with these circumstances."

"Am I able to see him?"

Beck immediately shoots up from the bed, looking concerned at my question.

"Of course you can. Feel free to come in any time this afternoon. Just be a bit cautious because Mr. McAllister has been a bit violent since waking up. We aren't sure if it's the anesthesia or the circumstances," the doctor states, weariness in her voice.

"Thank you, ma'am. I will be there in an hour or so and will keep my distance."

"There is an officer outside of his room. So, if you should have any concerns just let him know. Again, I am so sorry we weren't able to do more," she says before hanging up.

I feel Beck's eyes piercing holes through me before I chance looking over at him in the dim light of the bedroom.

It's ten-thirty in the morning. I haven't slept-in this late in years. Never mind this hard.

"Um... I think maybe we should have taken you in to be checked for a concussion," Beck snips.

"Ha-ha. Actually, I might have one. My head's killing me, but that's not why I think I need to go."

"You should go to the hospital and be checked out. Not to see James."

"I have to see him, Beck. I'm sorry."

"You've got to be kidding! You shouldn't be anywhere near James!" Beck says exasperated.

"I know but I need to do this for my closure. Dr. Huxley said a police officer will be there at all times. I'll be okay. James can't grab me if he can't see me."

"That's... He's blind?"

"Yeah. That's what the doctor called to tell me."

"Fine. But I'm driving you there and home, so I know you're safe," Beck declares, getting up off the bed.

"Okay," I say, not putting up a fight.

Because honestly, the thought of Beck being close by gives me the courage I need to go see James one final time.

*A*s I walk up to James' hospital room, I'm comforted by the knowledge that Beck is waiting nearby. I know it's his room because Officer Travis is camped out in a chair right outside.

"I'm surprised to see you, Ms. Archer? Do you prefer

that or?" he asks.

"Yes, I like that." I smile at him. Appreciating that he remembered my maiden name. "I was surprised when Dr. Huxley called me but she said James listed me as his emergency contact and wife."

"Yes. Dr. McAllister has been yelling out that his wife better be 'getting her ass here soon.' He is something else…" Officer Travis scowls.

"That he is. Is it okay if I speak to James? I'm going to try to stand as close to this door as possible. I imagine if he can't see me and I stand far enough away, James can't really grab me," I say trying to convince myself.

"I will be right here, ma'am. Try to stay at least 6 feet away from the bed."

I nod, before heading into the room.

Staring at James from a distance, he is seated upright in his hospital bed. White sheets are draped up around his waist. His eyes are wrapped in white bandages, minimal blood is seeping through at his hairline. His scalp lacerations look like they may have been glued shut.

James' hands rest on top of the sheets at his side, an IV resting in the vein on the top of one of his hands. His small fingers I dislocated are buddy taped to his ring fingers on both hands. James' right wrist is bandaged where I sliced it as well.

He looks impossibly small in his hospital bed. Like the smallest man who ever lived. Broken. Battered. No longer the greatest surgeon, but the patient. No longer entitled. No longer well-known. No longer able to lay his hands on me. Just a man. A weak excuse of a man.

Both disgusted and proud of myself. I feel empowered being able to stare at him and see him for who he truly is. Even more so since he has no idea we're even breathing the same air right now.

"James."

"Reese, baby, you're here," he coos sweetly. Sitting up a little straighter in bed.

Bile forms in the back of my throat at the sound of his voice.

He reaches out his hand for me, but I take a few steps back. I'm nowhere close to him, but I don't want him to even think I'm close by.

"Come here, Reesey," James demands, the slightest bit of irritation in his voice.

"How are you feeling?"

"I'm fine. I'd be better if they'd take these bandages off of my face so I could see!"

"So, you don't know?"

"Know what, Reese?" he asks, irritated.

"That they couldn't salvage your sight. You are blind, James," I say, not sugarcoating my words. Wanting him to really hear them.

"Ha. That scam artist of a doctor said that, but she's lying. I'll get my sight back. I just need to find a better doctor. Preferably a male doctor!" James yells out.

He's such a disgusting, misogynistic, entitled prick.

"Dr. Huxley is an incredible ophthalmologist, James. Very sought after here. There was too much damage. You aren't getting your sight back," I reply calmly.

"Well, it looks like you will be taking care of me then, Reesey. You'll need to come back to Boston and finish school so you can take care of us," James snarls.

"Here's the thing, James. I'm not coming back. The divorce papers on my end have been filed for a year. If you don't sign them, I have one more year before they can go through without your signature. I don't want anything from you, other than to be free of you."

"I am not signing anything. You are coming back to Boston, Reese McAllister," James barks.

"I'm not, actually. I wanted to give you one last chance to try to be a decent person, but I guess you're incapable. Goodbye, James," I say, walking out of his hospital room.

All I hear is James yelling but his words are jumbled as I tune out everything he says.

Officer Travis stops me in the hallway on my way out. "Hello, Ms. Archer, I just wanted to give you an update. Officer Tony called and wanted me to let you know, we are pretty sure we have enough evidence. If you press charges, Dr. McAllister could go to prison for several years. Unfortunately, he could get out early for good behavior. I just wanted to make you aware of that possibility."

"Thank you for letting me know. I plan to press charges. Please let me know what I need to do to move forward with this," I say before walking away.

The next day, I decide I'm going to try one last time to get James to sign the divorce papers. My guess is he's going to tell me to go to hell. I really don't want to wait another year if I don't have to, to be free of James.

Walking up to his hospital room, I'm met by Officer Tony today.

"Good morning, Ms. um…Archer?" Officer Tony seems

confused on how to address me.

"Ms. Archer is good, thank you. Good morning, sir." I smile.

"I'm surprised to see you. I heard you were here yesterday as well," Officer Tony remarks, a little suspicious.

Holding up my papers, I sigh. "I really just want him to sign these divorce papers. Figured I'd give it one more try."

"Good luck, ma'am. He's been...difficult. Just so you know, the nurse stopped by and said, as long as his pain is under control, they are planning to discharge him tomorrow afternoon. James will go straight to jail from the hospital," Officer Tony informs me.

"Good to know. Thank you, officer."

"Keep your distance in there. Dr. McAllister is definitely more agitated this morning," he says with a grimace.

"Are they giving him anything for the pain?" I ask. Wondering if that's why he's being worse than usual.

"They were and then they took his pain pills away. Someone was trying to cheek his pills and was hoarding them in the pocket of his gown. So, we aren't sure if James is really in pain or faking it to hold on to them," Officer Tony states.

"Oh, wow. O-o-okay," I almost stutter. A bit taken aback that James would do that, but also not incredibly surprised. James always needed to be in control of every little thing. He probably doesn't trust what the doctors are giving him.

Stepping into his room, James looks a bit better today. Less haggard. No EKG leads or IVs are attached to him.

James just looks like your average guy sitting upright in a hospital bed except for the bandages.

"James."

"Reese. I knew you'd come to your senses. Come here!"

James smirks.

"Actually, James. I won't come there. You will *never* put your hands on me again. In fact, you and I will never breathe the same air again!" I snap.

"Who do you think you are speaking to me like that. Get the fuck over here!" James snaps back.

I feel absolutely nothing for this man.

How could I have ever thought I loved someone like him?

How did I let someone like him dim my light?

How did I let someone like James beat me down?

He's just a guy. Nothing special.

"No, James. I initially came here to tell you that I forgive you for everything you've ever done to me. But I am done with you," I say firmly.

"Ha!" James lets out a laugh that turns almost maniacal.

"You forgive *me*? Forgive *me*? You're the one who ruined my entire life. You ruined my career. You humiliated me, Reese. You stole my sight. You took *everything* from *me*! The second I get out of here I will *ruin you*, Reesey," James snarls, slamming his tray table and violently pushing it away. His bucket of ice crashing to the floor.

Officer Tony immediately rushes into the room to assess the situation. "Everything okay in here?"

"I'm okay, thank you," I assure him.

He steps back out into the hallway.

"No one asked if *you* are okay, Reese. I'm not okay!" James screams.

Walking a little bit closer to James, close enough so only he can hear me.

"For the record, James, you can't ruin me because I already ruined you. And I'm not the least bit sorry that you can't see a thing anymore. You deserve fucking worse," I growl under my breath.

James almost roars in fury. Swinging his arm out to try and hit me, but I'm out of reach.

Officer Tony steps back into the room, nodding toward the door. "I think it's time to leave now, Ms. Archer."

"Her name is Mrs. McAllister," James yells, as we close the door behind us.

"The doctor explained to him again about his sight this morning. I think Dr. McAllister is in denial. He called Dr. Huxley every name in the book, but he is very much aware that he is permanently blind. Dr. McAllister is also furious they stopped giving him pain meds," Officer Tony states.

"I still can't believe he cheeked those pills," I stumble through my words.

"It's not uncommon for people with narcissistic tendencies to have suicidal ideation."

"You think that's why James was trying to save them?"

"I can't say for certain, but that would be my guess."

"I thought maybe it was his way of trying to remain in control. James used to have to control every little thing. I still can't believe that there's no chance of him regaining his vision. I didn't mean to... I just wanted him to stop attacking me." I frown.

"You did what you had to do to protect yourself. I saw the video footage. Dr. McAllister looked like a man out for blood. Odds are high he would have killed you. Try to forgive yourself," Officer Tony assures me.

"Thank you. I'm going to head out. If that's okay? Will you keep me posted please?"

"Of course. Have a good day, Ms. Archer."

"You as well." I smile.

*T*he next morning, Officer Tony calls me to let me know James is being discharged around four p.m. and will be going to the Allegheny County Jail until his trial.

I'm not sure why, but I feel the need to visit him at the hospital once more.

Beck is less than thrilled that I keep going.

I'm not even sure why I keep thinking I need to go. When I ran, I never wanted to see James again.

Maybe subconsciously I still can't come to terms with the fact that he's blind and it's my fault. It's like I feel guilty but I don't. There's a part of me that wants to see him suffering for once.

I have no plans to visit him in jail. I imagine I'll have to see him in court when our case goes to trial, whether it's for the battery charges or the divorce but for some reason seeing him one last time in the hospital feels final.

Walking to James' hospital room for the last time, I notice Officer Travis is sort of pacing the hallway and nurses are running in and out of James' room.

When he sees me, he makes his way toward me, pulling me off to the side.

"Hey, is everything okay?"

"We aren't really sure. Officer Tony told Dr. McAllister this morning that he would be going to Allegheny County Jail this afternoon when he was discharged. He smashed another tray table and Officer Tony left. About twenty minutes ago, a nurse went to check on him and he was unresponsive. They have been doing CPR." Officer Travis explains.

Barging into his hospital room, my eyes immediately go to James' lifeless body lying on the hospital bed.

"Ma'am, you can't be in here!" a nurse yells.

"She's his wife," Officer Travis states from behind me.

"You still shouldn't be in here."

"What happened?" I shout.

"We don't know. He ordered lunch an hour ago. We left him to eat it. When we came back to check on him, Dr. McAllister was blue, his face was swollen and he was unresponsive. We did a throat sweep and didn't find anything in his airway but his tongue is swollen. He didn't respond to CPR. We called time of death four minutes ago. I'm so sorry, ma'am," the nurse states solemnly.

My eyes are searching the room for any sign. Any clue to what happened.

"Has he been given any medications today?" I ask.

"Nothing, ma'am. They were discharging him today," the nurse states.

"James never yelled for help? Like he was in distress?" I ask, twisting back to look at Officer Travis.

"I was sitting right outside the door since my shift started this morning. Someone has been here 24/7 so he couldn't leave. I didn't hear anything," he states.

"You said Officer Tony left..."

"I just meant he left the room, but he came out here," Officer Travis confirms.

My eyes are searching everywhere and that's when I see the plate on his tray table, pushed up against the wall out of the way.

I imagine it was shoved out of the way so they could run their code on James.

There are crumbs like maybe it was a sandwich but I can't tell. The plate is empty.

"Can I speak with you outside in the hallway?" Officer Travis requests.

"I'm so confused."

"So are we. And I hate to do this, but I have to ask, since it's my job. You have been visiting him a lot, for someone who had a restraining order against—"

"You think I did this? I haven't even been here since yesterday!" I state, affronted.

"I'm not saying you did anything. Just making sure you haven't given him anything, or hid something in his room when you've been here. I did see that you used to be a nurse as well," Officer Travis remarks.

"I have not gotten close enough to James to give him anything. I was more so hoping he would give me some closure by apologizing to me. Wished that bastard would sign these divorce papers." I show him the papers I had tucked in a folder under my arm.

"Each time I've been here, he's turned it around to make it about him, and became the victim, so I left. I did not do anything!" I turn away, fuming.

"Ms. Archer, I believe you, but stick around. We'll be doing an autopsy this evening," I hear him say as I leave.

I've been walking in the park for hours. The same park where Beck and I had laid on the ground and came up with our truce after we got back from Vegas. That feels so long ago.

I'm not ready to go back and tell everyone because I can't even wrap my head around James being dead.

My phone buzzes in my pocket for what feels like the tenth time. When I finally pull it out, I see I have a voicemail. I press play and listen to it.

"Ms. Archer, this is Officer Tony, please return my phone call."

It's been an hour since Officer Tony called, which means I've been outside for hours and it's freezing. My finger tips are about as numb as I am.

I'm still trying to process that James is dead.

James. Is. Dead.

And I'm pretty sure that prideful, bastard somehow took his own life.

Rest in peace is the only thought that keeps creeping up through my mind. But it's not for him, it's for me.

I can finally rest in peace knowing James can no longer haunt me.

No longer hurt me.

No longer lay his hands on me.

No longer poison me with his words.

No longer dig his talons in even from miles away.

I don't have to look over my shoulder anymore.

I don't have to live in fear.

I don't have to walk on eggshells.

He's gone and I...

I can finally find peace.

I feel like I should feel guilty for feeling that way, but all

I feel is complete and utter relief.

And how do I explain that to my friends without sounding like a terrible person?

Sitting down on a park bench, I take a deep breath and call back Officer Tony.

The phone rings for only a second before, "Ms. Archer, the autopsy results are back," Officer Tony says immediately. "James McAllister's cause of death was severe anaphylaxis."

I wait a moment before I ask quietly, "What was James's lunch order that he requested?"

"A peanut butter and jelly sandwich with extra peanut butter. He must have really liked peanut butter. Afraid they wouldn't have it in jail?" Officer Tony questions slightly chuckling.

I'm completely dumbfounded.

"James had a severe peanut allergy," I state so matter of fact.

Silence. For what feels like eternity.

"Is there any reason you can think of that he would have ordered this then? Shouldn't a surgeon know his allergies?" Officer Tony asks.

"Oh, James knows his allergies—knew them. Was it not documented in his medical chart?"

"It wasn't. So again, can you think of any reason why he would order this? And consume the entire sandwich? Normally someone pulls the alarm for a nurse if they're going into anaphylaxis. Especially someone with his knowledge. There was an officer right outside of his room. He could have called for help. Officer Travis said he never heard a word. Not a sound. Dr. McAllister basically suffocated to death."

"Honestly, I don't think James could've gone on living without his sight. His career was his life."

"So, you think Dr. McAllister did this on purpose?"

"I really do, officer." I sigh.

The inkling I felt when I saw that plate was true. The humiliation of going to jail, ruining his career was too much for someone like James to endure.

James had too much pride to go to jail. Too much pride to be denounced of his status. Too much pride to go on living as less than.

So, James controlled his own script and manipulated the system one final time to work in his mind's eye favor.

I guess now we will both rest in peace.

39

Beck

Sloan has been staying with me for the past few days since James died.

She has been having to field phone call after phone call.

Sloan's also been incredibly hard to read. Usually, I notice all of her tells of anxiety or fear, but she's been oddly stoic.

We've fallen asleep together every night. I wake up with her wrapped around me like she can't get close enough to me but she has felt so distant.

I'm trying not to let old insecurities come up. Trying to hold space for her because I can't even imagine what's going on in her head. I would never know how to handle something like this but the disconnect between us is killing me. I'm trying not to push her to open up to me, and tell me how she is feeling. Hopeful Sloan will do it in her own time but I just have this gnawing feeling she's going to leave.

I have this impending feeling of waiting for the other

shoe to drop.

I'm coming in from a run, walking into my bedroom when I hear Sloan on the phone. I lean against the doorframe and listen in on her conversation. Sloan's back is to me.

"Yes, thank you. Just one day for the viewing and service please," Sloan responds to whomever she's talking to on the phone.

"Wow. In a week?" she questions.

"Um…how much does it cost to transport a body across several state lines?" I hear her ask with concern.

"Oh, wow. Okay. That's incredibly expensive," Sloan continues.

"A will. I never even thought about that. I imagine James did," she responds to the person she's speaking with.

"Yes. Okay, thank you, sir. I should be there within the week." Sloan hangs up the phone, tossing it on the bed.

The shoe is finally dropping along with her phone.

I don't even wait a second before I'm jumping down her throat. "So, after everything, you're running away anyways."

Sloan whips around. "What? Beck, no."

"I heard you on the phone. You're going back to Boston within the week," I yell, storming off. Ripping my front door open, I take off down the hall.

I hear Sloan running behind me but I can't even look at her right now.

"Beck, wait! Please! Can we please discuss this?" Sloan begs, her footsteps falling behind me.

My feet are tearing off down the stairs of my apartment complex when Sloan yells, "Stop!" Halting me in my tracks.

I whip around to face her. "You can't just use our safe word, Sloan."

"I just did, Beckett. Now come back inside and talk to me."

"Answer me one question, Sloan."

"I'll answer any questions you have, if you just come inside, Beck. Please," Sloan pleads.

We're having a standoff in the middle of the stairs of my apartment complex, just staring at each other.

We walk up the stairs to my apartment door in silence. I break the tension, ripping open the door and holding my hand out for her to walk through first. When we get inside, Sloan walks over and sits on one edge of my sofa.

"What's your question?" Sloan asks.

"Why? Why did you need to go see James every single day he was in the hospital? Why did you need to go see someone who hurt you? Repeatedly! Who tried to kill you, Sloan! I can't wrap my head around it. I have been thinking about it for days. How could you love a man who hurt you?" I grit out.

"Beck. It's complicated. Mine and James' relationship was messy. I thought I could get closure by going to the hospital. I hoped I could get him to sign the divorce papers. I thought maybe I'd feel bad for ruining his life. That if I stared at him in the state he was in maybe I'd feel some sort of remorse. but I never did.

"I don't love James. I'm not sure you could even call the relationship we had love. I'm not sure I even knew what love looked like until I moved here. In the beginning James was so attentive and said all of the right things. I hadn't been in many relationships to see the signs and then once we were married it was too late. There were times things got so bad at home, I didn't know how to get out of it. My parents told me to stick it out. That James was such a great provider and it couldn't be that bad.

"I was so afraid of him. There were so many times I had wished James would just die. A few times I wished I would just die. I think I've always hoped James would wake up one morning and see that I was enough. That I was worth loving, and he would apologize to me for everything he put me through. I thought maybe for once at his weakest moment he would but James in the end was still too much of a narcissist to take the blame for anything.

"I feel at peace knowing that he's dead, Beck. Almost euphoric and then I'm disgusted with myself for feeling that way about a man dying," Sloan explains, her face twisting in so many different emotions.

"So then, if you feel that way why arc you still choosing to run? If James is dead, why are you running?"

"Beckett, do you even hear me? I'm not running," Sloan says exasperated.

"But you are, Sloan. You are. You're going back to Boston. I heard you on the phone. I'm sure you'll go back home and remember how much you loved it there and stay. Leave us all behind. Why would you stay here?" My heart is breaking at the thought.

"Why would I stay? Why would I leave? I found a home in *you.*" Sloan points a finger at me. "I found a home with the girls. I found something I never even knew I was missing until I found it here with you, Beckett," Sloan declares.

"If this was your home, you wouldn't be booking a flight to Boston a few days after your ex died. You'd be staying here to start over with us. But you're choosing to leave us." My voice cracks.

Sloan gets up, moving to sit closer to me. Her hand

wipes at my cheeks and then she's cupping my face in her hands. I hadn't even realized I was crying.

"Beckett, I need to close this chapter of my life fully so I can start a new chapter with you. I'm choosing us. But I can't leave unfinished pages in Boston and just move on to the next chapter. I'm not going to just give you pieces of me. I'm going to give you all of me. That's what you deserve. Just like I deserve every piece of you. Just give me a little bit of time. I promise I will be back." She holds my gaze.

"How long is that going to take? How do I know you won't go back to Boston and never come back to me?" I whisper. All of my skeletons coming out of the closet. My fear of abandonment just leaking out at the fear of the unknown. The fear of being left again.

"As long as it needs to take. You will just have to trust me, Beck. Just like I've learned to trust you," Sloan whispers, gently pressing her lips to my cheek.

"How?" I croak out.

"If you feel what I feel. If you can trust what we have. If you think with your heart and not that overthinking mind of yours, you will know deep down, that I won't be able to stay away for long, Beckett. You've made me feel something I never even knew existed before. You make me want to be better for us. Trust that, okay?" Sloan kisses my lips softly and then presses the sweetest kiss over my heart. She gets up off the couch, grabbing her purse off the counter, and walking out of my apartment door. My heart in her hands.

When did loving someone become such a bloodsport?

40

Sloan

$\mathcal{S}$tanding in the airport with just my purse and a small carry-on, Quinn and Sutton hug me close to them before I head toward security.

"We're going to miss you so much." Quinn's voice breaks as she hugs me closer to her.

"I promise I'm coming back. Just give me a few months to get my life in order," I plead.

"So, what is your game plan?" Sutton asks, lacing her fingers with mine.

"Well, the funeral is in two days and I'm going to have to go explain everything to my parents since I ghosted them for a year. My old nursing program reached out after seeing everything on the news in Boston. They sent their condolences and asked if I needed anything to let them know. So, I asked if I could potentially finish my last few months of the program that I missed given the circumstances. They're supposed to be letting me know in a few days.

"My two best friends I left behind in Boston deserve an explanation too. I'll need to see if James had a will to figure out how to sell the house. Then, once it's all said and done, I'd like to come back here and make a life with all of you," I explain, shrugging my shoulders.

"Well, you know we support you. No matter what. But pretty please come back to us." Quinn squeezes me to her again.

"Yes. Come back. It won't be the same without you," Sutton whines.

"I will. But I have a favor to ask. You asked me to keep an eye on Beck when you left for tour," I say, squeezing Sutton's hand in mine. "Now I'm asking you to return the favor while I'm in Boston. Beck deserves to make it back to Vegas and take his title back. Make sure he doesn't spiral."

"I promise." Sutton squeezes my hand tightly, leaning her head on my shoulder.

"Me too." Quinn kisses my cheek.

"Thank you, both. For absolutely everything. I literally wouldn't have survived this year without you. I will be forever grateful." I squeeze them both to me.

"Bitch. Quit talking like you're leaving us for good," Quinn scolds me.

I'm cracking up through my tears. "I'm not. I'm just... I love you both so much. I'm going to miss you. Even if it's just for a little while."

"We are going to miss you too. But we'll text every day," Sutton says, reassuring me.

"We love you!" Quinn and Sutton both shout in unison.

"And I love you!"

Grabbing my suitcase, I make my way to the escalators.

I blow the girls one final kiss, on my descension to TSA.

Sutton and Quinn are holding each other with tears running down their faces as they blow me a kiss goodbye.

Once they're out of view, a sense of dread sinks into the pit of my stomach at what's waiting for me back in Boston.

*W*alking into the funeral home, a heaviness surrounds me. The weight is almost too much to bear. I feel like I'm going to be sick.

I wasn't the one who took James' life, but was the one who gave him a reason to. James can't hurt me ever again, but having this inner knowledge that ultimately in the end, only one of us was going to make it out of this marriage alive. I will never feel guilty for surviving.

The first half hour of the viewing was for family only. But James didn't have any family remaining, so I'm the only one here except for an usher who stands at the door letting guests in, and I'm grateful for that. I didn't exactly want people to witness my lack of emotions.

My parents are on their way, but they've been a lot to deal with since I got back to town. So, I asked them not to come early. To allow me space to feel what I need to feel.

I've been staying at their house with them the last couple days, because I just wasn't comfortable going back to James' house. I know I lived there with him, but it never felt like mine. My parents' house has never really felt like home either. It's like choosing which prison cell feels more comfortable.

My parents have been giving me so much grief for running away. And I get it. They had no idea where I was or what happened to me. I'm their only daughter but I could not trust them to know where I was. They thought James was the best thing since sliced bread since they met him. All they've done since I've been home is tried to make me feel guilty about leaving him the way I did. Said that none of this would've happened if I stayed. My parents have talked incessantly about how wonderful he was. That they 'can't believe their son is dead.'

My mother admonishes, "You could've come here to cry or rant if you needed to, honey. Could've taken a couple days for some space. But ultimately, James was your husband, you should have never run. He may not have been a good husband but at least he provided for you. You had a beautiful home. He always gave you those beautiful roses. You didn't have to want for anything. I never saw any bruises on you. It couldn't have been that bad. It's so terrible this happened to him. If only you had stayed here."

"I can't believe you haven't shed a tear since you've been home. You think you'd show some respect. He was your husband after all," my father states.

I explained to them that I was suffocating in my marriage. That I felt completely unsafe in it. That my mother might've thought she was offering wisdom but all she was doing was saying that it was okay to live in a society where we're so conditioned, that we believe we 'must' stay because marriage is sacred. That we're told that it's totally normal for love to become a prison. That somehow that's acceptable. That it's okay for a man to lay his hands on you or to emotionally and mentally abuse you just because he 'provides' for you. When in fact that's absolutely sickening and not at all healthy. I refused to be someone who normalized that just because it's existed for ages. Honestly, fuck the patriarchy.

I was not going to be my husbands' punching bag for his words or his fists so I did the only thing I thought I could do to protect myself.

I left.

And honestly, I refuse to stay here and be my parents' punching bag either.

When I finally get out of my own head and shake off the tension of the last couple days. I walk into the viewing room. I hold my breath, preparing myself to see James in a casket. The walls feel like they're closing in on me, as I approach him.

His professional photo from the hospital sits in a frame next to the casket. Always so perfectly put together at work.

Numerous rose arrangements adorn this room that I delivered myself this morning.

I ripped out every single fucking white rose from his perfect garden last night in a fit of rage. Letting some of the blood from the thorns stain the petals. Creating beautiful pieces that no one will know are tainted.

These roses have been my own open bleeding wound. A reminder of how controlling James always was. Haunting me for what feels like an eternity.

Now, they will die with James.

Along with the piece of me, he tried to mold into his perfect wife.

I'm staring at James' body lying in a matte navy casket. His lifeless frame, in an olive suit jacket. Foundation covering the gashes on his forehead and near his eyes fairly well.

As I stare at him, the only thing I know for sure, is I'm

ready to start this day and get it fucking over with.

It's going to be incredibly awkward seeing people from work that I haven't seen in a year. Gods knows what James has been telling his coworkers about me.

While I'm here, I will attempt to wear my best mask of a devastated wife mourning her brilliant husband.

Even though staring at his corpse right now, I feel absolutely hollow inside.

I whisper my own final prayer over James' body before the guests arrive.

Your demons almost stole my life. In the end they swallowed you whole instead. Now we both can rest in peace.

*T*he one good thing that came from all of this becoming local news in Boston was that James' estate attorney reached out to me. It probably would have taken me some time to find the estate documents and the will. So, the attorney reaching out was one last thing I didn't have to worry about.

After receiving the phone call last night from James' attorney, I have been nothing but a ball of nerves.

Mr. Motley asked if I could come into his office to discuss James' will and estate. I sort of assumed James had one but didn't really know anything about it. One of the many things he kept from me.

Sitting in Mr. Motley's office, I'm sitting on my hands trying to keep myself from chewing on my nails. Trying to ease my mind, my eyes follow the small hand on the clock as it ticks on the wall.

Claustrophobia was never something I thought I had, but between the funeral home and this tiny office space, I'm starting to wonder if I do. The room just keeps feeling like it's getting smaller and smaller.

"Good morning, Mrs. McAllister. I'm Mr. Motley, your husband's attorney. Thank you for coming in this morning. I just have a few things to go over with you and then you can be on your way," Mr. Motley offers, causing me to jump in my seat slightly. "Sorry to startle you, ma'am."

"Nice to meet you, sir," I respond, anxiously waiting for this discussion.

Mr. Motley starts shuffling around papers on his desk.

"I will cut to the chase. Mrs. McAllister you are the sole beneficiary on Dr. McAllister's estate and will. His funeral expenses will come out of the estate but otherwise he had no debt. You will be receiving everything left over after that is withdrawn. I will just need to get a few signatures from you to file this and get it processed. We will send the check to the funeral home. You should receive documentation for your assets in a few months at the latest," Mr. Motley states.

"I'm sorry, my assets?" I question.

"Yes, Mrs. McAllister. The house, the vehicles, bank accounts, retirement fund. It's yours to do with as you will," he rattles off.

"James had me listed as sole beneficiary?" I choke out.

Confused, Mr. Motley says, "Yes, Mrs. McAllister. You are his wife. As you know, he has no living family."

"I'm just... I was not expecting this." I struggle to find my words.

"I'm not sure any of us were expecting Dr. McAllister

to die so young. Such a tragedy," he offers.

"It is," I whisper.

"I just need you to sign a few documents." He slides the papers toward me. "Thank you, Mrs. McAllister. As soon as this is processed, I will be in touch."

"Okay. Thank you, sir," I nod. Still shocked and processing the fact that James somehow left everything to me.

"You said the house," I blurt out when Mr. Motley is at the office door.

"Yes ma'am." He halts, turning to face me, where I'm still seated in the chair across from his desk.

"Can I sell it?"

"Of course, you can. It is yours, Mrs. McAllister. You can sell it or you can keep it. It is up to you as sole beneficiary," Mr. Motley reiterates.

"Wow, okay." I nod, still completely in shock.

"Take care now, Mrs. McAllister." He walks out, leaving me sitting in his office completely and utterly bewildered.

James left me…everything.

41

Beck

Sloan's been gone almost two months and I miss her so fucking much.

We've texted and even FaceTimed a few times, but it's just not the same.

I miss holding her. Miss talking to each other curled up in bed or on the couch at the end of the day.

Even Mayhem seems lost without her. Searching for her in every room we go in.

Running on the treadmill in the gym, I can't help but stare at the weight bench where I had Sloan laid out for me. The pull-up bars where she trusted me to take care of her.

We had christened almost every section of this gym in the last month before she left. Now every fucking piece of equipment in this place reminds me of her.

Increasing the speed on the treadmill, I run faster. Trying to run from the thought of her.

I fell so hard for Sloan without even realizing it.

Without even trying really. This shared intimacy and deep knowing of what the other needs without even having to be asked.

Sloan could've let me storm off when I yelled at her and I would have deserved that. But she knew what the broken pieces of me needed to hear. I might've lashed out at her at the time. My mind only focusing on the "you're leaving," but I heard her.

When I first met Sloan, she never would've let a man like me anywhere near her. She also would've never chased after me. Never would've stood her ground and demanded to be heard.

Every day that woman gives me a reason to be so fucking proud of her. So fucking proud to love her.

The last few weeks with her prior to her ex showing up, we were inseparable. When we cooked dinners together, our shoulders or hands were always brushing. When we worked out together, we supported and encouraged one another. We fell asleep on the couch a tangle of limbs watching tv some nights.

Sloan just fits perfectly in my life. Like the other half of my puzzle piece. Without question. There's no second-guessing. She made it so damn easy to love her. Loving her was like breathing air--natural--you never had to think about it or question it, you just did it.

My inner beast wants to beat his chest, wrap Sloan in my arms, and keep her safe from everything. It's an innate instinct when it comes to her.

Sloan and I were a team. Where I struggled emotionally, she was a force, my goddess of wisdom. Where she struggled physically, I always had her back, I would never let her fail. We were always teaching each other how to be better.

It was time someone showed up for her.

The second I take back my championship belt, I'll be on a red-eye from Vegas to Boston to get my girl back.

I'm getting off of the treadmill when Asher walks out of his office.

"Are you sure you're ready for your fight in a few weeks? You haven't been training anywhere near as hard as you did last year to go up against Kenzo King," Ash states a bit concerned.

"What are you trying to say, Ash?"

"I'm just making sure you're ready. You had to take a break because of your concussion. I just want to make sure you feel ready physically and mentally."

"I'm ready. I've been training every damn day since the neurologist gave me the green light. I maybe missed two months of training. I got this." I smirk.

"Okay. I just—"

"What is your deal? I said I'm ready!" I snap.

Asher sobers. Not even trying to argue back. "Beck, you didn't..." Asher scratches at his head, uncomfortable.

"Obviously you were there. It happened to you, but when Kenzo knocked you out and you weren't responding I thought you were dead, man. Then after you didn't wake up for a couple days. If Sloan hadn't been there to keep me sane, I just... I don't want to lose my best friend. That doctor in Vegas said if you took another bad hit or if that hit had been any closer..." Asher shakes his head, turning away from me.

"Ash." My voice breaks at the worry in Asher's tone.

I didn't realize how much my injury fucked him up. It never even crossed my mind. I'm such a dick. Ash had to witness everything while I was unconscious. If that had been me worrying about him... Fuck.

"Ash. Look at me."

He turns to face me. A lone tear runs down his cheek, wiping it away just as quickly as it came.

"I'm so fucking sorry. I never asked if you were okay after all of this. My head's been so far up my own ass. I was so angry at first that I couldn't train. Then I became so fixated on training Sloan. I had to know that she knew what she needed to do to keep herself safe. I hardly remember that fight. I never considered that you'd be worried about me getting back out there," I apologize.

"It's okay, man," Asher replies, trying to brush it off.

"It's not, but I promise to do better." I pull Ash into a quick hug.

"All right. Sloan really is rubbing off on you." Asher chuckles, trying to break the tension.

"Real funny. But I do fuckin' miss my girl," I sigh.

"I was curious how you were holding up. You seem to be doing a bit better about this than you did with..." Ash cautiously states.

"What we have is different. I think it's because Sloan said something to me that's sort of stuck. She said if I trust what we have and listen to my heart and not my head that I will know that she won't be gone long. And if she could learn to trust us after everything that asshole put her through, I can learn to trust her."

"Damn. Sloan's good for you, man." Ash pats my back.

"She really is. Now I know you're worried about me fighting but I'm ready for my redemption," I say, smiling a deviously grin.

"All right, then. Glove up." Ash grabs my gloves from the floor and tosses them to me.

42

Sloan

I walk into the hospital, it's my last week of clinicals before I graduate.

It's crazy to believe that I'll finally be walking away from these walls. Freedom is so close I can taste it.

Thankfully, the house sold in forty-eight hours. I've been selling off everything inside and everything that doesn't sell by the end of this week is getting donated. I have no desire to take any of my old life into my new life. Staying in a motel after leaving my parents' place has been tiring. I'm looking forward to a fresh start.

I trade all three vehicles: James' SUV and sports car, as well as my old car, to get myself a nice all black Suburban SUV. I figured, if we wanted to go on road trips in Pittsburgh, the entire crew would fit in it.

I also put in an offer on a house just outside of the city in Pittsburgh. Not far from the café, but far enough that I can have my own yard and garden. Hopefully someday

Beck will want to move in.

"We just got you back, just for you to leave us again." Kailey sneaks up on me, pulling me out of my head.

"I know. I missed you so much. You'll have to come visit. Pittsburgh is a really cute city." I smile.

"Is it just the city you want us to see or…" Maria giggles.

"I think you guys would get along great with Quinn and Sutton," I reply nonchalantly.

"Anyone who kept our Reese's Pieces safe is a friend of ours." Kailey smiles softly.

"You know, I'm not talking about your friends. Even though I'd love to meet them too," Maria sasses.

"I hear you." I sigh. "I really miss Beck. We haven't talked much, but we have texted a little."

"That doesn't mean anything. Maybe Beck's giving you space," Kailey offers.

"You did tell him you were coming back here to close out a chapter. Maybe he's just letting you close it on your terms." Maria shrugs.

"Didn't you say Beck has a fight coming up too? Maybe he's just been training a lot," Kailey reassures me.

"I still can't believe you have been sleeping with that gorgeous fucking Adonis of a man. Not to be weird but I have looked him up online. Girl. The Big Dick Energy on that man!" Maria fans herself.

"Oh, trust me I know. That man can give me one look and I am a puddle. Beck doesn't even have to touch me. He just like turns on this aura or something and it's like *poof* there goes my panties. Sometimes I don't even bother to wear any." I giggle.

Kailey and Maria are both staring at me beaming.

"What?" I ask, chuckling. Searching both of their eyes but coming up empty.

"This is that fire we were talking about. Look at you acting like a hot little minx," Maria squeals.

"This"—Kailey sweeps her finger up and down at me—"is what true love looks like, my sweet girl."

"You really think so?" I ask, tucking my hair behind my ear.

"Yes. You are glowing. There's no fear behind those beautiful eyes. No discomfort or uncertainty. You are so in love with that man." Kailey squeezes me to her.

"I really am." I smile, tears forming in the brim of my eyes.

"Why are you crying?" Maria asks softly.

"Because I finally know what peace feels like after all of these years." I break into a sob.

It feels like freedom. It feels like hope. It feels like happiness.

The three of us stand in a huddle, crying but holding each other together.

*K*ailey, Maria, and I are standing outside of James' old house. We're packing up my black Suburban with the few things I wanted to keep. Like photos of me and the girls, books, and a few outfits that felt like the real me.

Staring at the house from the road, a giant red brick mansion stands before me, but all I see is time lost. Painful memories. Tears cried. A prison where the dreams of who I thought I wanted to be, went to die.

"Too bad we can't just set it on fire," Kailey shouts, standing next to me.

"Then Reese's Pieces wouldn't have gotten that giant chunk of change she earned. It's her justice being served after having to be married to that monster," Maria chimes.

"I still can't believe James killed his ex-wife," Kailey says in a loud whisper.

"You know I had always wondered if he did. Not in the beginning but once we were married and he really started showing his true colors. I had this suspicion." I sigh.

"And you never told us," Kailey shouts.

"What was I supposed to say? I had a feeling but no evidence. James always said no one would believe that he was hurting me at home. No one for sure would believe my suspicion about his ex. James made sure every mark was in a place no one would be able to see. He threatened to ruin your careers. So, I stayed quiet. And besides, he ensured I didn't get the chance to tell you." I frown, wrapping my arms around myself.

"James did try to ruin our careers and kept you from us. But fuck him. It was he said, she said. Yeah, he was 'respected' but James didn't have the power to get us fired. We didn't believe that you were in a mental hospital like he was telling everyone. So, we made sure to shut down those claims." Kailey rolls her eyes.

"We didn't know where you were though. We knew you were being distant. You had changed so much after your marriage, but we didn't want to upset you by questioning you either. When we went to your parents and they had no idea, we filed a police report, afraid James might've done something to you. I never would've guessed you ran, but

I'm fucking proud of you, that you got out of dodge." Maria slides her arm around my waist and rests her head on my shoulder.

"I'm proud of you for slashing that motherfucker's pretty face!" Kailey giggles maniacally.

"Shhh!" I shush her but I'm dying laughing. "Don't let my secret out of the bag."

"How did you know how to even do that?" Maria asks, laughing.

"Ash, Beck's best friend, but Beck too." I smile.

"Ran to Pittsburgh, banged a hottie and became an even bigger baddie." Maria shimmies.

"Look at you go, Reese's Pieces. I've never been prouder." Kailey does a little dance.

"You guys kill me." I laugh and then I'm bursting into tears.

"Fuck. I'm going to miss you. Promise you'll come visit. My new house isn't that big." I point at the mansion in front of us. "But it's big enough to have a few of my besties stay over for a girls weekend."

"We promise." Kailey and Maria cry, as we pile into a three-way hug.

"I love you. Now get your fine ass to Pittsburgh and don't leave that gorgeous man waiting any longer." Maria smacks my ass.

Kailey shuts my trunk and then walks over to the driver's door, pulling it open for me.

"I love you. Call us if you need anything. We're only a phone call away."

Hopping into the car. I pull the door shut and roll down my window.

"I love you both. It's not goodbye, it's I'll see you soon." I blow them a kiss and drive away.

I've officially closed this chapter, leaving my old life behind in Boston for good.

I'm looking forward to my future in Pittsburgh and for whatever comes next.

43

Beck

It has been four long months without Sloan.

We've been giving each other space. Well, I've been giving her space and hoping like hell she hasn't forgotten about me. It felt like Sloan needed time away to process everything she was going through and I can't say that I blame her.

Sometimes you really have to just sit with yourself, alone, to truly be able to heal. I probably would've never realized that, if it wasn't for Sloan.

It's hard as fuck and it sucks. Wow, does it ever suck but it feels worth it on the other side.

Looking back in hindsight at the way that I acted before was inexcusable. I'm honestly surprised my friends are still friends with me.

Instead of lashing out and starting fights, I decided it was time to spend some time with myself. To see why the thought of Sloan taking time away left me feeling so rejected.

Sloan didn't give me a single reason to lose faith in her. If anything, Sloan inspired me to want to be better for her. I never wanted to be someone who lashed out and scared her. I always tried my hardest to keep my temper under control. I never wanted to be someone who made her feel like she wasn't heard. I wanted nothing more than for Sloan to come to me, with everything—good or bad.

I'll admit I wasn't comfortable seeing a therapist, but I started journaling and writing down my feelings. Anytime something would come up when I felt the sting of Sloan being away, I wrote it down. I was quick to find that most of this stemmed back to my parents never being available and then my father leaving all together.

Trying to meditate was something new I started. Something Ash actually tried teaching me to do. Learning to respond instead of reacting.

I know I'm not a changed man yet. It's only been four months but I feel lighter. I feel ready to be the type of man that Sloan needs. The type of man she deserves.

The second I beat Kenzo King today, I'll be on a plane to Boston to bring Sloan home where she belongs.

I'm sitting on the bed in my hotel room in Vegas. I've been trying to remember when I was here last time, but losing the fight to Kenzo still hasn't come back to me. And maybe that's a good thing.

Every time I won a fight, I had hoped my father was out there somewhere seeing me on TV and proud that I was his son. I always wished for his validation but it never came. I was so hungry for attention that I looked forward to the phone calls from my mom, knowing she watched my fight, even though talking to her was often a painful experience.

Tonight, I want to win, but I want to win for me. Not to prove something to my absent father or my narcissist mother. But to prove to myself that fighting doesn't have to consume my life. Maybe I can find balance in fighting once a year but also live a normal life. That I can have months where I stay fit but don't have to have such a grueling schedule all the time. So, I can spend time with my friends and hopefully with Sloan.

Fighting was always an outlet to pour all of my rage into. Pushing my body to the extreme so I could feel physical pain instead of the turmoil always festering just under the surface and ready to boil over at any moment. But I don't want to feel that way anymore.

I'm realizing I don't need to seek validation outside of myself. That I don't need to fight all the time to manage my temper anymore. That I can confide in my friends instead of bottling things up. I know they will listen. That they'll be there to offer me guidance and be a safe space for me. Something my family was never able to offer me.

That I can fight because I enjoy doing it but not to just survive my rage.

A knock on my hotel door takes me out of my head. I go to get up and I'm hit with a memory.

Sutton coming to my door and telling me she was choosing August right before the fight flashes in my mind.

Another knock on the door, has me finally walking to answer it.

I hesitate, taking a deep breath before I open the door.

My Little Dove stands in front of me. Her long raven hair swept up in two space buns, platform sneakers on her feet, tight black leggings on her slender legs, and a baby blue T-shirt that says...

"Beckett Scott's Girl," I whisper.

"If you'll have me?" Sloan asks hopefully.

Reaching for her delicate neck, I pull her into my room, shutting the door and pressing her up against it. "Always, baby."

I crash my lips down on hers. Sloan melts into my hold, letting me coax her mouth open with my tongue. Kissing me back with just as much fervor.

"Gods, I missed you. When did you get here, Little Dove?" I ask in between kisses.

"I dropped my car off at my house and had Quinn drop me off at the airport. I came straight here once I got in. I missed you so much."

"Wait a minute. How did you know where I was?"

"Ash," Sloan smiles, kissing me again.

Pulling away from her, "Wait...your house? Your car?" I ask.

"Yeah. I bought a house outside of the city, maybe twenty minutes from you," Sloan offers.

"In Pittsburgh?"

"Yes," Sloan replies, smiling.

"So you're staying?" I ask hopeful.

"I told you I was, Beckett Scott," Sloan says huskily.

"You could've moved in with me. You didn't have to buy a house."

"I could have, but I wanted to do this for myself. I wanted a yard, a garden, a place for Mayhem and Khaos to run around safely. Your apartment is great, Beck, but it's yours. I wanted something that was mine," Sloan says nervously.

"As long as you're close to me, Little Dove, that's all that matters to me. Maybe someday you'll let me and Mayhem move in with you."

"Maybe I will." Sloan winks at me.

"Does this shirt mean you're mine, Little Dove?" I ask, raising an eyebrow.

"Only if you're mine, Beckett Scott," Sloan teases.

"You have all of me, Sloan. I'm a better man because of you. I promise to learn with you and love you how you deserve to be loved. I vow to protect you always, even though I know you can protect yourself. I will continue to work on myself for me and for you. So, you only ever get the best version of me, because that's who you deserve. I love you, Little Dove." I press my lips to hers.

"I love you, Beckett. I had no idea how to love. I didn't know how to trust anyone, not even myself anymore. You taught me how. You showed me through actions what love looked like. You proved to me that a good man would never use his words or his fists to hurt a woman. He will only use his hands to hold her and support her and his words to encourage her and push her to be her best self. You became the home I never knew I was searching for. You showed me a love and intimacy I never knew I was missing until I met you. I am yours, Beckett Scott," Sloan vows, kissing me back.

"Little Dove, I want to consummate our relationship with you only wearing this T-shirt, but I have to go weigh in for the fight," I groan, kissing from her lips down her neck.

"You can have me, in just this shirt, as soon as you win that title back, babe," Sloan purrs, nipping my ear with her teeth.

"Promise?" I ask, running my tongue up her neck to her ear.

"Promise." Sloan gasps.

"You're coming with me, Little Dove." I grip her by her

thighs and toss her over my shoulder. I open the door and close it behind us.

I carry Sloan that way on the elevator and all the way down to the backstage of the ring.

"Such a caveman." Sloan chuckles.

"Always for you, baby." I give her ass a little tap.

Sloan's giggles washing away the remaining nerves I have about this fight.

44

Sloan

I'm sitting backstage on a sofa next to Ash, while Beck weighs in. The arena is already so loud, the floor feels like it's vibrating from the volume.

Beck's hardly let me out of his sight since I got here.

"You can't stay back here during the fight unfortunately, but you'll be safe there. Promise." Asher pulls a ticket for a suite out of his pocket and hands it to me. "This is where you're supposed to be sitting as one of the girlfriends." Asher winks at me.

"Ooooh, like a WAG? Thank you, Ash. I'll head there now."

I take the ticket and pull Asher into a hug. "Beck's got this. You can breathe."

"Thank you, Sloan," Asher hugs me back.

"Quit hugging my girl!" Beck barks, making his way over to us.

"Good luck kiss for me, Little Dove." Beck puckers his

lips.

I give him a hug and a quick kiss and tell him, "Get your title back, Beckett Scott!"

I make my way out into the arena, looking at how almost every seat is filled. If James was still looking for me, I'd be incredibly anxious around all of these people. But for once I can just enjoy this feeling of doing something without fear.

I'm in complete awe as my eyes scour the room. There are strobe lights flickering overhead, with the octagon in the dead center.

A jumbotron sits directly above the ring, ever changing with the fighters and their rankings listed.

It's so wild being in the thick of it. Watching it on TV with Quinn didn't feel anywhere near as amped up as this.

The energy in the room is electric, palpable, and buzzing with excitement.

Making my way to the suite, I take a seat fairly close to the glass.

I know Ash is worried about Beck after what he witnessed last time, but I'm confident Beck has what it takes to win.

I believe Beck when he says if he wasn't ready, he wouldn't be here. I also think Beck wants to do this for himself, not for anyone else.

But I am slightly worried, because Beck may not remember exactly what happened to him, but the body remembers. I just pray it doesn't remember when Beck's in the ring.

The announcers' voice draws me out of my head. "Ladies and gentlemen. Fighting in our Heavyweight Division tonight is reigning champion, Kenzo King, facing

Beckett Scott who is here for his chance at redemption. We expect this to be a hard-hitting affair."

A video starts playing on the jumbotron, Kenzo King is walking through a hallway and *Beast-the Southpaw Remix* is playing.

As Kenzo's massive frame enters the octagon, a flashback of Beck's last fight with him runs through my head. He looks even more ferocious than he did on screen all those months ago. Reminding me how it took one hit and he almost took Beck's life. Knots start to form in my stomach, envisioning a repeat of that fight.

Don't think like that.

Beck was in a completely different head space then. I have to remind myself that his mind is clear.

Hopefully he wants to get this fight over with, as quickly as I do. So, we can return to his room and finish what we started. I hoped he would love this T-shirt. When Quinn dropped me off at the airport, she was also squealing about it.

The jumbotron shows Beck walking through the hallway to Knocked Loose's *Don't Reach For Me*. People are yelling and whistling, making the room feel like a live wire around me. It breaks me out of my thoughts of how this fight went last time.

The announcer starts talking about how Beck had been the champion for a couple years but lost to Kenzo King several months ago after a very quick knockout, which was completely unexpected. Beck took a few months to heal but is here to take back his title.

People are screaming, clapping, and whistling so loud, and my heart is beating wildly in my chest. Both at how nervous I am that something bad is going to happen to Beck and at how fucking gorgeous he looks in his video, wearing the hell out of a burgundy suit tailored perfectly to his body, and the sexiest smirk on his lips.

When Beck enters the octagon in tight little black shorts and no shirt, my body is instantly on fire. I haven't gotten to see or touch him in months. It's a gift to see Beck naked. My core clenches at the sight of him. All I want to do is run my tongue through every ridge of defined muscle on his delectable body, and climb him like a tree.

My eyes track Beck's every move. Every flex of his muscles. Watching him is like foreplay right now. *Fuck me.*

When Beck reaches his corner, his camp immediately starts taking care of wrapping his hands up.

His wrapping is...violet?

Huh, that's unusual.

"Ladies and Gentlemen, this is the main event of the evening," says the announcer.

The referee comes to the center and explains the rules. He confirms that they understand, both nodding. The fighters return to their respective corners.

The ref asks if they are ready, looking at each opponent for confirmation. Both fighters take their fighting stance. They touch gloves.

I notice Kenzo barking and snarling at Beck, but Beck remains expressionless. *What an animal!* My stomach twists in knots. Beck still demands the attention of the room, even in his indifference.

"Let's go!" the ref yells and steps out of the center of the ring.

Kenzo and Beck bounce around each other a bit, sizing each other up. Kenzo throws a punch and Beck dodges it.

I'm on the edge of my seat, adrenaline coursing through my veins, my knee bouncing with anticipation, so focused on every move Beck makes. My eyes never leave him. My heart pounding so hard I feel it in my ears.

Kenzo kicks Beck in the shin and Beck jumps back. Beck takes another step further back, as if he's preparing for something. Kenzo goes to throw a punch and I cover my eyes. Flinching at every punch Kenzo tries to land.

I notice Beck jump back again and can't figure out why, but then Kenzo's leg comes up in a roundhouse kick that would've gotten Beck right in the side of the head, but Kenzo just misses. Kenzo looks *pissed.*

Kenzo tries to throw a hook and Beck quickly dodges and counter strikes with a right jab, and a left hook that lands perfectly on Kenzo's jaw and knocks him to the ground.

I'm immediately on my feet, standing and holding my breath, with my fist to my mouth. I'm looking at the sheen of sweat coating Beck's skin. My body doesn't know how to feel right now. Worried for Beck? On fire for Beck?

Beck goes to finish the job but Kenzo jumps up and throws a solid uppercut to Beck's jaw. He shakes it off, adjusting himself, before dodging another series of punches from Kenzo. Kenzo is not letting up. He's out for blood.

Beck is finally able to get enough space that he throws a series of punches: a jab, a cross, and a deadly hook. Kenzo falls to the ground. Beck gets on top of him about to throw another jab, but the referee comes over and breaks up the fight and calls the knockout.

"Winner Beckett Scott!"

The crowd goes insane! It takes a minute for it to register that it's finally over but I'm beaming at Beck. So fucking proud of him for winning and for restraining himself at the end.

I am screaming my head off with tears streaming down

my face. My heart full of so much love and pride for this wonderful man.

I'm staring at the ring, when Beck's eyes connect with mine. Beck has the biggest smile on his face.

I raise my hands above my head and clap as loud as I can, whooping and hollering for him.

"That's my girl!" Beck mouths.

"That's my man!" I mouth back and wink at him. "So proud of you!" I blow him a kiss.

"I love you," Beck mouths back.

Before I can blink, I'm up and running to get backstage. The second I spot Beck, walking in from the octagon, I'm launching myself at him. Catching me in the air, I wrap my legs around him, grab his face, and kiss him with every ounce of adrenaline coursing through my body.

"You were fucking incredible, babe," I squeal, pulling back with his cheeks still between my hands.

"Thank you, Little Dove." Beck kisses me softly.

"I'm so proud of you. For real, Beckett Scott. That took a lot of courage, to get back out there so soon. But purple hand wraps?"

"They're the color of your eyes. I needed something that would remind me of you."

I swoon at his response, kissing him again.

"You two need to get a room," Ash says, coming up behind us.

"We have one." I giggle, nipping Beck's ear with my teeth.

"So glad we aren't sharing one like last time." Ash shakes his head.

"Adore you, but same, Ash." I laugh.

"You, this T-shirt, and nothing else, in my bed, in twenty minutes, Little Dove. I have months of sexual frustration to take out on this sinful body," Beck growls.

Making me instantly turn red at his comment in front of Ash.

The announcer comes in, just barely breaking up the sexual tension, "How does it feel to take that title back, Scott?"

"It felt amazing! But what's even more amazing is getting my girl back," Beck replies, never losing eye contact with me.

"Ah, I see! What do you think?" The announcer looks at me and then my shirt, chuckling, "Beckett Scott's Girl?"

"I'm so proud of Beck! It's well deserved!" I smile at the announcer.

"Looks like you're checking off all of the victory boxes, Scott!" the announcer states.

"Love isn't a game. It's inevitable," Beck says to the announcer as he carries me away to the uber.

I melt into Beck's arms. *It feels so good to be home.*

45

Beck

"Kick the door open, baby!" I tell Sloan as I try to carry her over the threshold of our hotel room bridal style.

"I am kickin' it!" Sloan giggles.

Fuck. I missed the sound of her laugh.

"Hit it harder!" I start cracking up at her laughing. The door is still not budging open. I'm trying to get my key to scan from my pocket without having to put her down. The light keeps turning green but we can't get the door open.

"That's what she said," Sloan snorts.

"You didn't just…" I'm dying laughing, holding her close to me.

"You set me up for that one, babe." Sloan's laughing hysterically, her entire body shaking in my arms. "Am I high?"

"Why would you be high?" I'm laughing just as hard as her.

"I don't know. Why can't we stop laughing?" Sloan

asks.

"I think you're just happy to see me." I flex my hips into her, as I carry her in my arms.

Sloan groans. "I am soooo happy to see you!"

Finally, the door clicks and we're in. Kicking the door shut with my foot. I carry Sloan over to the bed and lay her down on the comforter. Taking my time pulling her shoes off and then her leggings. Leaving her in only the T-shirt she made for me.

Staring at her, I take her in. "Can I take your hair down, baby?"

"Yes." Sloan smiles sweetly up at me.

"Sit up," I request.

Sloan sits up, crossing her legs. I gently pull at the hair tie holding her bun together. Releasing the one and then the other. Watching her long black hair tumble down her back, I gently running my fingers through it and shake it out for her.

I love her like this. At ease. Trusting.

Leaning forward, I give her a chaste kiss.

Eyeing me curiously, Sloan asks. "Can I make a request?"

"Anything," I reply.

"Can I..." Sloan hesitates.

"It's okay, Little Dove. Use your words," I coax her.

"Can I tie you up with your tie to the headboard?" Sloan asks, immediately looking down at the bed.

Surprised by her request, but loving that Sloan's being bold, I'll give up control to her for a little while.

Tilting her chin up, so her eyes meet mine. "Yes, boss." I lick my lips, smirking at her.

Shock flashes in her eyes before they fill with lust.

"Will you strip for me and then lay down, please?" Sloan's eyes are heated.

"You want me to strip?"

"Don't make me ask twice, Beckett," Sloan sasses.

"Oooh... Little Dove, definitely wants her ass spanked."

"What?" Sloan squeaks.

"I'll play into this for you, Little Dove, but then you'll do as I say after you've had your fun."

"I-I-I...umm," Sloan starts to stutter.

"You're playing with fire, baby. But I'm always ready with gasoline." I smirk, unbuttoning my suit jacket slowly. Peeling one sleeve down my arm and then the other.

I watch as Sloan's eyes become hooded. Taking all of me in.

My burgundy jacket falls to the floor. I tug at my tie, tossing it on the bed next to Sloan. She picks it up, tracing her fingers over the silk fabric.

Her eyes go a little bit wide as she watches me unbutton my shirt, taking my time.

I'm loving every second of watching Sloan squirm where she's seated on the bed.

My navy dress shirt falls to the floor. Flexing my abs and biceps just enough that Sloan notices, causing the smallest little hum to leave her throat.

Unbuckling my belt, I pull it through the belt loops and it clatters to the floor. I pop the one button of my burgundy dress pants and slide them down my thighs. My quads flex as I push them all the way down and kick them to the side.

I'm standing in front of Sloan in only my black boxer briefs. My cock hard as a rock, standing at attention.

"Please hurry and get on the bed now."

I push my boxers down my legs slowly, letting my cock spring free and slap against my abs.

I enjoy torturing her just the slightest bit by making her wait. I crawl over top of Sloan causing her to lay back on the bed.

"Beck," Sloan moans as she's panting beneath me.

Tracing my tongue up her neck, I let my cock just graze her leg. "Needy for me, baby?" I nip her ear lobe, before rolling over and leaning against the headboard.

Sloan works fast to get my hands tied to the headboard. Her fingers are trembling but she manages to tie it. The knot is fairly loose, but I let her think I can't move.

Resting my head on the pillow, our eyes find each other and so much love shines back at me through Sloan's eyes.

Sloan leans down and kisses my lips, tracing her tongue along the seam of my mouth. I let her in and she twirls her tongue with mine.

Sloan shocks the hell out of me, when she breaks the kiss and whispers against my lips, "I'm gonna sit on your face now, Daddy."

When she turns to face away from me, I'm speechless. As she slides her soaking wet pussy down onto my mouth, Sloan leans forward and takes my cock into hers.

Just from the taste of her, I groan into her pussy.

Fuck I missed her and I missed how fucking good she sucks my cock.

Fuuuck!

Sloan's tongue swirls around the head of my cock as she strokes the base. As she bobs her head, she takes my cock deeper down her throat.

I match her stroke for stroke, swiping my tongue through her folds, sucking her clit into my mouth and making her moan around my cock. Every time Sloan moans around my cock, it's like she's vibrating around it.

It takes everything in me not to come down her throat. Sloan needs to come first.

I'm flicking my tongue over her clit and sucking on it. I can't spread her any wider with my hands tied. I nip her clit with my teeth. As she comes hard, Sloan screams with my cock still buried down her throat. I can't help but lick every drop of her clean.

In minutes, Sloan is sliding her body off of my face.

Gripping my dick with her hand, Sloan lines up her pussy and slides down onto my cock facing away from me.

I feel my eyes go crossed at how fuckin' good she feels.

I watch as Sloan's perfect ass bounces up and down on my cock. Her hands gripping my thighs and nails digging into them as she grinds down on me.

Her long hair grazing my abs every time she comes down on my cock. It's feather-like against my skin, causing an unreal sensation. I feel my balls tingling.

"Fuck!" I groan, as Sloan picks up speed.

"Fuck, baby. Please let me touch you," I moan.

Sloan ignores my request and continues to rock her pelvis on my cock. Slowly moving her hips up and then slamming down taking me deep.

I can feel Sloan's pussy clench around my cock like she's close again.

Thrusting my pelvis up, I start to meet her thrust for thrust. Making her take my cock hard and deep.

"Beck, I'm so close!"

"Fuck. Be a good girl and come for me, baby!"

Sloan grinds on me a few more times before she's yelling out my name.

Her pussy clenches so hard around my cock, I see stars, before my release is barreling through me. Thrusting up into her gently a few more times as I fill her with my cum.

"Fuck. That was so fucking good, baby," I groan.

Sloan twists around, my cock still inside of her.

The sensation has my cock stirring back to life. I can't get enough of this girl.

Sloan leans forward to untie me from the bed. I lean up and take one of her nipples between my teeth, which has her gasping and her core clenching around me again.

Once my hands are released, I grab her around the waist flipping her so she's underneath me.

"Round two, baby. My turn." I suck her neck hard and slide my cock back inside of her. Fucking my cum back into her where it belongs.

"Fuck. I missed you," Sloan says, crashing her lips against mine.

"I missed you, Little Dove." I kiss her back. Putting everything into it so Sloan knows just how much.

46
Sloan

After Beck and I finally made it out of bed in Vegas. Beck, Ash and I flew back to Pittsburgh.

Within a week, my new home was furnished and decorated how I always dreamed mine would be.

The girls and I spent a lot of time at HomeGoods and Target. Going crazy picking out cute décor for each room in the house.

My living room walls are now painted a deep green. A gorgeous purple velvet sofa and chair fill the space. A gold coffee table, lamp and mirror accent the room. It even has a gorgeous cobblestone wood burning fireplace.

My bedroom has lavender purple walls. A giant king-sized bed with a sage comforter set where Beck, Mayhem and I fit perfectly. Almost the opposite of the living room, but so cozy and comforting to come home to.

My spare bedroom is lined with wall-to-wall bookshelves. Filled to the brim with thrillers and some romance novels. Something I've gotten more into because of Sutton and Quinn.

I have a pull-out sofa in the middle of the room for when Kailey and Maria come visit.

Beck and Asher helped me build a garden in the fenced in backyard. It's filled with fruits and vegetables. Quinn and Sutton helped me pick out beautiful wood furniture to sit out back around the fire pit. Fairy lights are now draped in the trees. My own little fairy oasis.

We all love having nights out here, but I think Mayhem and Khaos might love it even more.

The front of the house is landscaped with a mix of roses, dahlias and peonies. Lavender growing along the sides of the house. It smells like heaven outside. As I sit on my beautiful porch swing that Beck installed for us, I get to watch the butterflies and hummingbirds flutter around all of the pretty flowers.

Getting to wake up on weekend mornings and cuddle up with Beck while drinking our coffee on our porch swing is my favorite part of the week.

Sometimes I feel like I need to be pinched. My life went from an absolute nightmare to a dream like the flip of a switch.

*B*eck and I spent six months living separately. He and Mayhem spent most nights at my house, before they finally moved in with me.

I never thought Beck would want to move out of the

city. He had been in his apartment for so long, but he loves how quiet it is out here. Loves that Mayhem gets to run free in the backyard.

After I got settled into my house, I applied to several hospitals looking for a position as a psychiatric mental health nurse practitioner but nothing really felt like it fit. So, I continued to help out at the café a few days a week until I could find something. I honestly didn't even have to work with the money James left me but I wanted to use my degree.

One day, Quinn and I were taking one of Beck and Asher's self-defense classes and a woman we hadn't seen before came in. She was dressed similarly to how I was the first day I found their class almost two years ago now. The woman was incredibly skittish and quiet. She reminded me so much of myself when I first found my way here.

Beck partnered me up with her as sort of a kindred spirit to see if I could get her to open up at all. Kind of like he did with Sutton and me.

Before the woman had left that day, she had confided in me that she was working two jobs because her boyfriend was taking her hard-earned money from her for drugs. If she came home with less money than normal, he would hit her, shove her down, or kick her. Scream at her and call her worthless.

Her boyfriend couldn't keep a job. He would try and find one and end up getting fired because of someone or something. He sat at her apartment playing video games all day, taking pills and smoking weed constantly. Always high. Always cruel.

The woman wanted to leave him but she didn't know how and she was terrified. She had tried hiding money, but every time she did, he would notice and lash out.

She had told us her name was Remi. Beck and I had asked Remi to keep coming back to the classes. We told her that we would try to teach her how to fight back until we could come up with a solution to get Remi out of her situation.

That night when Beck and I were lying in bed, he asked me if he could move in with me. It wasn't even a question. I had wanted him and Mayhem around all of the time.

We were lying there in silence, just holding each other, when Beck said, "I want to keep the apartment though. For women like you, like Remi. I actually wanted to talk to you about that."

"Your apartment?" I question, confused.

"The complex actually. Mrs. Hazel wants to put it up for sale. It's getting to be too much for her and she wants to retire. After the water damage, several tenants left so there are quite a few units available. The insurance covered it but the stress was a lot for her. I've saved most of the money from my fights. I was thinking... What if there's a way for us to start a program for women who need help getting out of a bad situation? What if I bought it or we bought it?" Beck continues a bit unsure.

"In really bad situations, we may be able to get them out and put them up in the apartment until we can find a better solution for them? Teach them self-defense in the meantime?" I ask, thinking Beck's on to something.

"Sutton is leaving to go back on tour. You're looking for a job in your field. So, they're going to need some help at the café too. We could even potentially get some of the women part-time positions at the café with Q," Beck rattles off.

"I love that! It could help give them a purpose." I'm nodding, loving this.

"Maybe you can even use your license to counsel women. I don't mean this insensitively but who would be better at counseling women that are domestic violence victims or even survivors than you? You can offer them guidance, give them resources." Beck sits up in bed, fueled with ideas.

"That's actually a great idea. I can help screen them address any intimate partner violence. Once we get them in a safe environment, I could help them with any psychological trauma they may have. I'm sure I could find a doctor willing to come on board willing to help with that. Even if that physician is more of a telemedicine provider. Maybe find someone who works for one of the local psychiatric hospitals. That way if someone is really in danger or struggling with something that needs inpatient treatment, I could assess them and get them safely where they need to be."

"Do you think we could make it happen?" Beck asks, really thinking about everything.

"Honestly, yes. James left me so much money I don't know what to do with it. I thought about finding a charity to donate it to. This allows us to use it to help women in need. Use my resources and yours. I honestly love this idea. We may need to have it made into a nonprofit to get a physician on board. I can start looking into that tomorrow though." I'm beaming at Beck.

"Where do we begin, Little Dove?" Beck pulls me into a kiss.

It is our official opening day of Hope Blossoms.

It has taken us several months to get everything together but we finally did it. We had a few renovations done on the apartment complex. There are twelve, one-bedroom apartment units that are about 750 square feet. Four of the existing tenants want to continue renting from us, and they are aware that we are converting the complex into a women and children's shelter.

We lightly furnished each apartment so they are move-in ready as we need them. Having cabinets stocked with nonperishables, as well, will be another way to help them.

We set up an office area on the main level and had it soundproofed for medical assessments and therapy sessions. I found three incredible psychiatric physicians who are available on an as needed basis and were happy to be my supervising physicians.

It's in very close walking distance to the gym. Beck and Asher are holding weekly self-defense classes and it's free for all women. Whether they are part of our program or not.

Remi is our first tenant moving in. We were able to get her name off of her lease and her ex will be evicted upon us safely getting her moved in to the complex. She's also going to be quitting one of her other jobs, to start helping Quinn at the café.

Sutton and Quinn have small flyers on the windowsill at the café for our program, Hope Blossoms, for anyone in need of a safe space.

We started an Instagram page, sharing our hopes and goals for the program. WaggingWithWords and From Troy have been sharing it to get the word out.

As a survivor of domestic violence, I never knew who to turn to. Always afraid it would get back to my ex and make my situation worse. Afraid no one would believe me, because he groomed me into believing that. Losing trust and faith in myself, so how could I trust someone else to help me? Worried he had enough money to hunt me down, and James did just that. I know I took the first step in removing myself from the situation, but I'm not sure I'd still be here if it weren't for Beck and Ash teaching me how to protect myself. If Quinn and Sutton hadn't welcomed me in with open arms and become such incredible friends to a complete stranger, I don't know where I would be.

My dream for Hope Blossoms is that the second a woman takes a chance to get out of their situation, we are there to offer them resources, friendship, counseling, and the guidance one needs after being a victim of abuse. To learn to trust themselves again. Learn to lean on others in a time of distress. Learn to protect themselves. A safe haven to find their way back to themselves; mentally, emotionally and physically, and to get away from their abuser. A place to feel safe until they can get back on their own two feet. Just like these beautiful humans did for me.

Staring up at our apartment complex, tears stream down my face.

"We did it!" I beam at Beck through my tears.

"Actually, you did it, Little Dove. You made this happen." Beck pulls me close to him, kissing my forehead.

"This complex was your idea, Beckett Scott and it was a brilliant idea." I kiss his chin.

"I love you, Little Dove. I'm so fucking proud to call you mine." He leans down kissing my lips.

"I love you, Beck. We make a great team!"

Epilogue

Beck

Today is the day I ask Sloan if she wants to spend the rest of our lives together.

Sloan and I have melded our lives together in a way that I never expected to come as easy as it has.

Marriage had never been something I thought of. After watching my parents' marriage crash and burn, it never felt like something that was in the cards for me.

But living day to day, moment to moment with Sloan, made me realize that the right person had to come along. Our lives had just easily entwined as one, flowing from one transition to the next so effortlessly. We went from two untrusting, heartbroken humans, to learning about each other. Growing with each other. All I envision when I look at her is a woman that I'd be lucky to have as a partner and wife for the rest of my life.

I recruited Quinn and Sutton to help me plan the perfect day to surprise Sloan.

Quinn worked behind the scenes to get Sloan's best

friends from Boston, Kailey and Maria, in to visit for a long weekend.

Quinn planned an entire morning for all of the girls to get them out of the house. By doing this, Ash, August, Knox and I are able to get the backyard set up. Even Beau and Ty are helping out.

The girls started the morning getting mani pedis.

Sutton and Quinn have been texting the guys with photos to give us updates without making it obvious.

Sutton sent August a photo earlier of all the girls making funny faces with their nails done. Her caption reading, "New nails, who dis?"

Quinn sent a picture to Knox of all of the girls sipping tea, at a local tea shoppe. Her caption reads: Who says adults can't have tea parties too?

Sutton told Sloan they're doing a small charity at the café tonight and the theme is "fairy core." So, the girls are currently at the store picking out fairy dresses and then going to get their hair braided and flower crowns directly after.

Sloan has turned our backyard into her own little haven. It's almost like entering a fairy tale back here.

So, tonight, I'm really going to make it a fairy tale come true for her.

Since the girls left early this morning with iced lattes in hand, the guys and I have been working hard to make it perfect.

A wooden arch, draped in blush pink peonies and roses, baby's breath and greenery, sits toward the end of the backyard. Rustic lanterns with candles inside sit just next to it to offer some ambient lighting for this evening.

Flower petals create an aisle for Sloan to walk down,

as soon as she steps off of our back patio. Tiki torches line the walkway, softly illuminating the path. Fairy lights hang in several of the trees in the backyard carrying on into the white tent that fits about 15 people.

A burlap table runner with lace trim is draped over a large farmhouse-like picnic table in the center of the tent. Three beautiful arrangements of blush pink peonies, baby's breath and greenery fill gold vases that sit perfectly placed on the table. Two small bouquets of peonies and baby's breath are tied together with burlap string lying at the end of the table for Sloan to carry as she walks down the aisle.

Beau has a sound system set up, just outside of the tent and will be our DJ for the evening. Two microphones ready for Sutton and August to sing as Sloan walks down the aisle.

Ash and Knox have been in the kitchen the past few hours whipping up a taco bar.

While Sloan was in the shower, Sutton and Quinn dropped off carafes of lavender and hibiscus margaritas this morning as well as several different types of pastries from the café. We did everything we could to keep her out of the refrigerator.

Standing on our back patio, I just take it all in. This picturesque backyard I never pictured for myself but now I can't picture myself without it.

Two years ago, I thought I had been in love with my best friend, who was already in love with the man standing next to me. Now, I realize that love isn't just talking to someone 24/7, hanging out, going on a date, or just partying with someone. I adored Sutton as my best friend. I cherished and still cherish our friendship and easy companionship. The quiet comfort she offered me by never pushing me.

But loving, Sloan. Being in love with Sloan, she opened

my eyes to what true love really is. It's allowing someone in and letting them see the darkest parts of you. The parts of you, you try to hide from the world. The parts of you, you sometimes are even too afraid to look at yourself and loving them anyways. Loving them even more because that's when they need you to love them most.

Love is someone just being there for you and holding space for you when your world feels like it's falling apart. It's someone giving you space to fight your own demons but coming back and taking you by the hand so you don't let them consume you.

I'm not sure I knew what love was until Sloan allowed me to see her darkness even if they triggered her fears, and she allowed me to show her mine. Sloan fought for her life—for me. Now I will always fight my life—for her.

August interrupts my thoughts. "Sutton just texted and said they're leaving the hair salon. We have 30 minutes 'til they're here. Should we go get suited up?"

Turning to face the man who has become a close friend and who couldn't be more right for my best friend, I smile at August. "We shall."

*D*ressed in a light blue linen suit, I'm standing under the archway at the end of the backyard waiting to officially make Sloan mine.

It's a beautiful evening. The sun is starting to set, painting the sky like a canvas of deep reds and oranges, with a gorgeous golden hour glow.

There's a gentle breeze but it's still a warm summer night.

I'm a nervous wreck. I went back and forth on whether Sloan would love this idea or hate it. I know she felt almost forced to marry James and had been so unsure about it. I'm sort of springing this on her, but we've spent many mornings curled up together, talking about our future. Sloan has said that she never thought she'd even get married once in her life, let alone twice, but as our relationship has grown, she can't picture her life with anyone else and neither can I.

The girls start to make their way down the aisle easing my nerves slightly. They are dressed as the perfect fairies. They take their places to the right of the archway. Quinn in a blush pink tutu dress, Kailey in a sage green, and Maria in a baby blue, with butterflies and flowers sewn into their dresses.

"I don't think she was sus until we got back," Quinn whispers.

"Great." I grimace.

Knox, Beau and Ty stand to my left in sage green linen suits.

"It's gonna be fine, man. Don't worry." Knox kneads my shoulders.

August and Sutton stand under a tree not far from us, ready to sing the second Sloan makes her entrance. August in a sage green linen suit and Sutton in a lavender tutu dress.

As the perfect, obedient ring bearers, Mayhem and Khaos stand just in front of me in the cutest baby blue bows with gold trim.

It feels like it's taking an eternity for her to come outside.

Asher was supposed to be stalling her just to get everyone in position.

"What's taking so long?" I huff. I'm getting so anxious.

"Sloan's coming, Beck. It's okay," Sutton whispers.

I see Asher's frame in the glass door first and then he's sliding the door open.

Ash has his hand over Sloan's eyes when she steps on to the patio.

I hold my breath.

I can't hear him but he mouths something to Sloan before she nods.

Asher's hand lifts from her face. He gently reaches for her hand, placing it around his arm as he walks her down the aisle to me.

Sloan's eyes trace the entire backyard before they meet mine. Tears stream down her cheeks but Sloan's smile takes my breath away.

August and Sutton start singing a haunting rendition of *A Thousand Years* by Christina Perri but I can't hear a thing.

All I see is Sloan. My heart stops beating at her beauty. I'm not sure if it's the perfect angle of the glow from the sunset hitting her or if it's just her, but she's radiant, ethereal, almost angelic.

Sloan's dressed in a beautiful white corset tutu dress that's longer than the girls. It's grazing the grass, almost making it look like she's floating on air as she walks toward me. White baby's breath woven through her raven hair, braided in a crown on her head.

So fucking stunning. Breathtaking. So mine.

When they finally reach me, tears are streaming down my face.

Asher places Sloan's hand in mine and kisses her cheek. He walks behind the archway, standing at the ready to marry us, if Sloan says yes.

Sloan reaches up to wipe my tears, as I reach up to wipe hers.

"Hi." Sloan smiles.

"Hi, Little Dove," I rasp.

Clearing my throat, I get down on one knee, holding Sloan's hand in mine.

Sloan smiles so sweetly at me as I confess my love to her.

"Little Dove, I love you. I want to do life with you. When we wake up in bed together, I want to see those gorgeous sleepy eyes looking up at me every morning. I want to kiss each fingertip that you hold your iced toffee lattes with. I want to be the first person you share unbelievable news with and the person you reach for to hold you and calm you down when you feel like you're falling apart. I want to be the person who makes you laugh when you're feeling low. I want to taste your lips every second of every day and pleasure you every chance I get. I want to cook together and laugh together and travel together. Love on Mayhem together. I want to be partners in crime, taking on the world together.

"I vow to fight to protect your peace forever. With you, I feel like I could do anything. Reese Sloan Archer, would you do me the honor and make me the happiest and luckiest man and marry me? Right here, right now in front of our very best friends, our family?" I ask.

"Am I supposed to say yes or I do?" Sloan smiles through her tears.

"Yes and I do are perfect." I smile up at her.

"Yes, Beckett Scott. I will marry you, right here, right now. I love you." Sloan pushes up on her toes pressing her lips to mine.

Asher clears his throat. "I didn't get to that part yet guys."

"Beck, I love you. I want to do life with you. I want you with me, by my side, for the rest of our lives. I want all of you. You have held my hand in silence, helped guide me through some of my darkest moments and have reminded me over and over again how strong I am.

"You have been a safe space for me from the moment I stepped into this city. I will forever be grateful that I literally crashed into your gym. You effortlessly became the other half of my soul. Helping me find balance in my life when I lost my way. Always encouraging me. Never letting me give up on myself or forget who I am at my core. You are forever making me laugh. With you, there is only happiness. Thank you for allowing me to rest in a love that doesn't make me go to war. This is our place but you quickly became my home and I don't ever want to leave." Sloan smiles at me, tearfully.

"I think I'm supposed to say I do." I chuckle, my voice gruff.

"Actually, if you guys would let me read. You did this in reverse. This is like your vows." Asher comments.

"Okay, you don't need to read. We did our vows. Just get to the I do part and the kiss already," I huff. I just wanna kiss my damn bride.

"Always so impatient," Ash rags.

"Do you, Beckett Scott, take Reese Sloan Archer to be your wife? To have and to hold, from this day forward. In sickness and in health. To love and to cherish—" Asher continues.

"Yes! 'Til death do us part. For as long as I live. Yes. I do!" I say, rushing Asher.

"Do you, Reese Sloan Archer, take Beckett Scott to be your husband? To have and to hold—" Asher says.

"Yes, Ash! I do! We do! Can we please kiss already?" Sloan asks exasperated. Making all of us chuckle.

"Damn, Little Dove, when did you get so impatient?" I pull Sloan to me, crashing my lips down on hers. Claiming her lips as mine. My wife. My Little Dove. Mine.

"You can now kiss the bride you pains in the asses! You two better not be this impatient at your wedding," Asher shouts. I'm assuming pointing at August and Sutton, but I'm too busy kissing my bride to pay attention.

"I'm sure we will." I hear August laugh.

Everyone cheers as Sloan and I pull away from each other.

"Now, let's partaaaay!" Quinn shimmies, popping a bottle of champagne that came from who knows where.

We spend the rest of the night eating amazing tacos, drinking margaritas and dancing the night away.

When Sloan and I are getting ready to head in for bed, Maria grabs the bouquet wiggling it in the air. "No bouquet toss, Reese's Pieces?"

Sloan takes the bouquet from Maria and stands on the edge of the patio facing the door. All of the girls stand a few feet away from her in the grass.

"Sunshine, you aren't single. Get out of there!" August hollers at Sutton.

"Technically, we aren't married yet, Auggie. So, I can stand here if I want to." Sutton sticks her tongue out at August and we all start laughing.

"Neither are you, Blondie." Knox hollers.

"Shut it, Knoxie," Quinn sasses Knox.

"Okay, on three! And then we're going to bed." Sloan winks at me.

"One."

"Two."

"Three," Sloan shouts and tosses the bouquet.

Quinn jumps up, snagging the bouquet from the air. She whoops in excitement.

Knox runs over to Quinn, pulling her in for a heated kiss.

"I think I'm too young to get married, Blondie, but you might be able to convince me." Knox kisses her again.

Quinn's cheeks are flushed and red when she pulls away from him.

"I'm not too young though, Sugar," Asher says, turning Quinn around to face him, gently grabbing her by the throat and slamming his lips down on hers.

That kiss could melt steel, it's so hot.

All of us stand in the backyard staring at the three of them with our jaws dropped.

Everyone is standing, waiting with bated breath..

We are waiting for a brawl to break out. Except Knox is standing there, watching with a glint in his eye.

He bites his lip and says, "Sugar...I like it!"

There is never a dull moment with those three. Sure enough, it looks as if something intriguing and exciting is about to unfold.

Today is the start of our forever but the fight to our happily ever after was brutal, ruthless—like a blood sport—and isn't for the weak.

We survived, we're thriving and winning at love.

Bleed (Blood Sport Song)

Song Title: Bleed

Artists: Sutton Raven & August Wylder (From Troy)

[Chorus]

You'll be my demise
So break my ribs
Drive in your knife
Rip my heart open
With every word left unspoken
Every time I die
Everything inside me just screams
With you I feel alive
In your hands, I just bleed

[Post Chorus]

I just bleed
With no answer

[Interlude]

Another hour passes
Another day gone
Cardiac arrest she crashes
Her love for him lives on

[Pre Chorus]

Let me unzip your skin
Crawl into you
Breathe life into you again

Awaken you with all of our sins

[Chorus]

You'll be my demise
So break my ribs
Drive in your knife
Rip my heart open
With every word left unspoken
Every time I die
Everything inside me just screams
With you I feel alive
In your hands, I just bleed

[Breakdown]

It was not the end of times
But you can see it from here
Her fire would either burn us
Or set us free of all of our fears

[Interlude]

So keep me tethered to you
Ruin me, unravel me, I only bleed for
you
So keep me tethered to you
Ruin me, unravel me, I only bleed for
you

[Outro]

You'll be my demise
I only bleed for you
You'll be my salvation
I only bleed for you

Acknowledgements

To my beta reading babes:

You have been on this journey with me since Chokehold and I am beyond grateful.

Mum, thank you for reading and rereading my manuscripts, every single one of them. For the laughs, as we proofread sleepy, late into the nights. Thank you for being here for me and supporting my work. I love you!

Krysta, I have no idea what I would do without you from your love and support to our hilarious banter about different scenes. I always and forever appreciate your suggestions and love. I love creating vivid scenes and brainstorming with you. I love that you always push me to take on more challenges in my writing. Cheers to being one of my forever beta readers and ride or die book signing besties! I love you! @mamas.secret.book.nook

Mary, thank you for always supporting me and my crazy ideas. Your play by play commentary will forever be my absolute favorite thing. The belly laughs are top tier. Thank you for always talking me off a ledge and helping me work through the chaos of my mind and my need to always want to start a million projects. I am forever grateful I met my soul sister in line at a Bad Omens concert. I love you to pieces!

Kenzie, thank you for your outpouring of support and absolute love for Beck from day one. Your excitement has been contagious from the beginning. I am so grateful to you for becoming my PA and helping create our epic street team and gorgeous graphics for my books! I adore you! @ kenziekillswitch

To the rest of my family and friends, thank you for all of your love and support, it has meant the world to me!

To my editors Darlene and Athena, thank you for working so hard to make this flow smoothly and dealing with my impulsivity! You have been amazing to work with! I look forward to working on other projects with you in the future! @sistersgetlit.erary

To Cleo, thank you so much for always creating such beautiful designs and formatting! I look forward to working with you on many more projects! @devotedpages_designs

To Sarah, my cover designer, thank you for knowing exactly what this book needed to be brought to life! This is just as beautiful as Chokehold! I cannot wait to see what you create for book three. @enchantingromancedesigns

A special shoutout to: @highgravityaudiobooks for bringing Chokehold to audible! It was nothing but a pleasure to work with you all. My hope is to bring BloodSport to life in audio in the near future. Chokehold Narrators: @ amyhallnarrates @aidensnowvoice @gideonfrostaudio

To my Street Team, I owe you the world. Your support and excitement mean so damn much to me. Thank you for being here! I absolutely adore you!

To my Bookstagram and Booktok friends, you all are the greatest support and community. You have had me in tears with your outpouring of love and support. I wouldn't be here without you. Some of you have become some of the greatest IRL friends, and some of you have been the realest friends, even through a screen, and I hope to meet you in real life someday. I love you all to pieces.

To my Readers, I love you. I love you. I love you. Thank you so much for taking a chance on me and my book babies. Thank you for loving these characters and for all of your messages. Keep them coming!

You are all amazing! I love you. Thank you so much for supporting and encouraging the chaos, that is my brain. I will be forever grateful for these stories and these characters, that bloomed into a beautiful dream. The fictional world is a wee bit less stressful than medicine but this one ties both my worlds together. XXXXX

BloodSport and Chokehold take place in Pittsburgh where Britt grew up and went to college. She now resides in the beautiful mountains of West Virginia but is hoping to be off to a new adventure soon.

Britt enjoys writing stories and poetry. As well as reading a good book on a rainy day, BDSM style (big dogs snuggling me) cozied up under a soft blanket. She loves blogging about other amazing indie authors' books. (@waggingwithwords)

When she's not writing or reading, she loves to attend concerts with her best friends, travel to different restaurants or coffee shops in different states, or is singing and dancing around the house. She also has a love for the ocean and nature.

Britt also enjoys painting, journaling, reiki, meditating with crystals and reading oracle/tarot cards.

To stay up to date on all things Britt, make sure to follow her on her socials and feel free to shoot her an email or a DM.

Other works by Britt: Chokehold (Book 1), Will You Levitate (Poetry)

Links to everything on her website:
https://brittreignauthor.com
https://www.instagram.com/brittreignauthor
https://www.tiktok.com/@brittreignauthor
https://www.goodreads.com/brittreignauthor
https://www.facebook.com/britt.reign.23
https://www.tiktok.com/@waggingwithwords

https://www.instagram.com/waggingwithwords

The Foster Farm (is also very near and dear to my heart.) It's a rescue in Pittsburgh, PA that my sweet Leo and Hazel came from. With Emily's permission, I happily used their name for the book. If you'd like to donate to them. Please see the link below. It is also linked at the bottom of my author page. They help so many lovely animals every year and are mainly a donation based rescue.

https://thefosterfarm.org/how-to-help